SISTER CARRIE

SISTER CARRIE

a novel by

LAUREN FAIRBANKS

Dalkey Archive Press

© 1993 by Lauren R. Jagernauth
First Edition

Library of Congress Cataloging-in-Publication Data
Fairbanks, Lauren, 1958-
    Sister Carrie : a novel / by Lauren Fairbanks. — 1st ed.
    I. Title.
PS3556.A3618S57   1993   813'.54—dc20   93-18998
ISBN 1-56478-035-X

Partially funded by grants from The National Endowment for the
Arts and The Illinois Arts Council.

Dalkey Archive Press
4241 Illinois State University
Normal, IL 61790-4241

*Printed on permanent/durable acid-free paper and bound in the United
States of America.*

To Madan

Contents

SISTER CARRIE

Chapter 1

Otherwise Complete People

HERS IS THE INCONSISTENT TALE of an evangelist on the "born again." Believe what you (pleased and a little proud) want to believe. Some of what you believe will be the truth and some won't—no matter what you're fed. Some TURGID truths are more appealing is all.

Carrie explains her friendship:
What trips to mind? I think when we met she was working for Dial-a-Mattress—if you call them and want a mattress, it is TO you anywhere in the Metroplex, in less than forty-eight hours guaranteed. Her hair was tinted charmingly artichoke. She talked about things like infrared rays killing odor-producing germs. Called herself "Shiksa."

I was impressed with her knowing how to grow . . . what's that guac fruit? Avocado. She knew how to grow the trees from those big seeds. Raised Southern Baptist, she thought Jews had horns and asked every Jew she met, weren't they persecuted because they killed Jesus? The Lord.

I wasn't scared of Latrine because I figured if I knew anything, it was how to flee. Convinced herself she could read my mind. She couldn't. Yet she lived off what she thought she read there. Sustenance. She started me dressing her Barbies. I wanted to model. She agreed with Val, the soles of my feet were too hardened for modeling. I heard it from her first how Val got the city named for him. It made me start to trust her but not really. You can't. Don't.

I liked Latrine's sister Ludmilla. I also liked Grouse, her daughter. She was *"informant"* telling me all about Val and Latrine. I understand she's a Nazi baby now. I knew about their contacting each other even in Germany. I was in

Germany too. Val wanted me there. I wonder if Latrine knew I was there.

I used to think she was biding her time. Waiting her husband out. She confessed to being a perverted lesbian butch sis dyke who couldn't wait to be rid of Franz or Hans etc. Hard-hearted woman. I was the good he was the bad and she thought I was the afterwards when in fact it was herself in for the second time. This is all according to Grouse so I take little store. But hey—a rumor's a rumor! SOME validity.

Barbie wore toreador pants. Midge wore skirts. She had needs so we became very average boardinghouse keepers. We could tolerate each other's dating mistakes, but neither of us could tolerate marrying them. Slumming. I was under the impression the Double Nine cigarettes she smoked were opium-laced. We became ham eaters boiling our dishes. I felt like I'd been wheeled bloody across the finish line once too many times. Latrine was reading Burroughs and she kept buying sets of drinking glasses—so I ran. Not so long after that she met her own true love known as the "Buzzard of Berlin." There were insinuations of assignations until he put a stop to it all. Suddenly all insinuations of assignations stopped.

Got to the point where the sweat reek was that of a poet under glass. I refused to wait and view a calcified skeleton of what I knew. I hear she's off the goofer dust. So I'm back in touch with her. She said, "No one gets over being born eliminated." One day I heard about him placing her in the public square. I got her out of there. She still went back and never blamed him. He was a political scientist through and through—that is to say he beat her. She measures truth against early ancient relics of thought. I couldn't relate and seeing her made my stomach churn. I distanced. Felines lope around the edges of her life—but me—Xmas card. Period. Whenever I think of her I think of one of those thermometers nailed to an old wall; hot and cold, up and down but nailed to one sad somewhere spot by an ever rustier nail.

Like they used to say, "There is everywhere a depressing Iro-European respect for the white man's bedsprings no matter how busy howling and dirty (excuse my dust)."

Our fear is, though we are doubtful symbols of another world of womanity, covering as if by paraphrase far finer proud drum sounds and concealed streakers' symphonies in the street, a silent noise escapes. Our hope, which maybe is a result of that, is no longer to be silenced.

Having lost something once, I want to double then re-double on myself which will allow me to sink into self-deception. OK so you want to know all about the first time. I was sleeping with this Valmouth for the very first time. He asked me. He kind of mumbled "I love you" and then he asked me. I'm not so sure he said "I love you" but I HEARD it. Ignored it. I always think I hear it (people nuts on me) and then with so little to back it up, what WAS said? Maybe not much. I didn't say it back. Unrequited. He was a glubit kinda guy like Michelangelo, voice like a hornet in an oil jar. The distinct possibility rears its head—the request to requite may not have been voiced. His FIRST was someone he saw once a week for fifteen years rather than get pre-engaged. Poor girl. Advantage to being third—treated to a movie or two.

His talk was of church and wedding. His thoughts were short-term—one less than twenty-four-hour period. Mine were long-term . . . FOR THE REST OF MY LIFE. Like, BETTER be a fucking good party. At several Republican national conventions, he wore his black quilted tuxedo and was a hugely admired presidential hopeful. It's true. We expected, quite correctly, his matinal suit to be regulation Salvation Army. I thought about the wife murdering her husband, getting away with it, standing there grieving in strange and unremarkable languages. So I said no. The day he asked me I heated to red. My body heat was enough to blow and break the church windows. Stained glass COSTS. My courage. My rage. Beautiful young widows moping. . . . I picture myself in this shiny satin dress of undernourished cloth. The majority of you know more about it than I. Havershams all.

Yes it started when I was young. I've always had a strong pull toward presidential hopefuls (having lost something once), almost always drunks, can't be trusted, and yes they draw me.

I would spot one and decide I would be meet to greet. The first hard point of attraction is lighting upon rude electric health suggestive of rubies, elephants, and banghi. I often find my first perception in need of overhaul. People say, "Carrie, your first perception needs overhaul," to no avail. Listening to good advice is not one of my strong points.

My rainbow axles churn through many a red-tide infested canal. Then I know I'm in attraction phase II. Ageless witchery of women. I become haunted by the lingering barge of garbage. Whenever I booked a river or ocean cruise, there it was. Pithy reminder. The barge. (Same stinking omen which seldom elects to arrive.)

People I knew didn't have nearly the same worries. One girl's father (he had horn-colored eyes) put two mercenary armies to the task of getting her an occupation so she wouldn't have to make a sticky living off each toe. She (Latrine) landed a career as a secretary and believe me there is very little typing involved these days. But some.

This girl had no friends of any sort except Val and wanted none. She resigned from her day job (fronting a girl gang where members stuck needles into carcasses of passersby) and became a girl with outfits on a promotional track. Always smelled like she'd just been baking manna from heaven.

When she typed, poor little thing, she got her own pen to dot those *i*s. Black magic. If you knew her family, this would break your heart. I didn't know her family and it broke my heart. Black noise. We planned to do high tea at the Drake together. I walked into the dark little office (rabbit hutch) where she worked. The glare of dazzlement from the three carats on my finger caused her to avert her eyes to cowboy boots looking more and more like lonely pilgrims (pathetics) facing each other on a stepping stool. Read all about it. Besides there being no dirty glass in sight, all she could think about was how there had to be cherry pie for his (her husband's) dessert this night so he'd wag his Persian tail. (Iranian.) I thought yeah, as if he'd taste it. His usual habit of a bottle or two of Lancers and his ensuing trip upstairs to REPAIR is topic another day. Earthly affairs. Let's fix on divine affairs!

My position became one of peculiar difficulty and restraint. Never one to start a fight . . . I never refused one. I was not yet sensuously involved in a fat-modification diet. This may have contributed to my ill-preparedness for what I was about to hear. I refused at this point in my life to see chips were not good for me. Now I know them for the DRIPPING SATURATED fat they are. Through my lipid haze, here are Latrine Luissanne's words:

"I've tried to be triple thread as possible. WITH sex I was WITH irritations, without sex, my sexual organs were in unexpected constant motion. Bursting to have it, furniture was rubbed up against. I needed an outlet for my pent-up emotions. I would cook, bake pies, and iron shirts. Abstinence does everybody ELSE good. On my way to mourn my sins and renew my faith, I bumped into Mike the Mailman. We were IN, as they say, IT. Since that day I run home to do the matinal chopping or basting (on my lunch hour) and meet MY Mr. Mailman."

Narrator: Mr. Mailman is a nice Joe without any sort of *SIDE.*

Carrie: They used, in outrageous sexual acts, the food she would later that day serve to her hungry Persian husband. Then she caught on to takeout. The sky was the limit. So many lives in a life. No guilt. Her husband liked the tasty takeout better than her cooking—stupid meathead. Fresh food was saved for carnal recipes. While she and "Mike the

Mailman" were involved, she became a tigress with a banana—drawing blood directly. I've witnessed this. Impres-
sive. Changes one's relationship with fruits forever. If your
relationship with fruit is healthy . . . stay out of Latrine
Luissanne's way.

This was of course many years ago and we weren't even
girls THEN. Long distance does not permit me to be more
than a reader of Latrine's sexual treatise. Her sexual acts
are true works of art. I would lack manners to dare describe
any out of context but the rate of success a normal human
being has . . . let's just say, I have kicked myself around
some gutters searching for what came ever so naturally to
her.

I admit, the ones that excite most are ones in which "the
planned escapade" is broken. If the series of events is suddenly interrupted by the intrusion of some foreign element
or implement, my heart and other organs voyeuristically
quicken. Breaks your center wide open. The abyss charges
clumsily to greet one.

She breaks ground and falls once again through a large
hole straight to hell. Though strangely fettered, she has
found her niche. "Fettered" does her good. When she says,
"There's the wrong way and MY way," I gotta agree.

Let me bring you up to date: This friend of mine lives in
East Berlin now. It's a HAPPENING hot spot. She sits on a
toiletlike stool in a restroom. Business thrives in any café
with toilet. The customer waits as long as possible to use the
restroom. One usually drinks too much before attempting
the toilet run. It's a matter of huge pride with her that liber-
als frequent her establishment.

Latrine: "I only charge 15 Pfennig for use of the toilet . . .
washing hands 25 Pfennig. If they want to wash another
thing, of course we negotiate. ALL THINGS NEGOTIABLE
is our motto. Our toilet attendants enforce the rule that no
more than five and one half mosquitoes inhabit any of
these toilets at any given time."

Carrie: She's into trash of the highest quality; human
trash. Latrine is a New Age feminine role model. Chame-

leon on paisley. She rejected first country, first career, and
first man. This is a verbatim conversation we had before the
Wall came down:

Latrine: "I'll start with the man. You've heard of the Rat
Man of Paris? All the facts of his wartime are true as he tells
them, but he fails to mention having a Piccadilly weepers
brother. He has a brother. His brother is a Dundrearied
German. I'll explain the details later. I met this brother.
Fell in love. In Florida. Remember Woody's on the Beach?
Remember the unforgettable restroom setup? HAD EV-
ERYTHING! I'm into restrooms now. I think you could buy
coke from the towel keeper in there. Big sniff-sniffs in the
stalls. Doors scribbled with licentious notes invoking God
make me right at home because my philosophy is
Bardology . . . I'm talkin' peanut gallery filled with literati
hoots. This large handsome German was in Woody's.
Valmouth introduced us.

"It just so happens, he had seen very little of the West.
Strictly an East Berliner. He decided to take the service-ori-
ented (7–Eleven hits the bathroom) genre to market back
home. It's in production now. His dream was to have many
pissing men involved in his life. They were to be (in a small
way) reminded of him, whenever they tinkled. Or whatever
men do—men gush. That's who he is. What he stands for.
Sits for. The dream is reality. Rogue's End.

"It seemed almost decadent. He was red-faced over it. We
both were. Excited. I was stimulated by him. Absolutely wet
over the idea of taking Lysol Basin Tub and Tile Cleaner
over there. He said the most corrupt area of the U.S. of A. is
the county NEXT to Dade County. I decided then and
there my Persian and my mailman were out. I was going
with this strange retired East German policeman. As they
say 'I resolved to follow the stranger whithersoever he
should go.' I wanted IN on this venture. It was solid fact he
enjoyed a long leisurely session in the lav . . . studying up
. . . little did I know my life would be an ongoing Ph.D. program in waterworks.

"East Berlin is the place for me. We researched restrooms everywhere. We combined the best of everything in terms of toiletries, organization, and service for our enterprise, not to mention benefits for our employees. Don't get me wrong, Germans always pay to use the toilet, but now we're giving them the latest Japanese paperless toilet; you find yourself sitting on a warm seat, water is sprayed on your behind to cleanse you, warm air dries you and lastly your bum is disinfected and perfumed. Automatic! Choice is the unheard-of key; choice of perfumes, hair spray, etc. We have dental floss, toothpaste, even stockings if you get a run. In the men's room: condoms of all shapes, sizes, colors, textures, and flavors. Sometimes people come in to check out the variety. Tourists have a penchant for sheaths of rubber. Souvenir mania."

How old is your irredeemably infested Schlockmeister and company?

"How old?"

How old?

"He's seventy-eight. (*Long pause.*) We both wear pencil-thin mustaches when on Tigglywinkles duty. Our business is called the P.K.P. (Professional Kraut Pamperers.) We keep water closets clean. We're the only ones in the GDR providing such specialized services . . . opening a new frontier. Legislation may even be passed. Government jobs. We're looking into the new toilet technology that measures your body temperature, weight, blood pressure, and pulse while analyzing your urine. Hospitals are interested now. Taverns and private homes are next."

Any problems with the new regime?

"We're for it. We're against it. And we're neutral. That's official. A poor prosy substitute are we."

And the attraction? Any regrets?

"The chemical attraction is there. Well certainly, I wouldn't be human without regrets. Of course. He's in very good shape. His fiddle is fit. And when people stare at me in disbelief I say, 'Let me tell you about a dream I had last night. It has to do with two young men (consultants to terrorists) held in captivity against their will, a rescue opera-

tion ending in murder, a failed escape, a long waiting period and finally a TRUE walkaway.' Hopeful histrionics.
There—that's worth a moment's reprieve."

That's your USUAL response?

"Yep. Unusual regular response. I say I'm not sure what
language he speaks but we get along splendidly. Smells like
a cabbage so maybe he's Eye-talian. . . ."

I asked what keeps her busy the early evenings before the
toilet seat calls (before the café opens):

"Günther has lived in the same house for forty-five years.
Since nothing will grow in his front yard—and if it did, we
have little time to care for it—we sank 15,000 marbles into
cement. Marbles are cheap in what you know as 'Eastern
Bloc' countries. That was our project last month. It took the
entire month."

If L.L. says a thing at least four times, it becomes the
truth. EXAMPLE:

"I keep my eyes open and my ears flappin.

"I keep my eyes open and my ears flappin.

"I keep my eyes open and my ears flappin.

"I keep my eyes open and my ears flappin."

I've heard her say that at least five.

Latrine: "I'm also in a play. I study and practice morn-
ings. I'm Alice in Vunderland AND the Queen in
'Northampton' hairdos circa 1963. Surrounding me during
the performance are medical models of human beings
sheathed in clear purple tinted plastic. The performance
ends with the drum solo from *Moby-Dick;* wigged, padded
and bound I perform strange rituals with great enthusiasm.
This morning before work, free to pamper myself, I found
it a treat to facial, sauna, weightlift, do a voice check for
later, AND get laid."

How DO you do it?

"I've tried lots of things, like the Queen's Approaching
New Dress Agency. The sacred teachings of the vodun religion also work for me."

You don't mean voodoo or hoodoo?

"Not in the strict sense of the word—words."

How does it work for you?

"We have four souls each. One roams the streets while we slumber. A full life is had by all but forgotten . . . can't remember most of this life. Now tell me about you. How is Valmouth? Does he regret turning down the position with the Mounties?"

We'll . . . let's certainly talk about him . . . maybe later.

"I know! You want me to 'TEND TO MY SEPTIC YANKS FIRST,' am I right?"

More like SEPTIC KRAUTS. Tell me about the character of your until-moments-ago communist man.

"His sense of justice is off-kilter. Quite a long time ago, without any comparisons, he stopped judging himself as severely as he might. I don't know. There is a distinct lack of Western built-ins; guilt and dilemma and choosing between right and wrong. When right and wrong is decreed, there is no choice—life is simple but one is a child of the state. Sans choice—sans confusion. The Westerner might unconsciously stop himself five times every day from any number of acts after some degree of moral dilemma. He has none of that. Nothing to repent—all weightiness removed. He'll knock me over to get a really good long quiet look at another woman. The questioning part is removed, replaced with official answers. Someone should keep an eye on these people when they come West. Freedom is a very dangerous thing.

"Günther is a highly regarded framer of the New Freedom. The government appreciates his business foresight. I hold a special place in his heart, so I can still call him Zip the Apeman or the Missing Link, though no one else dares. . . . He represents a minority—the Austro-Hungarian Empire. How many of THOSE are left running around?"

Precious few and they are reputedly dangerous or very expensive.

"Priceless. He looks like a Viking god."

Or a Viking god's father.

"Conscientious hedonists abound. As a form of adolescence, this too shall pass. I met one man who simply could not cope with the fact his Coca-Cola glass could be refilled as often as he wished. Could not cope. His debriefing cost a bundle."

Is the Golden Age on its way?

"It's here because we know the Dark Ages are gone . . . never to return. Read it in a Hallmark card. They have damned pithy stuff. I often spend an entire day at the card store and consider it nothing if not time well spent. Edifying."

Is it true you were a former Miss Texas runner-up?

"A long time ago I went with a Dallas Cowboy."

Close. Do you feel, in any way, you are bettering the lot for your sex?

"I wanted to share myself with the women of the world (and men) so I entered the Pillsbury Bake-Off. I didn't make finalist. My vegetarian potpie has the cleansing qualities of a spa enema. The world's not ready yet. Do me a favor and get this strange man's hand off my knee. Oops you can't half a world away. We have a good life. My hubby feels most at home in Italy where he walks among the people giving audience to all."

Do you have a home there?

"A villa with gardens of box, quince, pomegranate, and lavender. There we don't have to 'play the tape' to know what happened to us."   ˋ

Could you explain?

"Whether we were in East Germany or in Russia, we knew we were being taped. If we had an argument about what either one of us actually said—we had a number to call and the tape was played back for us. This was officially illegal, but just knowing you can hear the conversation again reassures. No discrepancies. We'll have to get used to life without it. Our recent memory is getting exercised quite a bit."

I know you work for Fi Fi.

"Oh!"

I also know Adolfina is your child.

"Oh!"

Life is a puzzlement and with Sister Carrie's life we can
gather information from the "beleaguered willing to tell"
and then throw it out to you. Throw it up to you if you prefer. I thought yes Mama, with my omniscient narrator position, I would be like a god. Wonderful powers. A joyride.
Truth would out. The sole owner of the truth, I would then
spread it to the people using my superhuman abilities.

Trouble in paradise. Critics sprang up. I met with them. I
listened. They were unanimous in their conclusion—my
work was biased. That's why you're getting this total piece
of shit. Don't get me wrong—I stayed with the project. It
HAS NOT the smooth narrative of one who without question knows all. Sad. The witnesses' perceptions and half-re-
membered dialogues are juxtaposed in (shall we be frank?)
sloppy ways. Yunnerstan? I was taken to the mat for my
prank in the pharmacy but I fought to keep that (my favorite part) in. Yes, the pharmacy bit! They granted me that
one concession. It might mean future employment down
the road for me. I can work with these people no longer. A
little sense of humor would go a long way down here. How
sad but true that people born round do not die square.

By the time you get to my bit, you'll think I'm one of
those narrators who just interrupts and is basically another
character. Please remember I am omniscient. You want
truth you got it from you know who. Watch out for the
other characters. Like Grandpop for instance. He brings
me into the twentieth century kicking and screaming.

Grandpop: We are excitable and nervous. Went to school
with "crackers." Rednecks. So hurried at times, we put our
food in the blender not to waste time chewing. But hey wait
a second. An aside: it was a revelation to me that certain di-
rectors were intelligently and purposefully, in their own
films, reminding us of past films. History of themselves.
Don't you congratulate yourself upon recognizing a television commercial echoes a past ad? Intelligent people are
selling things. Kinda makes you proud. A honeymoon?
Yeah where do you want to go? Kiss kiss take a bath. Anywhere we can move product! I hope they're happy. When I

say past ad, we're talking SHELF LIFE OF MINUTES.

Narrator: What a card! Let's get back to Sister Carrie, not her acting profession. ("Profession" may refer to advertising. It may refer to prostitution. She was a well-rounded individual.) I told her folks she would have to wear her hair shaved on one side for a few years—and for her trouble, and theirs, she'd get a nice set of wheels. A deal was cut. Her tone is not sorrowful and lacks self-confession. More guilt can be added later just like salt. She may WANT to be alone but she can't live alone any more than you or I can. Any more than we can. One look at her face and you think (the common reaction) "Fungal disaster." The girl was successful; 85 percent of success is showing up, with or without a box lunch prepared—plastic-covered lunch meats as always remain optional. Remember she's the one who said, "When I think family, I think I'm linked to the tree of nervous diseases."

Why had she decided to leave this day and this time? So definitely? It had everything to do with the new moon. Something with a horoscope. (Carrie doesn't know that.) Does too! She knows because she doesn't make a move without reading the *T. & C.* horoscope. Had to use her mother's bathroom. Her mother had just cured herself one mean case of vaginitis and wrote a note in lipstick on the bathroom mirror: NO SEX WITHOUT FIRST MOUTH-CLEANSING WITH LISTERINE. The message was for Mr. (man of the house) Meeber. The message was the turning point. Carrie, who happened upon it first, was outta there like instantaneous weaning. Her mother, convinced her infection came from oral sex with a filthy mouth, used red fuchsia lipstick made by Chanel whenever she wanted words with Squeaky Meeber. Carrie heard the remnants of her parents argument :

". . . cesspool of rotting zoobies." Carrie knew this had something to do with Anthony Burgess—who he was, she had no idea—but Caroline knew, maybe by intuition, she, herself, was a person living in a germ-free environment. Hit her hard when it hit. You know the rest: SHE WAS OUTTA

THERE LIKE INSTANTANEOUS WEANING.

When Caroline Meeber parked her mother's VW Van of
Aquarius at the airport, she stopped to think about what
she had brought with her, besides her diaphragm, to start a
new life. Not much. But it's not worth going through her
suitcase just to satisfy our curiosity. Sensationalism. She had
some stuff.

Running away. "It is only our duty." Back at the beach
they all thought "Realtor Baby" was doing the responsible
thing—house-sitting. Her voyage (reveling in her own vocabulary, and if not her own, her sister's) had begun. She
had an address and words of welcome. She used them
thinking it was her last chance to grab a little life and took
to walking counterclockwise places where the pious and respectful walk clockwise. The airport limo brought her to
the nurses' housing; the carpeting had the same pattern as
the now-famous, hardly worn floor-covering in *The Shining*.

She recalled looking at *People* magazine during a recent
conversation with her mother (flashback):

There's Princess Caroline. Quite a playgirl.

Maybe I'll be a playgirl now.

You're too old.

For purposes of edification, we will often refer back to
the original literary legend "Carrie of Chicago": When a
girl leaves her mother's condo at twenty-three, either she
falls into saving hands cupped in prayer toward heaven and
becomes better, or she rapidly assumes the cosmopolitan
standards of virtue and becomes ever worse . . . But I own
you . . . [Blah blah blah blah] . . . Is that culture talking?
The cunning wiles. . . . The big-shouldered city uses forces
that allure . . . she wasn't cultured. When would she find
herself in the most loquacious, angst-ridden gathering of
her choosing? There would be no more prayer wheels or
flags to remind her of her Asian upbringing. Her destiny
would become weird corner interludes with gifts of gold
and slavegirls and many brewskies at Jimmie's.

The phone call:

Guess where I am?

Miami?
No.
Jacksonville?
No.
Tampa?
No.
Key West?
No. Chicago.
You're not serious.
The van is in 3E. America sees in collage. That's why I
called.
Get on the next flight and get back here. Right now.
Double clicks. A resurrection.
Instead of a momentary stay against confusion (temple
of unity), she wanted to stir it up. The sacredness of human
relationships would have to be put on hold or hung up on.
A stone adrift, she would come to celebrate passing wads.
Words. She would go incognito. She would dig a road
through mudholes and broken furniture debris. She would
make wads out of that. (The irony is that she would go hungry but eventually make her fortune manufacturing earth
earrings for the huge Earth Day celebration in her new
home, the city of her choice.) Her city windy and smelly
like wind pushed not of its own accord, through Swiss and
smelly cheese. Yes. A city proud and stupid to believe itself
unliterary. Yes but I own you. Is that the city talking? Merely
resurrection.
A tragedy. Everybody brings dessert. Nobody brings a
main course. Not a Greek tragedy because they know
enough to bring the lamb, the rice dish, and the dessert.
Carrie often made nothing out of something thinking she
was accomplishing just the reverse.
It would have been nice if she could wear black all the
time and pay dues somewhere, but there were no ladies'
clubs in Hyde Park. No armbands. No Woman's Auxiliary.
No Junior League. She let her politically correct life become an anti-German manifesto. Her usefulness was at an
end. She became another undocumented person. "My

documents are in Portugal."

OK, Carrie, since you are here, we have to ask you a few questions: Why is it when a forest burns, Germans spend all their time thinking about the deeper meaning of the fire? Rather than putting out the blaze?

Answer: Patriotic hyperbole combined with a congenital need for Louis Comfort Tiffany wallpapers. (When comfort is your middle name.)

What does joining the Shakers with or without the approval of one's family do for you as a young woman?

Answer: Whatever restores sanity to the realm. Wink complicitly. Work complicitly. What if I were interviewing you and wrote down everything you said or didn't say about the Shakers? They put pasta on their pizza for God's sake. Write THAT down. And don't give me any of that "IMPORTANT YOUNG MIND" expression.

Another mere deployment of words. Sticks and stones, Carrie?

I just wanted to be a regular old Joe and have become an interplanetarian.

Where do you find yourself instead, Carrie?

What?

What do you dream you've got in your hand and then awake to find you don't?

A piece of brick from Jim Jones's temple.

MERE resurrection, Carrie.

Would you care to talk to anyone else in the family?

No. Infidels all! Would anyone else in your family care to have a word with us?

Just one. Grandpop.

CARRIE'S BOCA GRANDAD AND GRANDMA (ON FATHER'S SIDE) TALK DUDEFEST:

Grandpa: That mysterious circulating windblown thing. May as well have the lightning-bolt insignias from Nazi uniforms on their collars. In Germany we are winning and winning and then losing. Losing we don't like. Yet we know the meaning of the word. Trouble ourselves to love authority. What makes us happiest. We Germans came to Boca. The German army was right offshore from the club. Took row-boats in from the submarine. War years! What screwing! What shopping! By nightfall, in our boats again, we rowed back. Forever "rush hour" out there. Shore leave was a de-light so sub-time we were clean-mouthed and in blood sports, lacking.

Home safely, a few years later, when it was all over, I watched my wife do the dishes, left my paper on the chair half read, came up behind her affectionately (in a way of familiarity beyond reproach in my own home), put my arms around her waist, then my fingers on her hips and softly said, "I WANT TO GET IT OFF MY HAIRY CHEST. (*Long pause.*) THERE HAVE BEEN HUNDREDS OF OTHER WOMEN." And how did she feel? She felt soooo crunchy on her way to the Gucci gas station. Designer water. Designer gasoline. She sang that (song?) the whole way "When a Mon Merries." She went, solely based on my description, to of all places, Boca.

Bleakbeard Ave. in Boca. And she took the babe. When asked about her decision, she answered, NEW BABES HAVE A FEAR OF FALLING APART or THERE'S BUBBLE GUM AT THE BOTTOM OF ANY YANKEE PURSE WORTH STEALING. Even baby said, AM LIKING IT WITHOUT THE KING OF THE ONCE-RANS.

The same child would grow up to run an escort service. All it was. Exactly that. Dinner and conversation. He had one working girl. One girl DOES an escort service make. Business went under but he married her. Let me be more specific: One girl DOES an escort service make UNTIL you marry her. Plenty of conversation. (Carrie's Ma and Pap.) Zenobia and her first husband. (Not Squeaky.) Life's upsom downs. They loved to march at breakneck speed. Marchers all. More children. Less Germanic marching. Number one grandson screaming at the top of his "special ed" lungs. Grandma (Zenobia's first mother-in-law) could be heard screaming all the way from Blackbeard Ave. "I

HEAR THE CRACKLE OF SAPPHIRES AND DIAMONDS SPARKLING THROUGH THE GREASE. IT TAKES LITTLE TO NO COURAGE TO HIT A DOG WITH A STICK. LITTLE TO NO Mr. Bigshot."

Grandma says she gave up on the idea of lovers because X-rated tapes and dirty rotten secondhand clothes were more than enough. She's a neck up person now. No more needles. . . . Disc jockey from hell. Don't you dare to change the station. Finds herself having to invent something— ANYTHING to scratch. When they ask about Grandpa, and they always do, she says, I'M NOT REFERRING TO THAT SWORDSWALLOWER. One could gather Grandpop was Germanic while on the extreme other hand Grandmother was Bavarian.

Were there ever any GRANDPARENTLY warnings to the girls, Carrie and Mary?

Yes. It went like this: IF HE'S GOT CHINCHILLAS IN A CAGE IN WHAT LOOKS LIKE A CHILDREN'S ROOM, AND YOU FIND A MOTHER'S DAY CARD ON THE KITCHEN WALL, YOU'VE NO ONE TO BLAME BUT YOURSELF. IF HE'S SURPRISED "OH WOW!" WHEN HIS KEY FITS THE DOOR, AND THE ONLY PROFESSOR (CONDOM) HE CAN FIND IS DRIPPING AND STILL WARM, BLAME NOBODY BUT YOURSELF. IF HE TELLS YOU GRAVEL AND LUGNUT ARE NOT HIS CHILDREN (GRAVEL IS THE BOY AND LUGNUT IS THE GIRL), CHANGE YOUR GOD DAMN ORDER. AND PLEASE, BY ALL MEANS, GET THE HELL OUT O' THERE QUICK. MEN—THEY'RE LIKE RED ANTS WHEN THEY CRAWL BETWEEN YOUR TOES AND GIVE YOU A REAL HARD BITE. . . . WELL I'VE ALWAYS FOUND IT TO BE MORE CONSTRUCTIVE TO STENCIL THEIR HEADS BEFORE THEY DO IT TO YOU. THEY'D HAVE YOU BELIEVE CATSUP IS A VEGETABLE.

LOVE,
your Bavarian Grandma

Chapter 2

Give Any Seed to My Bullfinch

INTERVIEW IN WHICH Carrie nods and shakes head often:
In her letter, "Helgi the Lean," special aid to the Eagle
Scouts, Missoula, Montana, tells all about the pair of you. I
see from her letter you need a job. We choose you Carrie.
This way dear. You wouldn't be part of the animal rights
movement would you now? Good. It's hard that is not easy
to explain what we do here. I have respect for the way you
carry or don't carry your rod. Yes, a hierarchy of sorts. How
many grizzlies have you killed?
Carrie: None.
Here's the basement where you'll find the ravined personnel in the southern part of the pocket. Have a nice day.
(Carrie got the job with guess who? Pimpo & Co.)
Carrie finds herself in the midst of this one-way conversation:
I'll pay for it. Won't BEGIN to tickle my bank account.
Proper time and place for everything. Wanted us to be
more than a teenage suicide fad. Death squads have proven
themselves to be very helpful in this region. However, one
bad public relations person and this parish sees to it you're
finished. Some things will not be tolerated. Which add up
hastily to a bum rap. One more thing Robinson Crusoe
could live without. Bad end. No future. Irony that Christo-
pher Columbus had no future.
Space for comment: (Carrie leaves it blank.)
The temperature? THAT would affect your choice in positions?
Carrie nods.
Well. One worker described himself "making my own
hell down here." Let's suppose it's abundantly warm. Or
abundantly hellish. Like I said, have a nice day.

Space for comment: (Carrie leaves it blank.)

Next Worker Bee: On the first floor, you'll find the shop. Please notice the sign in the window: "Shoplifters will be beaten to death." If you choose to work there—it is slightly cooler temperature-wise—you'll find Guru running the show. His operation is significant in that he turns the thermostat down. Less heat equals less sexual friction between the workers. I know he has been kicked out of Montana for some fraud or other but we welcome his expertise in our great state. One, maybe three wives. A showman. A businessman. A preacher. Just remember, whether you decide to go there or elsewhere, Pumpy Rodriguez is Guru's assistant. He says things like, "We shoot stylish graduates of Garbology school." What can I say? You'll catch on to the work lingo—like any job. We all catch on. His floor is invaluable to our total effect here. When he's gone . . . merciful Lord Jesus, give him everlasting rest. That's when WE will be sure to get some!

Carrie: Rest. Gotcha.

Casually ask him how it's going, ask him to stop sitting on the Catholic cross HE'LL HURT HIMSELF! He'll lead you to believe his day is filled with the pinning of society debs. And to a certain extent, it IS. The crux of the matter being, we need to know what manner of baby this is—what manner of grown-up, given half a chance, it might have become. If you choose to work with him, we'll have you start on our huge doll collection immediately. If this crosses your radar screen beep beep as interesting work, we'll call him in to discuss it with you further. We encourage you to initiate physical contact with the staff when either you or they are fully conscious.

I'll give you an example of a case on the floor right now: a youngster when asked *how old are you?* said "four or five." From this, we can deduct: 1) he has no interest in his own little age; 2) he is fully aware, insofar as it interests us, we'll either move or not move on it. How does he know his private truths may not be attended to? Most likely, we won't give a hoot. He knows, having arrived at this point in his life, the unfortunate and sad realization is that the facts of such a little life come to diddlysquat in the scheme of things. Have a nice day.

Third Worker Bee: My dear, as Pendergast said to Truman, "Work hard, keep your mouth shut, and answer your mail." You seem to have well-dressed ideas, and at the same time, remain unwealthy as you can BE without being in REAL trouble. I see it takes you all morning to dress and that's with the help of experts. May I be so bold as to volunteer Gucci? Their shoes are silhouettes of our race. We're into subtexts and symbols so your loyalty to the wrong sock manufacturer can and will destroy your credibility. No. We no longer douse one another with kerosene. That practice has been curtailed. Have a nice day.

Fourth Worker Bee: The second floor involves psychic connections to literary delvings. Family dynamics, if you will. We ask ourselves questions like How do we safely bring our children into the realm of exhibitionist? The artist as exhibitionist. Here's an example: 1) his mom and sisters dressed him entirely in little girl's clothes. Told him he was a little girl, so what does Hemingway assume he is ? Got it into his mind. Eradicate? No. Incorporate. Another example: 2) I understand your boyfriend's got $3000.00 worth of stereo equipment in the car and has anointed himself with oils. Hear him beeping for you? Thinks you're in a job interview? Mat down the hairs on your body. The pair of you. I know something about the young man's childhood. When he was fourteen, he gave soldiers cigarettes and asked for long slow wet kisses in return. No, not women soldiers either. Don't get me started on today's army. Sun and dust. Just have a nice day.

First Worker Bee back again: On the third floor we have a training spot. We train those willing and able (must be recommended). This is where and when you learn how to sniff out their shark pools before pouring your own blood into it. We don't want you to feel like a raisin at the ant-infested farmhouse spread. You will respond to these attitudes: "Sweetie, just cause they treat you like shit, you STILL act like pie." Here you would work on our study entitled *Why Females Have No Character at All*. This training is in-depth and prepares you for movement to almost any other floor of your choice. When you leave is when you want to shake your trainer till his teeth fall out. Shake him till his head is empty and yours is full. Transference.

Architecturally, it's the most interesting floor. Large as a warehouse unto itself wherein you'll find miles and miles of catwalks. You can help connect the disparate training areas. The walls are painted as black as Interloper's boots. One doesn't see the barriers. You know you're on one when you're thrown up against it. Dark as the inside of a cow. But sicker and sorrier. Pieces of sliced glass will be thrown at you with regularity by live figurines parodying the Last Supper. Here's your bag of glass. You may stick some into the wall. Then hit the pieces with this tiny hammer. This creates an incantatory melody along with the piped-in organ music. You'll find yourself asking the not-so-musical question, "How I felt about imprisonment?" Don't worry if your own glass cuts you, as this is often the case. We don't talk job hazards but . . . *reversed perks*. That might qualify as one.

Not to generalize—in a personal way. You. Yourself. Behind bars. You'll come to grips with quite a bit. At long last end of it your feet are so bloody you'll need a wheelchair to enable you. But it truly is over then. Did you find Venus de Milo any less magnificent with her arm busted? Think about it. Have a nice day.

Second Worker Bee: The new recruits (blue-nosed tragedians) all seem to want to be on the parakeet-training floor. Peer pressure gets the job done more than anything else. Now, let's break from all this and dine. A luncheon of duck and green peas. I want Key lime pasta in the nouveau Cuban style and two oat sodas to go. (Our small green way of hooking into an elusive state of perfection.) Always the best man wins. More on-the-job competition out there.

I'm spokesperson for my floor: "Professional Butchers." I say we're in the bone trade. Bludgeoned skulls and pulverized tibia all part of the job and we're PEOPLE for the job.

Love to put you OUT of work. . . . We're well-versed in the
biography of the man famous for writing the *Remarks on
Anal Pouches of the Armadillo.* You will be too. Study and
time. So don't go running off when you see horns and
skulls and body bits of animals (we do and don't eat) rush-
ing down the stream out of the hills.

This work area, which, predictably, involves a transsexual
hearse driver, reaffirms the old saw: if you're an itinerant
mass murderer of Jews, if you even LOOK the part, and are in
the market for a place to hang your hat, you can find life's
rewards somewhere "Southern." We won't get into "the
South" and what this may or may not mean to you and yours.

Just know in your heart, it's not Berlin SO LONG AS
THE WATER CRITTERS ARE EATING MOSQUITO LAR-
VAE, so long as whirlpool jets, nine jets blasting, lead one to
nirvanic relaxation. At one point after having received so
many threats from death squads (Pigsty Cleaners Union)
who had also taken early retirement in a manner of speaking, the cemetery director told one caller, "Sorry, we don't
take deep drawled death threats except between the hours
of ten o'clock and one. Call back later." (When WE DO.)
On our way this minute to find ourselves some regular
blokes. Not somebody whose grandfather has a cabinet with
bits of coral and a jar of water from the Jordan for baptizing
his children. You get to sign everything "P. Butcher." More
than five ways I personally know to skin a cat. You may come
up with more.

Narrator: Helgi the Lean shows up . . . saying, "I came
here to speak my piece in behalf of Sister Carrie in her job
search. I had to leave in the middle of THE ASIAN GAMES
or Snootsful. I felt it my duty to be here. Maybe I could
clarify some or even one of her pithy sayings. I represent
the Realty Group. As you have been told we're contemplating branching out—going global. We want you to listen and
observe our teleconference concerning Carrie with the
group from Malaysia":

Following on video: "My name is Ippolito de' Medici.
The omnivicarious (joked upon) Carrie, with or without

false eyelashes, was brought in after she said 'the beauty of intangible property is that it's unreal estate,' all this while she held up the tube mushrooms from her garden, put her foot down and significantly stepped upon centrally stipulate fungi. They were coldly defined by mycologists as terrestrial, fleshy, putrescent, stipulate fungi . . . which proves beyond a shadow of a doubt: she sees herself as the princess of Smolensk. Which incidentally happened to another friend of mine and THAT was, as they say, the beginning of the end. She was not, however, Parsienne or Beelzebub. . . . Dipping wings time. Armed with the FACT that puddle nymphs swim, she trusted the echo more than your FIRST OUT words. She's better off than the olives I'd like you to pass."

When we talk stipulate fungi, you say "Dinosaurs spit?"

Ippolito de' Medici: We didn't want your kind here for more than a week and you've been here two years.

We're talking herbaceous herds when he says "Spokes-nerd?"

Duct tape him.

Or reclassify him "The classic dead white male."

Sews to be bespoke.

Ippolito de' Medici: SUBCLASS.

Go figure.

Who are you really insulting when you say she's nine months and ten minutes apart from her sibling?

Ippolito de' Medici: Where you from?

East Fuck, Texas. Where our pleasures are equine and our desires—Alpine.

Give us a profound remark on the concept "LOVE."

Ippolito de' Medici: I'm taking my two weeks just about the time you're up. For two? If you want to join me, I'm going to the Lawrence Welk birthplace. It's a government tourist site Congress BESPOKE. Great country this U.S.A. I'll be nuzzling on a bucket of oat soda.

Congress canned it.

Ippolito de' Medici: This often happens to me—I find myself in such erotic fiascoes I feel like a dumb pachyderm. (As in not so smart.) Forgetfulness levels are a moot point.

Deliver me from the cul-de-sac. Makes an old man outta me every night.

We are grateful to Hackish females and the CEOs from the Realty Group; both groups took time from their busy day to share with us their invaluable insights into our applicant through the conversational teleconference medium. We are thoroughly enlightened. Hackish females had barely finished walking plenty of dogs before getting up a charity ball where they danced around tropical punches. This stirred up atomic vomits thereby urging us to help ourselves in our selection of a worker for this establishment. We want to send out a special thanks to both groups. We will adjourn to make our decision. Thank you. Special thanks to Signor Ippolito de' Medici.

Carrie: I fell to wondering what the job with Pimpo would be like . . . and went into a trance . . .

It was a dream but it seemed so real. There were pre-Columbian Indian male dancers surrounding me. They had huge hook noses and their skin was thick. They were decorated with yellow, red, and black paints. Hardened soles of feet. Their dance was soothing, hypnotic. I wanted to lay down my heavy head right where they were dancing. I did. I wanted to tell them this nursery magic is strange and wonderful . . . my tongue wouldn't work. The whistles of their clay pipes were hauntingly melodic. Much pomp and joy. The music stopped. I didn't want it to stop but my energy returned. I lifted my head at the start of their bloodletting dance. They pierced their groins with swords. Blood came gushing out into size LARGE wax-coated Dixie cups dangling on long strings around their necks. One who seemed novice lost his nose through sheer carelessness. I had a hard time keeping rhythm and missed a few steps.

I asked them in a dubbed-over and slightly askew way how difficult it would be to recycle those things (due to the wax). They ignored me and kept gushing. I was one born assassinated. UH oh. Their swords turned to spears. Their natural flight was toward me. My blood ran down gutters like mercury from a broken thermometer. It wasn't run-

ning so bad. What I was put on this earth to do. Then all
bleeding stopped. Mine dried up. Snack time. It was plain
they could be divided into Celts (grain-eaters) and Goths
(milk-eaters) before the soccer game.

When I described my dream I got "You'll never be the
same after a dream such as that!" *Same as always* is an interesting concept.

Then the worker bees came out with their announce-
ment: the position was mine.

I refused it for something more mainstream in the Prostitution Division.

IN THE WORDS of PIMPO and CARRIE while she is in his
employ:

Pimpo: My dear soul, first go to the street where we built
the Crystal Palace. Borrow my high-wire shoes. Since you're
a woman, add heels. If they're gathered round the fire in
powwow fashion, they will have their dicks burned. It's not
like we're taming enormous pianos. Dicks bums and green
peters. Parts we believe in. My golden pheasant, if the fire is
burning LIKE THAT what time of day is it? Perceive in the
deepest somnabulance the throes of entanglement's inop-
erative bad dream, and just a step beyond that, the hour of
awakening. . . . Hey get off him I said. These women will
wear out my men. Make 'em tired as pastry cooks. Keepers
of hatred. Classify each person.

Hillybillies . . . love the guys but they might fuckin' scare
away my women. Do you really want to add another color?
Crossbars are strong but at Cliff's Edge, hopefully this
won't prevent his shooting home the bolt. Never mind us.
Central planning gone mad. My jewel, if you would . . . your
plaid-suitcased impressions? Carrie?

Carrie: When We Talk of Death Decay and Drowning—
Call Me Schmatta, which is Yiddish for Rag. Or call me your
"Hostess Twinkie." Scattered. Cultivated appendages. Ferocious squints. Death. Death and more death. I waited and
nothing happened. They threatened, "If you're not going

to kill something, let's get on with it." Small animals. We proceeded to fall asleep inside each other. I could ask any old soak. Asked them to ask their own cocks. Something to believe in. Made me take it. Bound to you all by this strange tie of affection. Deluded by fine clothes. All mingles of combination. When I left, wasn't very much alive . . . a moving couch. Vexed now. What is that familiar sound emitted from your jowly grin?

Pimpo: Just me going again. Carrying on with lots of carrion. Carrion need acupuncturists too. Cures a carrion with a paralyzed esophagus. Like I always say, "A little more muscle and a LOT more stroke." Glad you're dragged back wrapped in a flag, sweetie. My sweet friend, how did you come to be with those people?

Carrie: You sent me. We all banded together. It didn't take me long to realize. There are very few people who truly care if your bird has a runny nose . . . if the bird is bored . . . or in the appropriate birdhouse.

Pimpo: Needles prevent them from being bored?

Carrie: Birds have neuroses too. In the long and short of it—this is exactly what brings people like us together.

Pimpo: I was under the impression it had something to do with DEEP DRAWLS and simian unpredictability.

Carrie: Does it help me at all that I once gave them a token? Does that count?

Pimpo: It helps that they were once GIVEN a token.

Carrie: A weapon?

Pimpo: Weaponry. It does not matter if it was YOU who gave it.

Carrie: I ONCE MET A MAN.

Pimpo: A purse from an elephant's penis, no doubt.

Carrie: Mine's simply a hairy-legged resolve with an ax at my side.

Pimpo: He's dead you know and just came in for a lapful of roses and pleasant society.

Carrie: Just a boy. A boy trampling the wild carrot. And it all happened in the town where Babe Ruth grew up. Clapotements furieux des marées.

Pimpo: They came to film his life story. He would play
the bewitcher. He'd come to the playground and quietly
darn socks then put on some blood-encrusted clothes or
whatever, white makeup over that black skin, scream his
lines, stick a knife in your ear—then quietly return to his
quilting and pantomime storytelling surrounded by orphan
children. He'd determine AFTER asking you whether or
not your room needed Hoovering. His few lines: "We know
who you are—you're the Antichrist."

We hoped more greasepaint and less talent was his
motto. His penchant for elbow-length black gloves added
credibility to his screaming, "Vott I like is boom-boom." IT
IMPRESSED.

Carrie: I HAVE MY OWN IDEAS ABOUT WHAT RE-
ALLY WORKS FOR THE LONG TERM. For example, did
you know the perfect couple is a pair—a tall black woman
and a short white man?

Pimpo: I knew the perfect couple was a flash-naked pair.
Pair of what? . . . thought I'd leave that for you to decide.

Carrie: I serve it right back to you and your friend Con
Woman Confusion . . . she'll get to it the minute she ceases
stabbing her belly button. (Outie.)

Pimpo: Truly a catch. Greatness and pain. We COULD
BE ideal . . . when she stops reminding one of farsighted
ugly mathematics stumbling into chaos.

Carrie: A sticky demented end. Pair of nubiles. Measured
to a half cup against infinities.

Pimpo: We've always been a laughing people.

Carrie: Populace. Before this is over, you'll get close
enough to get good and scared of me.

Pimpo: A ham in the street.

Carrie: You wouldn't know a puddle nymph if she
trimmed your nose hairs.

Pimpo: You think you're an actress?

Carrie: You think I'm a whore.

Pimpo: You acting when you're with me?

Carrie: Easy to fool one who fingerpaints in isolation and
daily demands half-open yellow rosebuds.

Chapter 3

Slumming without a Dinner Jacket

WELCOME TO AVOCADO BLOSSOM FLESHPOTS INC. I'll be conducting the interview for Pimpo and Carrie. (Carrie has been promoted quickly from within.) We have clean working conditions, no drafty stalls. We don't accept schizophrenic hayseeds. If you find any we expect you to turn them in. We will take it from there. The girls call the rooms poky holes. We have a vocabulary sheet for you to study at your leisure. We want the new people off to a slow start. In the beginning, what you will entertain is leisure and study more than personages.

Love it like hammers myself but I'm slowing up in my dotage. I've had my dignity dunked a number of times . . . who hasn't? Nonchalance is the one character flaw which will not be tolerated here.

I saw your video *Another Strawberry Dustbin* and was impressed with your "snatch a hatchet and run" assimilation. Interesting techniques. In our small viewing audience, you blew off a silk jockstrap or two. Very clever. If hired, you would hob the knob of the elite. When you sign you get a rainbow like this. Every client you do gets recorded by a knot in your rainbow. Adds up quick. When it's full, you fly to Hawaii—expense paid.

You are aware that your aura will be read? On a daily basis? (Good, because I would be unable to proceed until you had been through that leg of orientation.) The color of your aura . . . let's see, it's yellow . . . tells me where to send you—your area of specification.

If you have any questions about transportation, you can set up an interview with my auntie, who is in charge of transportation. Don't let her put salt in your eyes. We must see clearly at all times.

In many respects we differ from other firms. We want clients' dusks reeking of you. "Avocado blossoms." Each girl has her own method. If the detectable odor remains and reminds, the customer returns. Olfactories. Statistics. We're on the cutting edge of pheromone research.

Do you have any personal opinions or reservations concerning what invades your hole? None? Then may I assume you perceive the act as I do. . . . Strawberry says, "What was left of his head?" OK. Let me jot your response. Was that "Relieve themselves of their heads?" OK. That's very good. Original.

Overtime? I confess overtime is funny. One girl lives on it, picking off-hours and making them work for her. She's built up a wonderful supply of regulars. Finding her with a john after hours is like (occupational humor) finding a Mormon in Salt Lake City.

Our condoms may look different, yes, like balloon skins, but the important thing is . . . they're not.

Now I have to ask you to write down your answer to this professional dilemma after I've laid down the ground rules pertaining to it: Your predicament involves a customer, a guy whose tail bends sometimes to the right and sometimes to the left. Here is the complication: he is a deliberately balding man, allowed by our house law (which you must obey without question) to screw and run without payment. He is a criminal, so to speak, who served time for slicing an abdomen, unrelated (the criminal and the abdomen) to our corporate family. This Joe has recently been bailed out and has the gall to come running back to you and say "One lady's internment is a condom's freedom." Then he remakes your face with a broken half of an olive oil bottle. . . . What do you make of that? Please write your answer. I'll ring this bell when your fifteen minutes is ended.

I'm the Sri Lankan narrator. You've already heard from me. Heard!—but were you listening? Before I get lost in somebody's shuffle, I'm going to get a few words IN. Just so

you know me! You weren't really interested in waiting
around for the applicant's answer. Were you? A little bit of
Carrie's family background is warranted here. A friend
misremembers Carrie's grandmother on her mother's
(Zenobia's) side:

XXXXXXXXXXXXXXXXXXXXXXXXXXXXX but no
OOOOOOOOOOOOOOOOOOOOOOOOOOOOOOOOOO

THE GLUTTON UNIVERSALLY HATED AND RELIED
UPON assumed vulgar "Thigpen" accepted the challenge
to "any woman" and plunged some thirty-five feet on a
trained horse into a pool. Assumption correct, Thigpen
had to sue to collect her fifty-dollar prize. A long-admitted
slut to fashion, she broke her chanting down into eight
unmusical sobs when the crowd jeered "Fashion Slut"—
then she froze. Then SHE threw tomatoes. "Because," she
admitted, "it didn't sound aimed at me." She had remained
single beyond her second youth. As the story goes, when
her decision was to marry, she would tell her Aunt Edith
first. Her noble and ignorant response: "Is it possible this
regally magnificent person is my niece?"

The authorities confronted her with the decision flow-
chart, she had admitted her copulation considerations.
Contemplation of copulation was the norm in such instances. She and her chosen mate had to answer to the best
of their ability: IS IT A FAST DAY? ARE YOU NAKED? ARE
YOU A GLUTTON? IS YOUR MATE A GLUTTON? If it's
not and you're not, you may be given consideration for the
go-ahead if you can follow this "surefire" procedure: No
strange positions. (Yes, you know what we mean.) No enjoy-
ment. Wash yourselves and urinate thoroughly before and
afterward.

The authorities had to be informed . . . a previous marriage? A dead previous wife? A dead wife, such as she was in
fact a wife, and she was in fact dead, did need to be proven.
The marriage, however, did not have to be dissolved. YOU,
SIR, ARE FREE TO MARRY THIGPEN.

Her dream was to be married by an Elvis look-alike. (Elvis
Calabano.) He looked like Omar K. with slightly slanted

eyes. Two shall be as one flesh. Say what? The married couple went behind the curtain and a little Yeats was heard by listening passersby. Her voice rang loud and clear, "Stop Yeatsing me." He stopped. We needed to hear little after that. For no one could tell where they would find WHAT they would find. It is safe for us to assume they gawp down the maw of a Zeus-like figure of near-mythical perfection on a fairly regular basis.

We tend to lose track of people like those two. Years later I was reminded when someone had a partial quote by Thigpen. How many Thigpens can there be? The Thigpen who lived on the wrong side of Downing? Who got ice cream from cows' udders on rainy cold days? Who knew all about life in the bunker in and out of wartime? Who had a best friend in Al Capone's father? I wondered does she still sit like Goethe at her own table? When all was affirmed and I was sure it was the same woman, I asked them to please continue the quote.

The acquaintance continued: "If you can't say anything good about someone, say it in a book." We knew she would be on the Manhattan circuit and earn her 14.5 minutes BASED ON THAT ALONE. Excepting her, we all moved forward in a backward way. She was one of the few who hadn't deceived her brain and her body by committing a mass of idiocies. No end of atrocious things. And yet she is excluded from that picture encaptioned "WAITING TO JUDGE THE 4H COMPETITION IN RABBIT SHOWMAN-SHIP." The name of her new (back then) political party? "Guts for Garters." Or is that their slogan? It had to do with streamlining every American kitchen. Much later I heard she married a no-good Oriental type and had a daughter named Zenobia. I realize there are different versions to same legend but in all practicality, where do you think she found a name like Zenobia?

Magic in a magical land as told by Fi Fi Fixabelles (who runs the overseas bureau):

Baby capitalist's proposition, "Call this unlisted number to be eaten in the privacy of the home of your choice. We'll call you Pooh Bear if you like." Less imaginative than a baby capitalist because he's the big brother of a major baby brother capitalist. A nicked-up chipped-up shoulder for not crying on. Hate 'em as a gender . . . not in singles or the necessary doubles.

Bit of all right loquacious parrot. I was his favorite for all of twelve minutes. Preposterously punctual only cause I live here. Window is open at six. F.U.N. shortly thereafter. Brat thinks he can call at six for an eight o'clock. This time my calf muscles break HIS heart! I'll just rip the savage another asshole.

Thumb in his mouth as close as he comes to an innocent question: "Why so many redheads?" As in red. Blonde to black root work is too difficult. Henna. Believes the clink of every quarter is the buck of some nubile red-haired Goatessa. Green light baby. Let's go. Metered. Toll road's through me.

Yeah. His mutual room is worn just like any placard. Placard sandwich fantasies. Sucks more snake venom than any sheriff. Sucks more bullet than any cop. Le petite capitalist in all-consuming knowledge of two positions:

A) Drinking . . . he has the mouth for it.

B) Pre-dawn vertical insertion . . . we two have necessary rocketry. Tool to a no-strings release is a dirty crystal ball.

Am born. Beaten begun at some no doubt famous point. Working moments of rooms. Born to work rooms. Lucky to work rooms. Thumbsucker likes 'em with rubber dresses, stormer boots and G.I. Joe dolls. We play Ken and Barbie. Thumbsucker likes us. Thumbsucker likes US in rubber dresses. Concentration's the thing. On anything but the head of a pin. HAPPENED LIKE THAT TO ME ONCE—IN A VICTORIAN S.M.U.T. novel. Rode. Look no hands. Royal "wee wees" won't care for the hot pepper mixes or brand new colors. Saint Vitus part of both of us. Green teeth are my second spiritual inheritance. And don't ask me like everybody else when black teeth will be my third.

Last one groans: "How's the old vagina?" "YOUR JOB TO
TELL ME," says I. Ten trillion elated night crawlers. One
size fit all for years. Walls of Jericho. Raising of the razed.
Baby capitalist spoiler left over from the last good catering
job. Bouncing results of domestic thunders. Domestic
thunders send me napping. Capitalists remind me of my ad
campaign. My boy the capitalist. So raunched. Sees his parents happy and fast-headed to maximum security twilight
homes. So you're helping me with my advertising. Subur-
ban dentistries juxtaposed somehow, with poets' wives pos-
ing for Liberty dimes. Rewarding. Like delusions of being
filmed.

Light-sensitive Latrine Luissanne gets half. BLOODY
HALF. I don't care if it's counted out in praise-the-buffalo-
head nickels. She's a real nicks in the wood gal who added
what amounts to the mayo. on the chick. sal. sand. She
shook it. He bought it.

My beef? I wish she'd refrain from rippin' her head open
every ten minutes for all to see. Bit dulolly. Her big moral
question is mine . . . whether or no civility is the best MosT
eXpeDIeNt lubricant. What IRKS to no avail and all hell
out of me is the mistake on her left cheek for everyone to
see.

How can I honestly care where she gets the stuff? . . .
Long as she does her work. "Equal Pay" is my confirmation
name. The one I picked.

She claims there's less work if the undies are metallic:
"Less like wrestling naked." The fur pocket on her purse is
not for nothing. Cluck dolls drop like flies. Evil-eye-fingers-
crossed-hootchigootchee works for her. I plain don't care
how she does it but the girl's *requested*. I REPEAT "HALF
THE NICKELS" for much more than half the work.

All the baby capitalists think they dreamed her. She invented spaghetti wrestling for couples. Forget the vermin-
filled walls. Dream pies filled with Latrine Luissanne and Fi
Fi Fixabelles. Get Luissanne a well-froze vodka.

Was a runaway scullion in Grand Central. Rhapsodizing
weak-kneed on the subject of motherhood within five.

(Adolfina.) Rabbiting the underdog the whole turnip-picking time. Oh well. Tramps about like the rest of us except for her inexplicable hubcap hat and her mudfish google eyes of "storybook renown" as she tells it. I have to chortle chortle at her any drop of a hubcap cap BLASPHEMING. She's out with "gracious kingdom," and I think, if there's a God he surely dotes on her for that. And especially for the hubcap cap. But I wish she'd zip that yawp of hers.

Don't you just bust a gut to picture her FAST-MARRIED? Rumor never could keep a secret. The "Austro-Hungarian" groom is always in the Alps with Italian terrorists. One month of CONNUBIAL WHATNOT and she bleeped, "I feel like an imbecile married to a moron." The necro did it to her from the bottom up. "Praise backwards!" Like a corpse. I told her to rip him another asshole. He spoke Bislama—le langue de le sea slug. He's a story in himself. Right. Mr. Media Sensation. Oh you mean the time he set himself afire backyard of the White House at the CIA cookout? Set himself afire. Miss ah excuse, *MRS.* Latrine's calming response was: "Funny. He never did anything like that before."

Since Adolfina went to live with Ludmilla, I'm delegated KEEPER OF THE PETS. One hundred twenty-three baby chicks in a wire cage. Cluck dolls dropping like droppings. Give Luissanne the last Bronx cheer. She's an "asked after" desired place to be. Not for witchcraft alone. The job happens to fire some up. She'll be ready when you call. Hubby's recuperating in their loft deaccentuating busy bee hot pillow furrows and writing bathroom sink novels. Oh and I want business cards for my girls plus one for Adolfina. Of course we're international. What do you think I've been talking about?

Back to our adverts:

Convenient to the best shopping. A cheerful step away from mankind-captivity. Visit us on blatantly banker plastic . . . or corporate plastic while your wife's around the corner carmine-staining her nails. Great perks such as ICED PEPTO-BISMAL for better days after. HERE manly captives take a full minute to blurb back.

ABOUT ME? Fi Fi Fixabelles? Not much to tell. The belly rub's all I'll ever be about. A lifer. You kind of look . . . weren't you one . . . beaten begun at the same bulldozed point? It was minutes before the wives of all the husbands started to look like me? Your brother then? His tendency was to put a girl down like a picked-over tray of food. He was one of the strong ones. . . .

Chapter 4

We Poor Plebes

LET'S TALK WITH TWO OF CARRIE'S WORKFELLOWS.
Queenie (one): My incessant screwing is a whoompf and a groan. Whoompf and groan painless to automaton. What is your incessant screwing? Asses no doubt tattooed with no name numbers. Blatantly bankers as you call them think us smalltown. Leftbrained and a performing company. Think us. Think us. Heirs to great honesty. I'm a company woman. Traveling. Last Supper practically performs itself. Every night. Several times a day. Parody with as many extras as casting sees fit. Gallimaufry actors. Family. The family that goes to the dogs together is a PLEASURE SEEKS troupe only momentarily civilized by $$$$$$$$$$$$$$. "PLEASURE SEEKS" synchronize atomic clocks. "PLEASURE SEEKS" display goldembossed trimmin' o' women invites. Buying power. Timelocked red uniforms. Street fashions full of meaningfuls. Point-fiver alarm wardrobes are riots of red. REDWANTERS work gray pinstriped and meaningless so as to shoot us full of meaningfuls.

Outside the Grand Hotel, sorority-house tension is adventure for comingled self-absorbed byproducts hitting the avenues. Blatantly bankers smothered to off-color are just up from "what's nice." My specialty is the easy way up and down more or less the same sTaiRs. Whittler is a whittler into plastic art. Largest totem LOOMING intimidates blatantly bankers' KiNcH. Looming tricks a treat to different doorways. Hearthsides. Freudful psychographics ring doorbells places no one wants to live. LOCATION LOCATION LOCATION. Alltombing wombs and wombing tombs mean close the window already. My fear is chafing chains. Fear forced on large or small white walls. Old chum KiNcH. Old chum Totem. TOTEM. Totem reappearance relief. AHHHH. Red Egypt still down the block where liquid libations raise a

billy stiff and to extinction. Toast any slowblood's occasion.
Totems well up the failed ups. Into army cots. Like chit
chats. Well up dimestore endings. Drink plenty of liquids.

Her young friend (two) said: Let me tell you about our fair
city of Alarcon. Stars end the spires of our churches. Tom-
toms serenade us night and day. We are this far away (fingers inches apart) from the hour and the day of heaven and
fairy tales. The Castle you will love to visit is here within the
city walls. It overhangs "The River Formaldehyde." All the
windows of all the houses glitter in the sunlight while the
glass in the Castle is a shimmering diamond. Take the back
door off its hinges then I'll welcome you to your new life of
back-door-routes success. Easier route less taken. Don't
latch onto the modern for modernity's sake.
    Alarcon is where I ended up. Easy to count hides. My se-
cret is I am borderline retarded after accelerated crashes.
What fills a skull and bones. In an unusual sense, I'm a
product of the television generation. There was a show
aimed at matching hard-to-place children with suitable
adoptive parents. Folks involve a child with some form of
play for the viewing audience. The pet shop goes over big
in this instance. The interview shows the best the child has
to offer; see how nice the kid doesn't chew the ear off the
live bunny etc., then the phone rings, off the hook.
Framtidslandet. Swedish for "Land of the Future." You
don't need me to tell you all kinds of sickos watch TV.
    In my particular case, all responsible people involved
hoped the adoption home would not resort to this last television step. Cry for help at the eleventh hour. Had to do it
finally. Last resort. I was thirteen and a little sexpot. No tak-
ers until the weirdo. Man of affairs. Immune from accusa-
tions pertaining to his moral misconduct, he passed a lie-
detector test with flying colors. Got me. No haunting
attraction or parental abilities necessary—just the boob
tube and a phone. Little imagination needed to predict
what was going to happen to me when I left the home with

that man. It did happen. Such a cliché by now. Like the little Roman princess led off for rape by her executioner.

The involvement was cock talk pulled from Truck Joe's box of railroad slang. I shivered while he pounded. Sex is costly when you're paying.

You know how these days they're talking about Guam or some place taken over by snakes? Mildly poisonous snakes have been found 'round bawling infants, the critters mouths lock on an appendage in an unsuccessful attempt to swallow whole the babes? Snakes remind me of the snake him. Can't slay a virgin. Read what he carved on my chest. (Looks like illiterate scrawl.)

On his way to bed needing a slap and tickle he'd "excite" me talking "laid to rust." "Excite" a thirteen year old? Word games saved me—removed me from my situation.

My sustaining desire was to reduce the English language to its necessary components. I reduced it to two sentences that sum up the entire American language:

1) Good luck scratches through your underwear.

and

2) The American people never forgave Rudyard Kipling for not dying in New York.

When I ran out of things to occupy my mind, I went in for suicide fuchsia hedge style. Bought that bestseller. Tried starvation but, clad in polyester glad rags, he fed me intravenously. I'm a hard stick and he fancied poking me with needles. ALL IN FAVOR OF BURYING YOURSELVES ALIVE! Tried to get me to do awful things to him all the while calling me Saucy Black Angel. When I wouldn't, he'd say, "But you considered it so you will be punished for contemplation alone." Posturing Pig. During punishments I wished I HAD done the things. Swore I would not be turned into a demon by this man. What a blurred-at-the-edges wonk.

One day, just outside his house upon the overhang rock, worried about my skin freckling, he ran for silken awnings to protect me. Freeze-dried moons. The ensuing day the bastard busied himself branding me with dull kitchen utensils (ejaculating his poisons all the while) like a slitherer. My orders are to call him "My sweet Muscovite" or "My rousing Cossack."

Tells me his original plan (to adopt then murder) has been mitigated into a marriage plan by circumstances beyond his control. Plan B. Cheap Mother-Fuck-Agent-of-Contagion adopts me one year wants to marry me the next. What am I, his mountain cousin? Miserably bad at it. Yodeling folk for Moses in horned helmets? Here for his comfort, his continuity and communion? Here for his emaciated feet and hands. I used to pray his zeppelin would explode over Vienna. Hard-core hate trip.

In his soggy mental game, his name was Lucius Norbanus Bulbus. Meat Man, charmer and rake. I became the three Caligula sisters. It was up to him which of the three personalities I was permitted to be and when. Merely two aspects of his own personality shone because the schemes: 1) conceived by a madman—were 2) executed by a fool. "Secrets of the Deep Roman Orgy" were his favorites. I don't know if he watched public television or read a book once, but this was his wicked penchant. Calling. He sacrificed flamingos to the gods so we would be blessed with a child. A man willing to settle for love. Fertility rites. I had to drink the blood. Tribal. I was similarly occupied flinging filth instead of eating everything from my cut-up plate. That paleface milk thought I was finally getting into his debauchery. Figured I'd be happy to hear (straight from his *How To . . . Roman Orgy Book*) what he expected our suckling babes to do to his cock.

My regret is I got out of this warm familial arrangement without a particular piece of him broken off into my hand. Can't say I didn't try. Partridge and sausage sauce if you know what I mean. Long hard shuffle to the car for him but I got away and he never caught me. Gotta get away . . . can't buy a ticket? Steal one. To steal is to own. Last brass taste. Stole away from Monkeyland. I figure it cost him at least seven milking cows.

You start thinking of yourself in terms of a half-crabbed

disemboweled abortion's sexual gratification and that stays with you. He was an abortion. Incidents prevent my returning and finishing him off. Can you see snipers in French Lick firing at the cretin? What would The Bird think? All I could do was more of the same but different. Alarcon, close enough to the big city derives benefit from a big-city clientele. Take. Make. Then rot. Shadow of a different fear.

Pimpo's OK. Carrie carries her batik sunbrella and teaches. Physical gesturing is encouraged and that helps. Things are looking up. No bones of contention. Just boners. Scattered parts.

Recently I read up on depraved Mr. Bulbus when he came before Cook County Judge Bean. This time Fuck-face tried to adopt a young boy. Told the adoption people I was away at school. My carping age. It was the where and when of it didn't match up for the authorities. Uncertain customers. Don't be surprised they gave the boy to him anyway. After an exciting pre-adoption weekend the boy accused him of trying indecent tub-learnt things. Couldn't paint a stache on Jesus Knabe. Sex got away from the great citizen brought low. I have to say we citizens of probity and restraint are shocked and amazed when any amount of justice is done.

Carrie encouraged me to write it all down. Especially the part where his sickness abated into sissified involvements such as quilting—his all-time model was an antique Virginia reel quilt. She was laughing and screaming bloody murder when I told her about his painting entitled *Pig on a Whitewashed Pile of Buffalo Bones.*

Carrie likes my past peculiar tense. When I had trouble ending my paragraphs, she gave me a writing tip: "If at a particular moment in your writing you can flush a toilet, end the paragraph there."

I'm skillful as the next guy at repulsive love for gelt. A long day of ravaging and wildly slaying the pissed and whipped land into deification makes me want to drink liquid from a felt-tipped pen. We aren't ALL to die victims of mass imagination.

I'll never forgive him. War is a great possibility. He's stuff to fill a graveyard. Wrathful or no, it's God's job to forgive types like that. Not mine. Mine to hate 'em.

Chapter Five

They Lived on a Planet Scarcely Bigger Than Themselves

A GLIMPSE AT CARRIE'S IMMEDIATE FAMILY:
From Your Dad My Dearest Carrie, With Love:
"Carrie, you are in the hands of the Philistines, where eponymous Saint Valentine worked the land where lemon trees bloom and fish without hair and feathers are eaten and dammit, I sent you there.

"I'm sorry. Devotedly, professionally disappointed, bony knock-kneed Dad. And remember—don't ever feel like your entire generation has arrived onstage about five minutes after the audience walked out. Don't ever feel like one of many cherished, petted courtiers. After you try to tell the truth long enough, you'll be a cynic and you STILL won't be telling the truth. . . . Don't try to communicate . . . mere sixties hogwash. The true beginning of happiness is less communication. Benign neglect."

My unusually nosey dad (Squeaky adopted the three of us), Carrie innocently explained, might remind you of George Bush, if either were alive. His story can be summed up in a train ride Squeaky Meeber once took. Said to a fellow passenger Hitchcock: "What's that package up there in the baggage rack?"

"Oh, that's a Mackintosh," the other answers, turning to wink at Hitchcock (no laugh there).

"What's a Mackintosh?" asked innocent Squeaky.

"An apparatus for trapping possums in the Scottish Highlands."

(*Abashed:*) "But there are no possums in the Scottish Highlands."

"Well, then, that's no Mackintosh." Hitchcock smiled to himself, relishing previous knowledge. Incidentally, he got the scene on film.

Since that incident, his "epiphanic moment," my dad goes around with quizzes for everyone. Puts his own statistics together based on similar queries. Example: "This one is for all you genetically engineered orgasms out there. Hippie or a Digger? I can tell by your food preference—choose one for the psychological study. Pâte in a drum or pigmy chickens in a shoe box? Think carefully about your answer and I'll get back to you soon as your dust settles."

Carrie lost track of Squeaky for years, then, pointing to the most important box in the history of the world, Carrie announced, "This morning, I turned on the TV, in search of weather, whereon I beheld written in bold white words— the weather. The weather show's background, for something completely different, was LIVE FROM THE ZOO. Monkeys in the zoo. Monkeys mating in a tree to be exact. Then whose voice do I hear?"

My father's distinct voice in the background: "The guy in charge of such filming used to write for the *Jersey Shore Herald*. MY particular expertise comes from freelancing out of Puerto Rico for a bowling magazine. As a fully realized man, I say, with uncharacteristic self-absorbed verbosity: Any charismatic person conscious of his own mythic potency and the value of undemanding SUPERMAN OR SPIDERMAN SEX, awakens a basic hunger in women and pays reverence to it at harmonious and inappropriate sonic levels. Call it charisma. Call it Canadian. Some see it for the dread disease it is. Do a twelve-minute drum solo here. Let's blame this on obesity and blame this obesity on old-fashioned gluttony and sloth. Think of these as sadder fatter years. Just finishing the job of destroying myself. Strangers won't believe this all happened in a town where people still work for a living. Grandma's over there dripping beefsteak all over her running shoes."

"That's my dad," Carrie said. "I needed to talk to him so I phoned the station."

Carrie: I care about you just like I care about your shirts.

You need shirts. So what if my INAPPROPRIATE reaction is to straighten a stranger's tie?

Dad: I hate to say it, but he could have sent his suit that night. I'm always asking myself that unmusical question, "IS THIS THE YEAR WE GET SOME KOOK?"

Zenobia: Then I ask myself that musical question, "THIS IS THE YEAR WE GET SOME KOOK."

Dad: Troglodytic lunacies. I'm afraid you're always right.

Zenobia: Some kook who looks presentable yet inappropriate as Mrs. Selma Schubert in a yellow dress trapping butterflies under glass . . . then BORN AGAIN HARD. If not this year . . .

Carrie: The one who bothered me the most was the socialite. Officer in the Knickerbocker Grays and card-carrying member of the "Children of the American Revolution."

Dad: That's what you get for living in the South.

Carrie: On the South Side of Chicago.

Zenobia: She called him Ambassador. Protocol. He never had a neighboring country of his own. She pretended he would never leave her side.

Dad: I wasn't there for her . . . forever on the verge of other employment.

Carrie: Was she his meat for the moment?

Dad: She was deep and throaty-voiced and he became even more stiff-pricked at the visuals. Maybe next! Carrie have you been listening to a word your dear father, beloved of all fathers, has been saying to you?

Me: Yeah, Dad. How did Mom get on the party line?

Dad: She's entitled.

Zenobia: I had become a tough little animal. He wanted me to promise "never to unman any man."

Carrie: Resulting in her beautiful body being manhandled and beaten. The Tossing Of Trinkets Will Leave Us With Zero Defects. Throwing them will strengthen the upper arms.

Zenobia: You need that physicality in your life. Your guarantee is a lovely burial . . . my little Soldier of Fortune. Come to Mama. All quiet on the Western lice-infested front.

Dad: Bammy-Lamb, it is my not unhealthy desire to murder (your grandfather's) culture. Call me Holy Lord, Gentle Glory, His Eloquence, His Compassion, Learned Defender of the Faith, but don't ever call me "Ocean of Wisdom." And I superbly quote: "reifying the material with an analeptic bulimia of quaquaversal literary, psychological, political, physiological, sociological, and culinary references in a flow of finely ordered dialogue. . . ." Then just as reliably, I unquote . . . in order to get on with a life of ordinary enough toughs.

Carrie: Where do you get this stuff, Dad? Tell me on our way to Club Fuck.

Dad: The present era is rampant with five forms of degeneration, the erotic fiascoes, in particular. Destruction and renewal are intoxicating. Air and light exhilarate.

Carrie: But don't listen to me, pass the cappuccino. My grandfather, born on the same day as myself, forty years previous (the day of the Louisiana Swine Festival), finds meaning in HIS life.

Dad: May he fall unconscious into the lap of a eunuch.

Zenobia: A good eunuch is hard to find. Who are we to say?

Dad: Hair farmers?

Carrie: Yeah. They mosh good. Here comes the guy . . . does he really know all the songs?

Dad: Felt it his duty to learn them ever since his fans started to look like him.

Carrie: Isn't there one member of our family who has been the subject of varied publicity lately?

Dad: We're checking for any relation to me. I know who you're talking about. He's one of "The Munificent Men and their Flying Latrines." His avocation is to set afire and hurl porcelain toilets soaked in gasoline good distances at high speeds. Same last name.

Carrie: If he IS related, you want to get him for Grandpop's band?

Dad: Exactly. So long as you stay away from any ethnic derivative of two "emotional" races.

Carrie: Where did Mom go?

Dad: Speaking of emotional races, we lost your mother AGAIN?

Zenobia (*purposely, philosophically distancing herself from the other two*) says (*mouthing both parts*): Like the old Russian adage:

Z: I caught a bear.

Dad: Bring him here,

Z: He won't go.

Dad: Then come yourself.

Z: Won't let me go.

Carrie interacts with her brother Nick George (literal translation of George is "Plow the Earth") Adams. Bro, who is the prime minister of the County of Nogs, is in the midst of directing Carrie's latest artistic piece.

Bro: She's one of those girls carrying a Japanese black box instead of a regular lunch of skinned cats and dogs . . . so there's a lack of nutrition at the onset. I don't like the hair dyed again or the powdered vampire face. Carrie, dear, our lines are not irretrievably broken.

(*In response to his producer:*) Her total outfit? I simply refuse to comment on that. L'oeil Espiegle. Working herself up to a truly Shakespearean flaw. Abracadabra. Reference to not being cross-eyed several times in her life.

(*To Carrie about her character:*) Billy pain so sweet. Tree does wet her up. The brachet stopped pushing wood for a moment. She climbed atop the wheelbarrow and said "LOVE AT THE WHEELBARROW. LOVE ATE THE WHEELBARROW. Now Standing On Same Wheelbarrow Before You, I Bring Forth The Doubleness."

An actress heard but not seen: "Tired (*in a Southern accent*) of such occultation of the heart?"

Space for answering . . .

Bro: Precisely because. That goes for the doubleness and that goes for occultation. A plenitude of biscuits and wine. Who's picking nits?

Narrator: The green thing brought once again into realistic focus. Focus of a woman with pursed lips. In moments of stress. White wrinkles. Old lady pops out for a look around. Brandishing old lady's props. Poetry and the juice man. Supertruth laughs. (The narrator, who is none other than myself, is omniscient because that's the only kind who will have anything to do with Bro.)

Bro: Carrie, when you leave the green think of the symbolics. Lessons too obviously learned the hard way. Don't miss it. Not any. Cranking need to know the time more often. Get to know the characters. Consider you've made it when your next-door neighbor's pet's shrink has his own agent.

Carrie (*rehearsing in a monotone*): Distancers marrying distancers begetting voids. Solitary intelligence in involuntary swim.

Bro: Your favorite song is "Turkey in the Straw." You are one of the unidentifiable girlfriends masquerading as wife. If the plane goes down, your dental records mismatch that of the genuine wife who thrives in Muskegon. To his chagrin. Eventually? All in good time? Think about the mistress living in Peoria eating exotic fruits from California. One whose brain is "una función electrica." She has bleached-out hair and an old-fashioned hairstyle. She's the first to admit having gone to a welfare dentist so the records of her teeth show a lot more work than was ever done. "Voids" are the subject of another future treatise. Trotskyites falling out of trees don't quite cut it. Think.

Carrie (*rehearsing*): LET'S GET THIS PERFECTLY STRAIGHT: ONE MUST HAVE CHAOS IN ONESELF TO GIVE BIRTH TO ADVANCING STARS. This man, if man he is. Then my reply, "This God, if God he is." Zeal and spleen.

Bro: She didn't find cleanliness inconvenient. In your full-flavored Southern accent, YOU TALKING ABOUT MY BODY? MY STINKING BADGE OF PIETY?

Carrie: My final response didn't capture the disgust.

Bro: "Your ablative excesses." Your shirt should be dirtier if you're honest. Where on earth do you think you're going?

Carrie leaves her "brother/guardian" alone in his agitated state to figure it out for himself. She walks to the drugstore where a strange man (Interloper) has some kind of staring game at her.

Brother searches the script to see if and where "going to the pharmacy" is indicated.

Carrie: I'm in the drugstore to purchase a product which will allow the insect carcasses to die and fall off my body and this slug (Interloper) is figuring how to get MY panty hose over his head. I answer his queries in ladylike response: "Want insect carcasses hanging from your private parts? Dick? What you'll get from me Dick." Stand aside, this is the thing called higher-level shopping, something to experience only as we forever leave this drugstore.   •

Narrator: (If we ever leave this drugstore.) In transcendence of life's conditions, attack them in their self respect, resent that stinking love of theirs. The stench is fearful. Resent it even more. Yes. Yes. But maybe no. The thing disfigured. A thousand years without a bath—oh but of course we're not talking Middle Ages.

Carrie: I may be a Caloosa Clogger but whenever they ask me what I do in my spare time, I have to say I read my own diaries. Pyrogravure. The ladylike bird I most resemble is the egret. Known to play in the sugar . . . the reason I admire a carnelian honey bowl. The lapis lazuli one is butter-filled. How much mammalian excreta did that particular recipe (per pound) require?

Bro (*working still*): What one is reminded of is so minuscule, so earthshattering, and such a lie to the person now reading it, as if God had created a brand new person to inhabit the body of the long dead one; man with a hoe and a breakfast of two tomato mayonnaise sandwiches and a yawn. Convenient how the new person has little acknowledgment of the old . . . as if we too are so high up in the nosebleeds with the cheapest of tickets . . . the great unwashable peeping at couples engrossed in spaghetti wrestling. Like purchases bought so dearly.

Narrator: No. I won't be the lonely sicko who passed water in a bathroom down the hall, out of earshot. Strigil me clean.

Bro: Accelerating history as pressure accelerates water. Freebooter. Very fast. Dropped zip zip. Weighted lightning breaks through this paperweight . . . which reminds me . . . if the wrong color cock is in the wrong orifice of the wrong sex, we are up in arms but what about God's cock? Try and tell me it's not a cock. Try and make like it's God's vagina. Who are you, snacking on swamp cabbage, kidding? Clears the head. Ask yourself four times a day. When asked a question answer "Cuz." Be like me in my query: "What's the entertainment of any bodily appendage?" Ask yourself every day then ask yourself four times a day.

The Narrator who is dressed as Bro dressed as the pharmacist, working in same pharmacy has much to say: "One time a very long time ago, a stranger came to be sorry he accosted my kin. She looked like such a nice girl."

Thinking the pharmacist was her brother, Carrie responded with something like: "You know that sick sixties green enjoying popularity again? That is your color green with black background in an East European brocade. Your suit coat and fez-shaped poll cover. Pillbox hat out of same. Yep. The very taupe hammered-pique-and-organza shift with the scoop neck and drop waist you have been seeking, I bought for $38.95. Your favorite game—the beast with two backs. Entering with you into your wine in fashion. A thing not at all against nature."

Interloper: Hmm. A pretty wench with a good mug on her, sucks it. Stuck to suck to the substantive marrow of our narrow bone. Certain to be descended from certain chambermaids.

Bro (*still at the studio*): Carrie is a slipshod piece of cloud who gave an onion peel when they asked "How much for this man?" Seemed more than satisfied with the exchange at the time.

Carrie (*still believing she's talking with her brother dressed as a pharmacist*): The dirty part the cook couldn't even throw in the pot of soup. Contumely. Muddy soups . . . what the man wore. And the fish was good. Yummie. So I asked, "What do you call this fish?" They answered, "Jimmy." Swore to the Greek gods and all the plainclothes firemen at the fire station on East Mountain, "Never again!"

Narrator: So you find another example of a silly woman thinking whatever she wants is hers. Not my kin Jimmy the Fish. Asked for no pity everywhere. Got no pity at home. Asked for no pity at home. Got no pity everywhere else.

The stranger with Carrie in the drugstore (Interloper): Look lady, I just thought you might want to go out for a beer sometime. I usually don't try to pick up ladies in THIS section of the drugstore (anti-fungal and lice-ridding), but you are cute and I'm happy in an argument when the other is in opposition to the point of perfection. THEN I must totally agree that WAS my point exactly, when in actuality it was your point.

Carrie: Human nature changed in 1910.

Interloper: I vehemently disagree with you and say that human nature changed two years earlier in precisely 1908. When we were wee, we played this game in which we were children of eminent Victorian intellectuals. Such fun I don't recall having, in this decade anyway. Mot triste. A poem with actual sounds. The hardcover edition is in a book covered with hairy cowhide. Like that hairy place below your belly. Your friends thought you were home when in actuality you'd come in to see if anything needed ironing and your presence reassured them. If there were any questions on Burroughs, why I was there and made quite a good showing. Stopped the laughter and turned it into horror. Live like a bourgeois and think like a demigod.

C: Are you a white-lips writer too?

Man: Yes (so I can bring it up), I'll pretend it reminds me of the time watching Turkish television. Turkey's cuddliest creature, who looks a bit like Rushdie, lies decoratively in the background, then jumps to his knees, rolls almost imperceptibly forward, and sinks his fang into the famous cook's Albanian leg. The song dissolves in a shriek. This is all between sips of the house drink which tasted like ouzo to me. When I asked if the fish was fresh, I was shown the still-pumping heart.

(Pharmacist strips off the pharmaceutical garb to reveal himself as noneother than Bro.)

Carrie: Gadzooks!

Narrator: Fish can't get any fresher than that! Telling stories is always a political act. The orgasm behind the orgasm. Instead of being amazed and leaving what I found, I'll stick it in my backpack. You wouldn't want me to forget certain things. My desire is to disfigure other things . . . mostly the easily recognized, thereby acknowledging it a truly amazing thing.

Bro comes running in saying: "Sis, get back to the studio." (Looked like Bro.)

(This "Bro" rips off his second skin to reveal himself as Narrator, who is in fact bodiless.)

Narrator: THE THING DISFIGURED. I digress. Too.

Carrie: I know you want to be all things to everyone but don't you have enough work being omniscient?

Narrator: A workaholic's wet dream.

Carrie: It's getting old. I'm going to tell you a true story about my life and I hope it helps you. The problem with these last few pages is . . . there doesn't seem to be much truth or anyone willing to get on track. I can make excuses like we're acting now . . . but hear me out. Many years ago, a man I never knew how much I cared about, but who loved me in the most extraordinary way, made me realize what true love will and won't allow.

Narrator: Spare me.

Carrie: He wanted to see me the time I was laid up in the hospital for so long. They wouldn't let him in. So he wooed and married my nurse all in a matter of days. Into my room he'd creep. I was delirious. Yet I knew someone loved me. I recovered. His life has been screwed up ever since and probably even before that—but he gave me back my life.

Narrator: Wants you to believe that. These people are not even the slightest bit fuckable.

Zenobia at Carrie's:

Zenobia: I'm glad you're finally off the phone. Doped and buttoned. You're lucky I have no expectations left for you. My charms? I don't know what it is to be an actress anymore. The sanity level isn't there for me. At this age anyway. When one is a talker . . . there are so many you don't want to be stuck with, seen next to, or across the table from . . . one loses the desire to be involved in the same old proverbial word exchange. When I DID act, I left 'em somewhere between laughter and tears. In life . . . find me poised there. Until I'm bored with it, yes. Then I'm off the wall over the top. Ankles just a little too sexy. Too private. I'd have to say brilliant elbows and long arms. Play up your best features.

Carrie: Your laugh.

Zenobia: My laugh? The insane scream-laugh. We're machinists shaving off the last ten-thousandth of an inch. No one ever said your mother wasn't hip. You know how calculating it looks when your daughter is so accurate about her age—especially in this profession.

Carrie: Hip self-parody.

Zenobia: Remember when we were filming in Scranton, we advertised for someone with "Scranton written all OVER his face?" Look what I found—a picture of an applicant who plastered the name of the town on his forehead and shaved it into his scalp.

Carrie: A picture memento to cherish.

Zenobia: Try to remember (*with a touch of dignity*), we're selling body parts here. Like stylized food, body parts have to be displayed. Body parts to the front. See and sell. If you're the prettiest girl in the class, who's gonna know it? Your mother? That won't even do me a BIT of good. I don't mind telling you, a lot of this was lost on me. I'm only now catching on. But you will have had a mother in the business. Lucky girl. It'll save you twenty years finding out for yourself. Some things haven't changed that much. You are the subject of desire who should not allow herself to be prey. You cut your god-damned mass of hair so you would HAVE to be "personality" or maybe "talent." Best feature . . . shit!

You remind me of your father when you make it hard on yourself! You entrapped with your blue-black mass of hair dyed realistically auburn and after vows—snip snip. Shit! That's why your husband split . . . could no longer recognize his wife.

Carrie: That's ridiculous.

Zenobia: Fear of what you might become pushes you to the brink of some resolve. Cute the way it sticks up in the air . . . what's underneath? In the computer? (*With this Zenobia points to her head the same spot she saves for knocking wood.*) I feel sorry for you because you never had a female companion warning you not to stare fulsome into a man's eyes. You would do it anyway; first, to see if it really worked, second, to see if it works ALL the time. Unshakable habit by now. A good friend of mine told me to just stare big-eyed into them. Ask a woman (indirect compliment) how she gets men (strokes) and she'll (flattered) tell you.

Carrie: Indirect compliment then strokes. Gotcha.

Zenobia: Don't forget that aspect. You are a mighty tight squeeze. So take this jockstrap and put it on. You have to wear it over your breasts. We'll figure out a way to get the most concealment possible. We cover the rest of you with green slime. It's actually got avocado, lots of vitamin E. Then you push this book cart half-filled with books but mostly with body parts through the crowd and onto the stage. Help me get this off.

Carrie: Do this . . . to . . . it. Turn it. Unstuckness. Precision in the procession.

Zenobia: Wait, honey. I'm trying to understand it AS I'm reading it. I'm not sure . . . if fear touches you or the chainsaw touches you . . . oh . . . it's the fear. Fear caused by the chainsaw ripples through the crowd until you feel it too. Is that so terrible? The actors are not in danger. The audience is. They won't let anyone in unless they're agile. Fast and lucky, if you ask me. Sounds like the perfect performance for New Jerseyites. They don't read the notices though. Then you have to take your jockstrap off. And get in the tank. They'll throw cut-up body parts at you. You'll

like it. This is where you get imaginative with the meat. You
don't save any of it to make a coat or anything.

Carrie: MOTHER!

Zenobia: Don't Mother me. You wanted this career. I
wouldn't have you risk "cosmetic skin" for any part. Think
submission. What I find most unpleasant is the mouthful of
gizzards you have to spit at someone in the audience . . . not
anyone you immediately dislike, but someone who won't
retaliate in any way. Elephant innards were cheaper so we
went with them. Not an easy transport in our Coleman
cooler. All you have to say over and over again, with blood
dripping down your face, is "Bucky balls." You do that for
half an hour max. It is hardly scatological. I'll let you read
yourself what comes after. Think about the needs of your
audience . . . an audience interested only in your failure.
Stories of failure go over. Any success involved—let it be
theirs. Reward their ability to pick a good show. Begging
back for more. I won't be able to coach you forever, you
know. Hmmmnnn. . . . Then you dress like an Englishwoman in the countryside. Cashmere cardigan and pearls,
you find yourself seated at the breakfast nook with all your
finest handed-down silver. You read the paper seeing the ad
for customized canine toupees between $35.00 and $150.00
(a range wide enough to be inclusive) and you say, "They're
out of Tokyo where dogs lead very stressful lives, resulting
in hair loss. This, apparently, will be the case on our own
continent more and more." Your husband enters played by
Rupert Ames and says, "So it could be time to open up a
franchise. Franchises have yoga lessons for the dogs in the
back rooms. A dog deli in the middle. . . ."

Carrie: Japanese ideas.

Zenobia: Don't look at me cross-eyed, young lady. We've
been affiliated with worse than the Japanese. I've been affiliated with your father for Pete's sake—"The Manass
Mauler." Don't forget your name was Dusseldorf when you
were born. After that you're supposed to say the only out-
door game you play is dominoes.

Carrie: Result of a good upbringing.

Zenobia: You don't have THAT cross to bear.

Carrie: Which?

Zenobia: A good upbringing. It says here, at the end of the performance, you detach your mind from accepting a humdrum succession of moments then magic ensues. In other words get over the CULT OF THE HOME. It's an inaccurate concept. So is family. Time for you to get clear-headed and repeat MY life. Exactly. Step by step. If you regret the monkeys then forget about them. It's bad for your posture. All the frowning makes you look older. How old do you want to make me?

Carrie: An old decrepit woman.

Zenobia: All I need. If you feel dejected, think of the house we'll build from dead neon and brick. Nature's no compensation for our bestiality. Cover the beast in a beautiful home. Then appear on the beach as Raggedy Ann if you like, though personally, I find that unpardonable.

Carrie: That's not bestiality.

Zenobia: Then Fauvism. I'm a woman of stout heart throwing it up for discussion. I don't leave the ground early like you. Learned a great many things in order to abandon them, thank you.

Carrie: I'm keeping my eye on the horizon. "Lineness."

Zenobia: Don't let your ego isolate you in the name of protection. Remember when you're acting, make yourself perfect then paint it, then describe the painting . . . circle warily around the audience until you feel the loneliness go away. . . that singular idea arising in the crowd; the idea of befriending your character. . . . Oh. The time! I have a decorating job after this. I'm leaving shortly.

Carrie: For whom?

Zenobia: An Englishwoman whose husband left her. She wants no reminders. He bid farewell to no one, left her half the money in the bank accounts, dressed for a day of butterfly-catching—and was gone . . . what came to be forever.

Carrie: Put it all behind him, eh?

Zenobia: No hitches in his giddyap. He's been to my nightclub several times (whenever we have a rumba band), always brings women who smoke; big rings of smoke envelope their beautiful faces the same way fuck-me sandals adorn their feet. They inevitably have that "black lipstick film noir" attitude. Said he got fed up with a staid life where all the men of his acquaintance called themselves Bruce and his wife never noticed when he hadn't shaved. Got to him.

Carrie: I thought not shaving was some retro fashion statement.

Zenobia: Something ruthless and "beautiful day" about it.

Carrie: Any decorating ideas for her solidified in that multifaceted pea brain of yours?

Zenobia: The whole family needs years of decoration therapy and I'm willing to stand by them every step of the way. Before I leave I'm giving you the shoe index, and the jewel index. Pimpo has the holiday index. I wanted to make sure you learned your lines before I gave them to you but honestly I have little time for that. You have to want to learn them yourself. I'll leave the lists here in the your silver butler's tray.

(She was gone.)

Carrie finally got around to looking at the lists and here they are:

Foot apparel for all participants. To whom does each set belong?

1) Slipper-mules with pom-poms.

2) Gold lamé fuck-me sandals (all heels and toes).

3) Boar leather oxfords (waterproof).

4) Canvas sneaks with the toes ripped out for total comfort.

5) Roller Blades and kneepads.

6) Hush puppies.

7) Weeboks.

8) Orange plastic ballet slippers with large metal daisies over toes.

Jewelry List:

1) 18kt bracelet made of x links with one gold and ruby cabochon lady-bug charm.

2) Gentleman's yellow gold wristwatch with rectangular white enamel dial, black enamel roman numerals, steel blue hands, sapphire crown and gold brick link band.

3) Cornucopia earrings of carved ruby, carved sapphire, carved emerald with cultured pearls and briolette-cut suspended diamonds.

4) One pair of signed Cartier calibre-cut emerald cuff links.

5) A purple cabochon heart crisscrossed with gold ribbons and gold ball ornaments.

6) One ring with an enlarged Moses carrying the tablets (looked like a buffalo head until the diamonds were put in).

Carrie greedily read both lists but what she really needed was a clue.

Narrator: I have clues, like: Emerald strengthens memory, reveals adultery, offers eloquence and controls optical disorders. And the pigeon's-blood red Burma ruby is emotionally powerful; the color red, due to chromium impurities, glows luminescent while absorbed light plays in "wavelengths."

Stuck in between the jewelry list and what she hoped would be the holiday list, Carrie found this "confession" among the papers:

"I was just beyond kisses in the moonlight. Our fortune secured, I designed our mansion which came to be home. It is somewhat loosely based on Versailles and successfully conveys that 'feel.' It has the look of the Sir William Orpen painting of the Peace Treaty at Versailles where the reflection in the Hall of Mirrors distorts and crooks all crooks. I only had to reconstruct thirty-five rooms. I don't need a flotilla of battleships to get me home. Destroyers all . . . the way I live. When bundles of fur sally through the portico, I call the people who in turn call the dogs OFF. I remember only one time in my whole life when I refused to concern myself with what they required of me. Some wanted the girl in the Parthenon frieze to step down and cavort—I want to put her up and out of the way forever.

"I'm cognizant you need a description of the art though you don't deserve it, here it is:

"Neo-classical busts juxtapose broken Parthenon pieces which juxtapose old black and white photos of doomed or famed historically moral bankrupts.

"1) First I have a picture of Hitler in jail after a coup attempt in 1924. He's taking a break (writer's cramp) from *Mein Kampf.* The most important artifact in the background of the photo is a Nero-like laurel wreath just his size. This circular vine on the wall makes me wonder did he tend to dress up like Caesar or is this some basil drying for stew?

"2) The next photo is Rodolpho Alfonzo Raffaeli Pierre Filibert di Valentina d'Antonguolla. He liked potatoes with his potatoes. What can I say? I shiver. I grow weak in his presence. I feel faint in spite of the fact he inevitably screws something out of the other person before falling off his barstool. Hurts himself.

"3) The third is one of Miss Mae (been on more laps than a napkin) West. She was found guilty. Morals were corrupted. A police officer observed her doing a belly dance. She 'moved her navel up and down and from right to left.' Jail became her spot. The photo is interesting to me because Beulah drops a peeled grape into her mouth bringing to mind the famous line 'Beulah, peel me a grape.'

"4) The last masterpiece has an unknown happy child as its subject. A sweet little girl. All her needs met. The poor little fuck—will she ever be this happy again? Is she enjoying it at all? Probably not enough, we all tend to think there is MUCH MORE."

Carrie: How strange.

Chapter 6

Paradise

The Island
Seaweed legs.
Woman all the way down. A gone chick. Rainbows uncover held-up doom.
Sloe-eyed smiles.
Your mind. Filled with ancient stupidities.
Few to no holy people around. Haitian and Jamaican suns are never selective. Hottest. Cruelest.
Voodoo man has what we call the yellow slash blue eye. Is it the light?
Position is gigolo. Position is "Retainer of Pot."
A more persuasive selling tool would be meat on your bone.
A family of hill people will have moved in. Wearing hill people tams.
Freakeristic. Under puey yellow tree. She stands, our little bit of a squirt, on Mathilda's corner.
A live goldfish swims in the heel of her wedgie shoe. One one coco full basket.
One day she discovered the lake full of pitch. Dewormed her.
(Fat and toothless effect on me too.) She lives on "dug up" in from the garden roots.
Dig? Where living well is stealing well. Takes her highness down. Rips chick feathers on any bird. Right out. Presto. Another Dougie. Works behind the Jerk Pork neon sign. Can't miss their mom. Looks like Whoopslie with a coke. Not original recipe. She, ha ha, can't tell the difference. EXODUS after limited growth.
There was talk of a monkey making the long banana climb. Talk of meeting me on vulture hill. Beyond Wag

River we ate mangoes in our bathsuits. Pineapple CLUNK
on the head is a sign of welcome. Here come the career diplomats. Protecting some dignitary. PULLED ME OVER
TWICE. Career diplomats walk in on zona rosa brains. Always like to think "you killed a man." Career diplomats say
things not unlike that while carrion carry on.

Don't worry, little miss. Strength returns as if by magic
after you shoot the glass off his poll. The pain's all gone. I
was going to use it for Kava and it looks like I still may do
that.

Carrie in Jamaica (as rumors of her death circulate).

Log entry:

Not yet had the whale disgorged its belly.

Not yet had priceless merchandise broken loose to mid-
day cements.

Not yet had I been brought to some inhabited land.

Not yet had I traveled in the lands of men.

Not yet had "laid to rust oranges" with crawling things,
their unique chance to stink green.

Just before I was the first in our family to receive a crest
of heraldry, I met someone else who changed my life
and in the night
and at the fading.

He sustained me.

He threw away my nuclear weapons. I said good-bye once
and for all to misfired pricks and dicks. Said he used to be a
peeler in a coat. Was I in any position to argue or wonder?
Could this stranger on the beach become "the best and
most indulgent of husbands?" Yes, you remember correctly,
I met Valmouth at the beach too!

Swim swam swum. My body was voluptuous. I wore an orange neon suit plus perfectly matched orange zinc-oxide
on my nose. He noticed. He had this funny ethnic joke—
What did one nameless Swede say to a second nameless
Swede? I was chuckling when he became curious about the
bug repellant I carry in a crystal perfume bottle around my

neck. Here in Jamaica, mosquitoes could spoil my beauty.

Gossiped the scalp-tingling live-long day we met. Lots in common since we both work for Pimpo in New York. His bakin' head was red, so we went inside for reggae. Asked me how hard and long ago I fell. Not hard to pinpoint . . . though the mind works wondrous erasing. When did I fall? When did I fall? I said, "I used to admire my father the businessman who handed out rosaries at every board meeting but then breaks were made and suddenly all breaks were made. I'd been busy making them."

When did you stop resigning yourself to the will of God?

"One sultry day with wind and bamboos. Palms and cotton trees resign yourself to yourself . . . nothing to tie to oneself."

He was happy no ladies came . . . no one to entertain. One elderly man came for me; the old in-out quick and over so Chuck and I happily resumed. One old guy on orders from the clergy kept bugging us:

What were we doing here?

Scouting locations for modeling shoots.

My boss got word to us he was interested in business expansion. Needed us to remain on the island for what could turn into six months. He would join us when he could. Orders: we should take jobs sent through the New York or Chicago office—no others. Our moll buzzer had spoken. Gotham and costermongers far away, we were alone together. Time on tanned hands. Our depravity was behind us back in Chi Town.

Chuck's little gem for me: "They want you to have a child, Carrie. You would be paid well to be fat while fishing. It's up to you to pick the guy. You might never have to work the Bagnio again." Visions of me sitting with a big belly caressing my thighs. It had to be me and it had to be mine. Pay alone wouldn't choke me to do it. Fi Fi's words haunted me: women like us don't have children. Fi Fi had informed me: Chuck Bioff is the best at what he does. Presently, on the island of Jamaica, there was no one of my acquaintance to contradict her statement.

We made it our business to see the whole island. Chuck
didn't mention a baby again. One night in Montego Bay we
discussed our own sex drives:

Mine is nonexistent.

Mine too.

Work is work is paid. Work is work. Slushing and otherwise.

I thought lusts were cleared and cooled but no. Room
must be left for fantasy levels minus bullshit levels. I found
myself involved in the wildly exciting physical closeness of a
scummy couple. Couple of prostitutes. I blew on his neck
and kissed it until blood dripped down the side of his face.
Sorry. He asked, "Is that a sweet girl-next-door kiss?" We
held hands. Just for him, I became "Hollywood's Autono-
mous Adult White Woman." We ate, lounged, played in the
water . . . it got to the point where
. . . sex with him . . . sex with him . . . sex with him . . . SEX WITH HIM
was on my mind more much more than my father's rosa-
ries.

Chuck looked stunned when I asked him was he interested in being the father? I read his mind then. He thought
"Where's the enthusiastic audience for a 3:00 A.M. card
trick?" Chuck said, nothing personal, he would love to love
me occasionally, but THAT he would have to consider. He
thought, "I'm selling prayer beads while I'm sleeping." A
week and a half went by. Chuck was inevitably out when I
(to complicate his life) came by. We were living in different
hotels. Jobs came rarely. I felt like I'd done the pistol to
three human skulls. One skull had yet to be conceived.

I saw him on the beach in front of my hotel one night. I
went out. We kissed. He left a cough lozenge on my tongue.
I said, "Chuck, nobody wants to steal your army of little
metal warriors . . . so what if you've decided against . . ." He
said, "Carrie, I was hoping you wouldn't be at all interested
in their proposition, but if you are, I'll help you. Let's not
talk about it. Let the juices begin." I said, "That won't be
hard. I've been saving myself for you my whole life."

He laughed and we got to work in what I call our post-

Vatican Council era.

We got an apartment. Invited no one else to sup. No jobs were coming in now. Fewer rats. More corn. We're both talented at doing two with heat and ease things at once. Turned bookends into doves. In the middle of a long involved philosophical conversation, we tested who could go the longest without begging for entrance of an organ (depends on who's screaming). We both enjoy screaming so we didn't have to wait incredibly long.

Every morning Blue Mountain coffee and orange juice comes with breakfast. He gargled with the juice and chased me. I'd smell like oranges. Then we'd swim. Then rum punch on the beach. Then back to bed. Chuck Bioff took impregnating me as seriously as any job he ever had. Our major monstrous fashion statement was love. After stinking ourselves up with exotic island oils we attended the Chinese opera. Life hadn't cooled to "restful dreamy and vague" yet. He told of his life, how he grew up in JA., moved a lot, learned his "trade" roaming Tripoli at night in a beat-up Cadillac.

I read his mind only to come up with a blank hum but that moment I got a reading and confessed to him, "I know your angle. This arrangement is a setup. You're an ant with a waist if ever I saw one. You conned me. You may smack of the entire Eastern Church but you weren't my decision."

Their decision. Carrie, I knew you wouldn't like it when you found out.

I don't.

It was the choice of a lifetime. No matter whose idea. I didn't put a hitch in your giddyap no matter where. I wanted you to be sure about it.

You made me decide under false pretenses. Rapidly used-up world.

Don't you see that behind this freedom is the worst slavery? I did sign a contract with them before I came here. I was having impotency problems. My choices were limited. I had to go back to being the corner butcher's meat man, which is agonizing because all the housewives want FOR

NO BUCKS to screw you. Pimpo knew you could work on
me and look—I'm cured. Carrie, they've dealt with women
in these situations before. No one trusts a woman when her
child is involved.

Tell me about the time I asked you and you left . . . how
often did you think about me?

No, Carrie. Leave it alone.

They knew that interim would work with someone who
thrives on excessive courtesy. Someone like me. Did you peruse their psychological work-up on me?

I had ripe thoughts about you every two to three minutes.
It was that old baked-beans-from-a-can geezer, your client,
the guy with a many-nationality accent who just talked . . .
he of whom you spoke. He'd flex his rabbinical flab and
flush . . . plus he knew how NOT to get his mind read.
Pimpo had him teach me . . . worked until this minute.

Mr. Seltzer! He encouraged ME to talk! Said the life you
save may be your own! He had me building larger realities
out of social rituals. My curse is "Ice pick scribbles on everything he loves!"

He's on Pimpo's payroll—a psychoanalyst . . . the bad
breath and sour stomach were the only genuine parts to the
man. The idea was for you to concentrate on his foul smell
—and spill your "wild radiant" guts.

Trinity of impotent men. Gave him lots of space. Regur-
gitations. What DIDN'T I tell that poor old Giggleswick
creep who couldn't get it up?

You got him up, all right. He had to see another girl right
after you. Catching a Japanese train.

Tell me the girls were in on it!

I really don't know how it worked. I suppose they were. I
think Bootlaces was.

You don't seem like part of a con. The strength of your
work should win you Pimpo's estimation for life. Stop fid-
dling with your hatband.

I wanted you to think it out. Pimpo was sure you'd pick
me . . . I hoped you'd want someone else or you would
change your mind altogether . . . I gave you time to make

the decision . . . right for YOU.

What now? I feel it's not so easy to do a primal scream with peanut butter stuck to the roof of my mouth. I suppose you feel like some stud? Is that the point of this exercise?

My job to feel that way. This baby is theirs. They know things about its genetic makeup we don't want to know about our own.

I want this baby, Chuck.

You signed this one away before conception. Let's have another baby on our own.

This is the child I'm able to love. They did this to other women. Didn't they?

Maybe you could be hypnotized into believing it was a dream. Think of it as having freedom from the necessity of earning a living.

Licebrain. We can get our psychoanalyst in. You're a poetic memory now. Love begins with metaphor. You oxymoron.

If you think about it, the way they're predicting your reactions and planning around them, they must expect you to get ugly with me and disassociate. You've been totally predictable for them, Carrie. Let's be dangerous to them. Together we contend.

Maggot! Ambitious unworthy. You pretended . . .

I pretended not to know things outside my province but now I know what I know. You know.

Bombafu. I've experienced an infinity of unconsummated loves. That finite number—infinity.

Falling till we hit. Special madness doing Rough Boy Pimpo's bidding. No place is home. There's but a narrow neck on Pimpo's bottle of mercy.

Falsely philosophical eyes. Let's go back to a brand new room. Kaaribu come, you are welcome in your pink pith helmet. Trickle down blush fathoms deep. You remind me of what I hate most—a Costa Rican cattle rancher I once knew. First man capable of inspiring a sincere . . . one of us is too smart for this.

You were ready for the process. Don't rush to put your

boots on, Carrie. Think of something.

What if I gouge Pimpo's eyes with a conveniently con-cealed copper eye-gouger? Minutes later I'll calmly deco-rate our tropical Christmas tree with eyeball-clotted mops. Why me, Chuck?

Wish I knew . . . I met a higgler woman today. She takes pepperjam to America and makes $300,000 a year.

Amazing. Like nailing your visiting card to the door.

Democratic. She said it beats keeling over in a room and having to pretend you're haphazard or pregnant rather than sleep your ganja break.

Are you saying we should start some kind of export? Get the baby out that way?

Ouch. What was that for?

Your chin is a face bumper. When I mislocate, I'll miss your mean hose but watch your own step or I'll bake your fat head.

Not like I was happy as a two-tailed dog over here. Present at the conception, I'll be present at the escape. Then my ambulance chaser won't have to contact your am-bulance chaser. All but one of my fires is out. Let's throw gold out all the windows and doors.

Exile! First I have to trim these hairs around my nipple. I wouldn't want the baby to choke on them.

Try a french braid.

Then let's get married at John F. Kennedy the Baptist Church. I'm finding myself out from under previous im-pressions and obligations.

Were you "under" the impression I didn't know what was going on?

Don't flirt with me now. Let's get to the church—the guy over there gives great sermon.

We can name our children Perplex, Duplex, and Stuplex.

Where's the dark third of us?

In the dark, handing out glow-in-the-dark rosaries.

Interviewer: Carrie and Chuck think they're on their way to safety, but their pilot has been hired by none other than me. Who might I be?

The empire is not at stake. Someone exists to take over immediately.

I: A pattern emerges. The airplane pretends to take off. What is their bodyguard's name?

Guillaume Tell. The lingerer . . . asexual like a young boy, the women were all attracted to him. He was to choose one from all who strutted before him. Told our girls he wanted neither countess nor cossack. One would guess the one who got him did so purely by politics. . . . eventually shattering his smug.

I: Was he won away from his cause?

We needed him. It would help us to revise the constitution. He is our "never in public" favorite politician. Put fangs on the Mona Lisa, if you know what I mean. Suits her. What a babe.

I: Did a woman entice him?

When they finally got him to come in, he knew precisely what he wanted: "One Minoan virgin refusing to blush at size and delicacy." Like the boss says, they come for their own body parts as well as ours. No previous frame of reference.

I: I see no Minoans. Which girl did he choose?

The white-skinned strawberry blonde. She entertains him as only an educated person could. Close as one comes to a neutral color. Blue anklets to bluestocking literary. Drug him in.

I: What about her hysterectomized womb?

He didn't even guess. For all we know, he believed her to be a virgin.

I: What was that noise?

A human construct. Blood making noise inside of you.

I: Pray it's yours. When you visit a certain relative, what is complained about?

How she can't kill herself with knives and forks. How she has to turn them in after each meal. How the disgusting

food does a number on precarious health. Makes her fire-
breathing dragon breath sulfuric.

    I: Maestra. She's must be an anti-biologic cockroach.
We're all on a yearlong detour. Any objections?

    No.

Chapter 7

Informants Included

BARTENDER (ORM GAMULSON): Hold on, man! Let me listen to my choices to be with you momentarily.

(Beeps and Meebs for the Overeducated or Orm on the Phone)

Press a button!

If you are a SWM seeking intimate chats with coeds, press 2.

If you are a DBW or a DWW wanting to make a special female friend, press 3.

If you are a gay or bisexual man seeking some Latin spice in or out of your life, press 4.

If you are an endangered species, Successful Literary Lady who wants younger man, press 1 then 4.

Whatever you are or think you are, if you're verbal and irreverent, press 1 then 5.

If you are a SBW seeking some Latin spice in or out of your life, press 4.

M or F looking for a musical Amazon 140 lbs. or more? Press 1.

Want to talk about your mild case of herpes? Press 2 then 3.

If you would like to rent a villa in Tuscany close to Etruscan/medieval town, press 6.

If you're a F defense analyst seeking a currently employed air force pilot, press 7.

If you want to embrace the tiger then return to the mountain, press 8.

Bartender: I'm off now. These businesses put you on hold and keep you there. As you were saying. Yes. There was a chick who spent a lot of time in here. Fits your description now. Said the arrow of hair on top her head kept her pointed in the "correct" direction. Looked not a thing like this Baby Sweet Pea in your photo here.

There was something about her and all the free haircuts got us worried. Rumor had it she'd collect a ball of your hair and do hoodoo practice with blood and chicken bones. Management calls in the bouncers for that type of thing. As you can see, we are a biker bar located in a small university town which allows us the freedom to intellectualize on many realms. But we're conservative. For instance, we have Kierkegaard night etc. Look and you'll see Jimmy Stewart types everywhere. Big thinkers. We had an econ. guy in here the other night, said his laboratory experiment —COMMUNISM—was finally over. Gotta chuckle.

I actually had the hots for this chick. But I must reiterate, she looked nothing like your sweet pea photo. No former Miss Occidental. No former Miss Oriental with manicure and pearls. Would say she was a few years shy of the age of consent. The one time we two conversed, she said if she collected my whiskers for sixteen years she'd have enough to form a one-pound ball. When I asked, is that a marriage proposal? Little snot. She walked.

It made me wonder where the muskrat pelt on top of my head really came from. My mind was in Nazi Germany thinking about the weight of roomfuls of hair alone. Gross. All I could hear were strains of Wagner backgrounding screams from tortured Jews, Gypsies, and Catholic priests. I was holding that thought when her big "boyfriend" came in, picked me up, and put me on the meat slicer and would you believe, turned it on? Knife-styles of the bar. I would much prefer a life of leisurely days dedicated to avoiding unpleasantness. Unfortunately I have a history and an imagination. Multiplied fruitless endeavors.

I: What do you do to your own hair?

I oil it up towards the ceiling. That bitch was a nuclear perfume sniper, if you ask me.

Bartender's assistant: I know stuff in direct relation to how much noise is a-flappin. Look up easy answers in the *Journal of Sound and Vibration*. Don't come talking to me like you're the protagonist in every soul-searing book you've ever read. I'm no absent paper doily. I'm not the "visiting from another country" cousin kissed passionately on the way in. You and your constant talk of erectable brushes. You people conjure me up as an invention to satisfy your public thirst for me. Insatiable. Pond Stink is my recording label. Ask me about THAT. Some men need a country to represent. Some men need a country to represent them. Shamed when they don't have one. Others with two, wouldn't know what to do with a small parish. Monies from this I dedicate to any fine purchase. Name me one.

She's interesting. Keeps the place hopping with discussion, but let's meander over to the next personage or celebrity on your first and probably last visit to our biker bar.

Personage 2): I'm a devoted biker. I beat my woman regularly. She thanks me. I was just at the point of crowning her lucky mug with my lucky fist when you interrupted.

I: Your tattoos?

P2): The tattoo is typically an attempt to make permanent that which is fleeting.

I: I see you've devoted the left side of your body to Archie comics and the right to Loving Mom.

P2): And I drink my beer bottle from a brown paper bag. People don't mess with the tattooed. My stomach section has moths drawn to the flame. Symbolics. Basking in the light.

I: This biker bar is a social institution. Tell me what is socially redeeming about it?

P1): Strange bundles of passion and vague desires.

I: Sensory satisfactions?

P1): Erotics if you can get it in the door.

I: And on to the next invariably agreeable patron. A chatterer without a word of his own.

P3): I'm a plebeian. Of plebeian blood.

I: Is it true, with lust in your heart, you talk about other women in front of your "woman"?

All: Yes.

I: Why?

P2): These women are factory workers. It makes them

feel worthy if we return. The foreman is the true ogre in their life. We look good to them because prowling is part and parcel of the life-style.

P3): We buy them whatever they need for biking. If a guy's woman isn't decked out for the road, it's his fault and seriously frowned upon in our culture. You think we want the girls' hearts revolting in shame for better clothes?

I: No. Have you ever seen this woman? (*Picture of Carrie.*)

P3): Whoever tells you they haven't's lying. When we don't see her on *Most Wanted* we see her on the news.

I: She used to come in here.

P1): No way.

I: Her hair was different. It was kinky permed and sculpted into an arrow. Ring any bells now?

P2): Lots of black eye-makeup?

I: Could be.

P1): Well . . . talk about a resurrection . . .

P3): She looks like an Oriental schoolgirl. . . .

I: Who is this man? (*Holds eight by ten glossy.*)

Bartender: Beats me. Stinkie? Stank Stunk. I have seen him. You could tell he was a man of Falstaffian excess. One of those dilophosauruses. He came with this five-carat diamond. Said he earned it writing the definitive book on scruples in Palm Beach. I thought, "Could have done a better job." We had a deal. Figured I'd clue him in—the price was right. My wife has been buggin' me since day one for a rock, so nonchalantly, I was all ears. I'd be "going with myself" if she wasn't wearing one or more blinkies soon. "Yes, dear, you're absolutely right."

My wife may be bad-tempered and too thin. But believe me, illiterate cowboys ride three hundred miles to be caressed and bask in the aura of my long-suffering warp-speed spouse. Old familiar surface. She's like the mustard on my sandwich. Spicy and yellow. I can sum her up in one little anecdote: She wanted to name our child Whitney. I says, Honeybunch . . . but . . . why? She says, "Whitney is an abstract idea to be rid of then exchanged for something more substantial when the time comes."

Anyway he was one of those paramount chief guys with NOBODY inside his clothes who complained the weather on the Riviera was pooh-pooh. I mean, his concerns are not my concerns. I had to make it simple and classy. I had to appeal to this pretentious fop pretending to be a blue-blood person. He suggested "GOOD FRIEND FALLS DOWN STAIRCASE TO HIS DEATH." No. We could do better. I needed a little time . . . I felt a great idea coming on.

Said I'd get back to him after a little research. I'd seen his type before and since there are seven relationships in the world, it's the seventh I seem to be having over and over. Well this guy isn't exactly fighting for a cause like the "United Front of Abandoned Women" or something. (Frente unido de las abandonadas.)

I have this consultant—friend in the business: "Purple Sediment of Sorrows" Ludmilla. She says we should create a sect to round out my big con idea. I agree. You know how Russia is freeing up now and anything goes? She thought a kind of well-established Russian Hare Krishna sect "flavoring" would be just the thing. In order for my part to work we had to have a Brit because umbrella shenanigans are crucial. We also needed a large group of formerly regimented types unafraid to work with phantoms, one holy man, and a large meeting room where the formerly regimented lose themselves in high energy states before being rocketed to another chosen dimension. Goose-stepping was not required but a plus.

I found our holy man outside the book store at Harvard, gesticulating madly, excuse me, ENERGETICALLY, inches from a (no longer willing to be there) shopper's nose. Some people's space-invader. Once he left Jesus out of his mudslinging, we were set and could NOT have been happier with his performance.

My job was to implant one of those East European poison metal balls in the bottom of the umbrella. His mission was to get close enough to the victim and prick the man's ankle with the umbrella—seemingly by accident. Our holy man didn't know the umbrella was poisoned. We told him our victim is diabetic and this is the way to get a new formula of insulin administered once a month, as our patient (victim) enjoys his matinal walk in a crowd. I says, "It must be when he least expects it and administered by a different stranger each time because this man refuses to take his medicine voluntarily."

Thought we had this kook thinking of himself as "care-giver." No one the wiser. He had this kind of fundamental plastic honesty which corresponds to no perceptual logic; a real gem. After the elimination (job done) I'd get my five carats and our holy man would be splattered over some-body's wall somewhere. Our bodies were turned inside out with our hearts pounding on top of our skin when he wouldn't buy ANY OF IT—damned Christian Scientist. No care-giver he. Holy pope moral superiority we don't need. Next guy, first question—RELIGIOUS PREFERENCE?

I drank the white electricity and it elucidated the earth. It clarified at once in moments. Short on fact and long on interpretation, we had to come up with something else.

Ludmilla wanted one of her relatives to benefit. I didn't like the sound of it from the start, but since my creativity isn't what it used to be, I heard them out. She brings in what looks like a little boy and turns out to be a girl. I thought it was a sick joke the kid was made to look like Hitler . . . gave me the willies. Forelocks greased to the side, Nim Chimsky is this "baby stormer's" name. The best thing I can say about her is she's a clean kid. Goes as "Adolfina" and goes as "Grouse."

The plan gets complicated here but suffice it to say, the guy we want to murder lives with his mother who happens to be redecorating and—this is where it gets weird—she needs an exotic bird to match the decor of her living room. The bird is strictly furniture. The baby neo-Nazi works in the pet store this woman frequents so we have a tie-in there. Endless possibilities with that one. I just didn't know about bringing a Nazi into it.

My particular contribution to the oeuvre is to take a

murky poetic twist, lend it precision, and refine into a work-
able murder plot. I'm the originator. I predict the out-
come. I push selected events. We're not going "mauler of
ol' ladies" or "relisher of infant flesh" routes. Being subtle
here. "Subtlety," our motto for the nineties . . . no use tack-
ling a swarm of lethal stingers.

Finally, we called the whole thing off. Too many people
were involved. High-risk operation. I don't do *High-Risk*. So
my baby's still wearing pink cubic zirconias.

What is the name of the man you were asked to kill?

Valmont. Or something like that.

Skunk (narrator) and Macaroni III (interviewer) and Interloper, in their as yet unsuccessful search . . .

If I give you a list, an incomplete list, a rough sketch, will
that do?

An approximation? Since all three of us are trying to find
her?

OK?

OK.

Shameful red hair and not ashamed. When she came of
age.

Heritage?

She's Oriental. Broad. Would have answered Russian Jew
and English on the census. The Oriental part looks Mongo-
lian. The Russian Jew part appeals to her. She wears a yam
yarmulke on her head when they make love. Mezuzah on
the door. She was raised part of the time by a Baptist grandmother. No dancing allowed.

And her male counterpart?

He was partially raised. Feels himself a convert to Islam
every time he marries her. Now he's learning some unnecessary dance steps. The Baptist part is, in his mind, philosophically, not that far removed from Muslim parts. Feels
they go together. Maybe it's the *not dancing part*.

Flush-warped. Looks unfit for fidelity.

Epiphanies. Could be bad.

No one knew what she did in the war. When she came of age. Could be good stuff.

A psychic told her someone was trying to steal her job. . . .

Who would want it? And which one? Shamanistics. (All three stare at the pretender taking dictation.)

She wailed to the trash. When she came of age. Could be bad.

Said this one or that one gotta hole in his or her stomach, when in actuality, 'twas a mountain on fire. Find the bright side of that.

WRITE THAT DOWN BITCH.

Verified she was a hippie love child by her mother testifying "Oh no she's not."

Does admit to lower intestinal grumblings. Admits to little else.

I find them crestfallen as a group. Sans croup. That's bad. Need to talk about gut leakings. And related guts leaking. That's professional. What a people these Americans are.

I haven't talked to her for two years since she called me a son of a pope. Like sticking a man while he's praying but something much worse to a woman.

And when is she expecting her Irish toothache?

Starting in November.

That's good.

Come to me when you're prepared to talk enserfment.

To the great disquiet of the population and like a juggler with his balls, she was never seen at the wrong end of a pickax on the right side of town.

Nothing extraordinary in that.

The worst thing she ever said was, "He is a poor translation." After she came of age.

Decisions? Why make them?

Why wake them?

Exactement.

Ah yes, didn't Carrie have large Russian feet and ankle bracelets of an Indian princess? Her second dad was the

king of Denmark, so of course there are the incessant lessons for her while the rest of us worry the whole time about
her mandarin sleeves. When she comes of age.

After she has bore him a boy child, if one says he walks
light and a little ahead of himself, is that the same as saying
her "mom's" heart's big as a washtub?

But more directed? With a touch more direction.

End of evening brings women solemnly dancing away
from one another.

Things one learns in the Rotary Club; on your fast way
down you're stumbling over same important somebodies
you glazed over (saw) on your way up.

She had a dream where Hell's Angels get on like a pair of
Rotarians—Harvard men who in a pinch know what to do
with a vacuum cleaner and say things like, "She will come to
naught."

Sucking one another up. Into the vacuum, THEY come
of age.

We're both fond of sentences, so shouldn't one of us find
another means of expression? After all, how many sentences before we're in shards? You know that line where the
rose is red for the first and last time in the English language? Can't forget it backwards.

Where is she now? Cutting up pumpkins for the cows?

More under her hairdo than a brain . . . and spreading.

What can we do together?

Lots of lusty Russian nose-blowing.

When I needed cheering, Carrie whispered, "They may
have more to say to me when I stop inventing the quality
umbrella."

Carrie lived for gamps.

Pooh Bear. Somewhere far away Carrie is alive. Opening
a new gamp to a lusty wind and hailstone rain. Morgen
kommt der Schornsteinfeger. I majored in that too.

Mall head to you, Bub. No woman. No poems.

What IS it you promise never to forget . . ?

About you? Consider yourself forgotten. So is Carrie
Meeber . . . tomorrow the chimney sweep cleans for your

naked nerve of a female relative . . . doesn't mind having to work this spot but draws the line when it comes to shopping here. If you decide you truly want to *find* Carrie, come get me. We'll search together. The two of us.

Not three?

Not four?

Right-o. Let's start now. I'm reformed and my wishes are clear.

OK.

How's it going?

Slowly.

OK.

Sure you're ready to find her? One thing merely to look. Your straight-warped frequent that shop. Like that one there pretending she's a Vulcan chomping on thinsulate pizza twirl-dough (fake pizza skin molded from a safe non-toxic substance—a secret polymer to look and feel like real throwing dough). After throwing, one simply wipes with a damp cloth. Voila! Relieves customers' "waiting in line anxiety." They think it's Old World pizza—so it's worth your while to keep them waiting. Watch the show. Regard the faces of the people waiting in line.

I don't see her. Are we on the right path? Primrose? Garden? She would love this. She's surprisingly handsome when animated. Animation after British pizza dough throwing. If it's a glass harmonica, I will be told, won't I? Mmmmn the menu is interesting. That particular pizza flavor is like something one's ex-husband would eat. Where oh where is Carrie? With what devotion she would watch her thinsulate pizza. With what care she would guard her thinsulate pizza, with what fervor she would hold on to her thinsulate pizza. With what prudence she would bite. With what affection she would break it and with what diligence she would suck it. Hey! That's her! She's shaping each pizza into an edible United Kingdom; her small, delicate way of expressing the daily island life of Third World English people. "Carrie! All this time I thought I understood ALL aspects of your politics. Why ENGLAND?"

Carrie: I was meeting the same people wherever I went. I was unconscious. . . . What in the name of something-or-other are you doing here?

Looking for Jack-the-Corpse you.

Told you opening our eyes we'd find her. It's my opinion "you know who" should be "you know where" with "you know whom."

C: I tell the truth now but SLANT. My cause is "Children of the Ruling Class." My battle hymn is "Take No Souvenirs." I haven't seen you since you married a man who went religiously to a "clothier" who had little time for a second customer. He sewed a number on the back of every tie sold to "alleged" husband which corresponded precisely with the number on the coordinated suit. Without the code, your "alleged" husband was a nervous wreck.

That clarifies a bit. Sold a suit for every tie? A tie for every suit?

I'm suddenly made aware of the danger we are in. Immediately quickly and quietly walk out of the sunshine and back into the light. I'll buy you both vile drinks at the Marxist cash bar. On me! Hurry!

C: Stop taunting me with your pushes and adulation because . . . frankly . . . it works. And frankly, I like it.

Now I'm prepared to answer your queries. After I answer them and you are satisfied and return home, what I promise always to remember about you is your continually blocked nose. So Carrie, sweetie, be a good girl and tell us where you've been.

C: I really don't know. My head is crammed with useless information. Historical.

Hothouse world. Put her under.

She's ready. Carrie. Just talk.

C: I'm the Queen's historian, the following full deck of vice is all according to me and I am one of the few with the privilege to say "in the words of the Queen. . . ." I love Albion, my new homeland. Not an abundance of caveman stuff hereabouts.

Has she been time-tripping?

Quite possibly, maybe.

Perhaps.

C: In the words, like I said, of the Queen: In the tenth year of the reign of Queen Elizabeth I, records were initiated for Royal purveyors of muttons, "veales," "beeves," and fish. History marched on. . . . Though a palace document from 1775 listed the Royal Rat-Catcher and the Royal Mole-Taker, it failed to credit the Royal Bug-Taker, an oversight that caused one Andrew Cooke to complain that he had successfully removed bugs from numerous Royal beds. (Same bedbugs, crickets, and grasshoppers from this period can now be viewed in Cooke Memorial Museum.) The man saved everything.

She's a walking ad for a museum. Or a present-day historian talking about the past.

C: The Royal Rat-Catcher smells a rat, the Cookes are starting to smell like a bank. Andrew just this minute said, "I probably smell." I retaliated: "Probably. But not like a bank."

My dear. As-Salaam-U-Alaikum! Cowabunga with a K? Now she seems to be IN the past. Do you think she heard us?

Shrug.

C: The Queen, by her existence, makes me define genius. I need to describe the Queen Mother. I like to use the little brat's expression "stellar and undiminishable something" to describe what she has. Have we ever known anyone else like that?

With that certain something? No.

We have not.

But we can throw a date on her now. That's Emerson.

Why would she quote an American?

She wouldn't.

C: The Queen's humor from brutish beatings is cold-blooded and purely mental.

I recall saying something like that myself, and in the same vein I recall disbelieving it.

I wonder can this be attributed to her ability to read up-

side down? My two sisters (both of whom slovenly, grandly,
and innocently married into crime) are endowed with this
same talent. I guess that makes them doubly talented. One
is a prostitute and the other, a poet/nun.

My personal favorite, in terms of an adage, was the time
you said: "Half-breed is grace personified is a high nose
with scarred moled nose is peanut butter on banana. Is
grace personified."

I said that? Does it have anything to do with catting
around?

A very important point but more important are the val-
ues of courage and persistence. The Chinese tell us when
we are tired, or ill, or unhappy, or skinny, "Do not go out in
the streets." Bamboo munchers—not. Unhappiness is a
communicable disease.

C: Let me leave you with this: "If the Queen's corgis nip
at the ankles of the household staff—ain't she got problems
and won't those dogs be better off after a visit to the dog
shrink?" I may not be a professional exquisite, but more
than a few Bullyshits I have known. If you were a bright
young thing, you'd hear me talking to you.

We can't exactly squawk against this idiotic bit of crypto-
fascist self-regarding rube knee-deep in the Ganges para-
noia.

C: Don't be a tamarind bottomless monkey but, knowing
he's imbecilic and anti-biological, use by all means a
condom on your wedding night.

Could she be channeling for a historian? Historian lost
in a time warp?

Beats the crazy-head shit outta me. We can work by the
orange light of her hair.

That's her aura, Fuckface!

I thought her aura was yellow!

Carrie dear, when is the baby due?

C: Last November. The child has been born. Safely. Without disease or infection.

What have you been up to since we last met?

C: I contracted AIDS. After birthing the baby. The baby's

safe, thank God, or he'd have been a live bomb on one of
my missions. Chuckie would have been given up to a great
cause—not a painful, stupid, deadly disease.

Tell me about your mission.

C: I decided I had to go out doing something momen-
tous. I say no to being reduced to a potato sack of bones in
a hospital bed or an ad for orange jeans. I'd been research-
ing that human abortion Saddam. My plan was to attract
him. Then blow him sky-high.

He likes blondes. I know how to dye my hair. My mother
taught me something. No longer "titian." Heil myself. I
dyed it and went looking for him. Anyroad Baghdad.

I was to get the first postwar interview. I figured Diane
Sawyer would be game. I loved the idea of blowing myself
up in front of forty million people. She had to see how close
I'd get before she'd commit her program. I found the
hangout for his men. Said I wanted to fuck him. Had to
fuck a bunch of them first. I hope they all die painful slow
deaths. Seems Saddam doesn't like Orientals—saw his
mother that way—and, smart bitch Mom was, she tried to
abort him. Anyway, mission failed—I came to England for
more elaborate rituals—where it's damp and cold. Suits my
mood.

What about a cure?

No time to hope for that. I have one more mission first.

Jesus, Mary, and Joseph! You need to go to the girls' seer if
you want answers.

You said something "simpering in the night." What's going on?

I never said that. What simpers? Wimps do. Children do.

Is there a child or animal, perhaps a pet involved?

A mouth too large and improperly controlled. Crying
will make you thirsty. Don't make yourself a thirst-maker.

She wanted to have a child and she DID have one, didn't
she?

What if she did? Do you find that such an uncreative solution?

Perhaps. Perhaps not. Sounds extremely creative. Are you saying she did?

No. I'm NOT saying that. Would you please excuse me?

Interviewer: I remained and panked my wet hair in the direction of my lopsided downturned mouth. Looking at my bloodshot eyeballs in the window's reflection, I considered deliberately balding.

It would be somebody's obituary and a child was somehow involved. The girls dislike coffee-suckers' caffeine—too acidic on certain body tissues. The girls dislike Condom Man. Reminds them of their own mortality: "HOW WE COULD ALL WIND UP." The girls dislike pretty tits—theirs are not. Thought the girls disliked babies. Lopsided simpering.

Copo (*after following Interviewer, Chum, and Carrie back from England*): You're under arrest.

I: For what? I didn't even hear you come in.

Copo: Not you. YOU. For harboring criminals. Don't say anything until you're read your rights.

Chum: It need not hinder me from going about my business, Kafka.

Copo: Do you receive visitors at day or at night?

Chum: I waitress in the day.

Copo: And at night what do you do with the onion's scarf-skin?

I: That's what I came here to find out.

Chum: Peel and eat it raw.

Copo: What use are these toothpicks?

Chum: Relevant for hors d'oeuvres. I get all the Calabans.

Interviewer: As opposed to . . .

Chum: Irrelevant. Poetic clairvoyance.

Copo: Where do you get this stuff? Tell us about your leisurely sessions.

(*Carrie jumps from the back room, confessing:*) I didn't like you even when it was possible. No longer possible, so tell, why me? Honeythroated Rainhands. H.R. blazed your ass a few times.

Copo: So you did. Rode me stead o' worked me. Lifted your dress up so the sun wouldn't come near your ears.

Carrie: So you did. I mean so I did. I can feign any century's lunacy in order to fit in. I abandoned my inner goals that created a line's excuse. Wrinkles everywhere I don't want them. I dropped any squareness, any straight line. Neglected my future and erased my past to survive each moment in a different selected identity; any helpful identity.

Chum: Started when I visited a local psychic in Peru. We ran the unwed mothers home. I taught the unweds how to unsmelt iron.

Interviewer: This one talked to me about unrelated things: Central Park Zoo, the Duke of Windsor's garden, unphotographed hummingbirds, and other things too disparate to be grouped in a cohesive way. I said, "A burpy gusto anyway. Why should ancient saints have all the fun?"

Carrie: I rejoiced in it. Life had a fluency. The psychic told me if I didn't feel comfortable wearing Jesus' costume, then I should at the very least accept one certain doctrine and spread it; that I am one of the chosen. I even relinquished when it came to the costume. I wear the robes at home. Loincloths are comfortable. All I wear to bed when I'm alone. I am Christmas. I invite ALL to share in my arrival. The procedures are long and involve straw-hatted Italian ladies and these necessary items: Texas or Texas-style cockroaches and sealskin-lined coffins, made of lignum vitae wood.

Chum: You have to reel in the vows of the original water drinkers if you want to qualify as a member of the eternally devoted.

Copo: What about that nagging itch in your nose?

Carrie: I scratch.

Copo: And if someone doesn't get the whole lineup?

Carrie: Sorry lots are sorry lots are sorry lots. Truthfully they're worse off than if they had never tried. It kind of works against you and fortunes won't be made on paper.

Without a backward glance you must steadfastly gather in order not to feel wet or vaporized. I'm not your company you know. I'm free to Buddhaheadyou go. Verlaine was part of the same conspiracy and medical emergency team. I don't scare easy.

Copo: Buddha. Head. Me. Dead by decapitation. What's that painting on black velvet behind you?

Chum: The Sacred Heart. I have a better one on my bedroom wall—more blood. Radiates vibrating stamina needed to endure. Don't you think? Like his soul-patch?

Interviewer: Between a yokel and a gentleman I want a few measly questions answered. Can you forget about flying cockroaches and vaporized telegrams and tell it to me straight without so much as a backward glance?

Carrie: There are certain rules which must not be ignored. When a white man passes, dressed for the English countryside, don't expect to understand. Realize. Certain places enable you to wear certain clothes. Neon black differs from sunshine black. Do you hear me? One grows tired of face down soft things. Works but ill. Ornaments from any old thing hardly count. Pillar of salt. In a single day one must initiate conversations. Convalesce and do not doubt the details of yourself. Hold on tight. Nevertheless and still, take Mefisto the pig and hilarious fortuities will be yours. In a green place somewhere, long before we're forgotten, life's work is done. Light up a tooth if you must. If you see no other way out, dilute and warm the beer, make it stretch, drink from the coiled rooftree goblet.

Chum: All planned preparation for the wicked breeze.

Interviewer: A tested tried following for Stepmom's tea.

Copo: Amen. Carrie, the fact is there was an adoption.

Carrie: Sure. Of course. That's why you're here. When Valmouth found out, he got this Irish look of white skin round an especially drunken face appropriately topped off by a red fright wig. Milk actually started up in my breasts so you know my heart was in it more than your regular adoptive parent. Two for suckling now. Maybe three. Real birdies don't run on batteries and who's to say what's what? So from him it was a well-placed cigarette on my neck. To bring me out . . . make me less than anxious, the cretin knocked the furniture about my head a while for sport. Whenever any of this got close to the kid we both panicked. What I tolerated for myself, I wouldn't tolerate for myself as THE KID'S MUM. He watched me read the child his book holding the iced foot rubbing my baby toe with my thumb round and round over the top over the little nail. Round and round. He'd say, "Wear your religious collar, but kiss my throat or better yet the back of my neck before I go." I never saw the snake again.

(*Interviewer and Copo leave the premises together.*)

I: She had it sounding like SHE was the adopting parent.

Copo: I come away from fugitive Carrie without arresting her and with one piece of her amazing story. I guess you went to that fern bar and talked to her friends there. Well nobody over there knows how she spent her free time when she had an uncontrollable itch. Hah! I've got you interested now like finger sex. Have you heard of the Kamikaze Club? When I REALLY needed to find her and the other haunts were exhausted, I'd find her at a game called pai gow, which uses domino-like tiles and is often a bewildering blur of betting strategies and tile combinations best played in Cantonese (she's learning). Her second favorite game is *super pan*—ripping good fun. Why she needed money so bad—hundreds of thousands ride on a single hand. Losers get gift certificates for tattoos. I sometimes wonder if the rumor is true that she has slept with all seventy-three security personnel employed by the Kamikaze Club.

I: She's in with the Asian Mafia?

Copo: Not necessarily. She's had her dealings. She's not party to "home invasion robberies." She flies to California on occasion to "tour" the card clubs. Some have been in California since the nineteenth century. Likes 'em big— like the one that's 80,000 square feet where she rents a $55-an-hour seat. As you can see, gambling is her "national" pastime as represented on her flag here. We have every reason to believe she's had to pay back a loan of $900,000 at an extremely high interest rate under the threat of force. Might explain a lot of her behavior.

Narrator: Her childhood chum would continue to harbor her. Pimpo's threat of throwing boiling water on her newborn was unquestioningly believed by all concerned. She continued to serve Pimpo his coffee in a glass watching and waiting. A few months would pass—she would hunger for him. When he came to her, sausage first, apologetic, she heard him out. One cold kiss for the longboned. She got one in return. Perhaps Valmouth is dead. Perhaps the opportunity for a great getaway occurred. Forced him back into sidewalk cracks.

Interviewer: Pimpo never had anything nice to say about her friends Studs Bioff, Chuck Bioff, and Valmouth. I quote: "Your experienced-in-holes traveling companions will cost you. I catch you either handing someone his grumbling thunder burnbag or them handing you a just-shared burnbag, believe me, you three will squeal like pigs." Said it might disillusion his fans if he slept with one of the others, so he'd continue with her as he saw fit. Fact is, they couldn't manage to get him pointed. Not one of them. Only Carrie. He tried all the girls. Every single one. Even some of the men. Didn't want to depend on Carrie. Nice for a while but then IT would start up. Certain hours embrace turned into slow encirclements up to their ears. Working his calluses alone would make a full day's pay for any other girl. I come away with what may turn out to be Carrie's last log entry:

A MALE WHITE ERMINE MOTH GROWS AN APPENDAGE COVERED WITH HAIRS EXTENDED FROM THE END OF ITS ABDOMEN.
    Our last exchange:
    Would you like the same skinful?
    No, thank you very much.
    What's the child's name?
    Clucks Bioff.
    Go figure.

This baby will grow up to believe in two types of men: pimps and pimpish. Happy "wid de big drooms mon."

A lot of dissatisfaction there?

There's hope where there's new life. Branching out. Religious beliefs in a life. I'm on a commercial basis with my butter-tongued God. We drink wine together on the grounds it isn't Coca-Cola. My general comment on any general comment is to bring dripping points to bed saying, "I am fucking you, Krishna, so stay fucked." Kaffeeklatsch philosophy.

(End)

Interviewer: Will we ever know who that "last exchange" was with? After our conversation I knew her murder would disappoint only her mother (in the midst of securing an insurance policy on herself. Who's the beneficiary?). The irony of that maternal position fills books. Her murder would not disturb the rest of us beginning to see the light. Or was it murder? And if so, whose?

Nine Lives Nine Lives Nine Lives Nine Lives Nine Lives

Carrie (*left behind*): I'm not from here. Applied for many jobs. I got some. Mostly shit. Even shit jobs are hard to come by . . . I took the personality with me. Personality comes too. Like a shrunken head in a plastic voodoo carrying case. Weird ain't weird no more. I wouldn't go for the kind of job where you need clothes. Having clothes is admission of guilt. Admission of a past. One interview for a magazine, I borrowed clothes and, looking great, walked right by where I didn't show for the interview.

Latched onto a survivor and did the survivor thing. The reason I totally dropped out and started in the amusement park businesss is because of this flamer. Thinks he has some inalienable right to my child. He beats Chuck. Chuck is safe now, my mother has him—as long as I'm "dead." If I were alive, so to speak, that flamer'd be stealing my son biweekly. So people think I'm dead. Hard on me thinking about kill-

ing myself. Never having been suicidal . . . this "charade" is
a new concept to me. I made one decision when I was pregnant—the worst way to go is smothering in your own vomit
or choking on uncontrollable saliva (dying because of
something your own body manufactures). Scary. Those
routes must be avoided at all cost.

Narrator: At that moment Carrie picked up her Daum
dresser statue of Madonna and Child and began to mastur-
bate with it. "I have necrophilic tendencies. It's cold. It's
dead and smooth."

Chapter 8

Occupation: That Human Construct

IN THE WORDS OF A FELLOW PROSTITUTE "Brocade":
Carrie builds herself to be missed and mourned . . . great
talent in making everybody sorry for her . . . always planning what they'll say about her after she's worm food. Such
planning dictates one's actions.

And Pimpo?

B: He insisted she be called Grace.

Did she volunteer anything about Pimpo?

B: "Pumpkin screwpenny man in gleaming oil" is what
she "volunteered." Carrie quoted Pimpo, "Little can be said
of the mind." Said "He never knew exercise to do anyone
good." Belief was in red meat. May he choke on it. When
asked a tough question, he refers to someone else's notebook. (Successful life most successfully gleaned from the
pages of some "Magnificent" with furnace tastes.)

Acting on the architectural level, Pimpo (Puck with a ci-
gar) oversaw the entrance with a keykeep's sense of over-
sized church savvy. By architectural, I mean thrice stainless
and skirting disaster. Architecturally speaking, if I may continue in this vein, he wipes his nose and it smells like lem-
ons over fish in a badly kept building supply store.

Was into beating his girls with light fixtures. His threatened thrill in terrorizing her, scared the very day. Broke
her nose and her hymen! No one had to catsup her sheets.
Off-white and pulverized forgotten, they are an additional
high-rise fatality. Dirty hands make clean money. Furrow-
ing animals. Others leave their women somewhat alone.
Assured he allured all, he parceled indecencies out to his
girls screaming, "No pleasure in a gaping hole. Bestial
bondage. Open wide to get the same all over my wine-col-
ored Persian rugs."

It didn't shock us when they came together as an

unstoppable team. It was July 1. "International Cherry Pit Spitting Contest Day." I won't forget. A war room, designed to map out entrepreneurial strategies, was situated next to the Hot Pillow Hotel. Priest of hands-on indecencies, pleased to meet priestess.

Laplanders in need of more vitamin D. Life was climax anticlimax, climax etc. Turin papyrus wallpapers the map room. Symbolics. Pharmaceuticals know Pimpo. Would be ready for bed except he just ate seven hits of speed (type thing.) Baby dope fiends for succor. Madman mirrored in the hunter noiselessly cocking what used to be his wife. I used to feign we were more than hood ornaments to the pair of them.

She used to be his wife?

B: In his dreams.

What did he do for fun before her HOWLING BITCH, SQUASHED BROCADES, SPARKS-INTEREST APPEAR-ANCE gave him courage to make a go of the business?

B: Invented a wardrobe for her before they met. It con-sisted of oyster satin drapery ball gowns and plastic rainhats for accent. He learned this would pay for her time with his grandfather. The old man needed encompassment twice a month. Made Pimpo feel "funny sometimes." Her smolder-ing shoes made all three stars of the mock masterpiece. Life, unfortunately, had little to do with "heart." They took destructive pleasure in that fact.

Asked when Carrie became "Pimpo the Second," this is what Brocade said:

1) Reputation same as Alexander (both "conquerors" of the world).

2) When the realization came that the world was no longer a safe, sane, civilized enclave, Carrie developed an attraction—the fresh for the stale. Just about that time (in fact, simultaneously), Cupid tipped his platinum head.

What came along and sliced one of his Herculean loser heads off?

B: What always does. Hotspur like such and so many bird-ies. Work with me to work up sickness. Audience is a good audience is a silent respectful audience listening to screams.

In other words . . . he squeezed blood from a green pea.

B: Sweet Pea! Can't escape what you did cause you're doin' it again. Pimpo and Carrie flirted with the limits like Fred Flintstone ALWAYS on his way to the Grand Order of Water Buffalo meeting.

Could you be more specific?

He dropped acid on a regular basis. She was game. It was his fault she had such a bad trip the first time. He never hallucinated and resented her hallucinating. He didn't believe her when she relayed her experiences. Maybe he didn't even believe in hallucination. Makes you wonder why that was his drug of preference. She saw him as a cubist Joker, half his face purple and the other half with a ghostly white heart painted over his cheek. She knew it was him and yet had a hard time going near him. Couldn't seem to get her shoes on.

I surmise feelings of neglect. Show me the fruits of your struggle, or the designs you women have come up with.

B: Here is a fine example, a set in sterling called the Eye of Horus.

It has little eyes on top.

B: Yes, top center are fish eyes dried and enameled. Dishwasher safe.

Who designed it?

B: So So Guerrilla Gal: a mall rat with none of the despised calculation of the whore. She has tolerable weirdness as a New Age barefoot hippie who LOVES TO SHOP. Likes it when Pimpo threatens her with her own knives and forks. Many women delight in some chosen form of subjugating themselves to Pimpo, subtle inspiration for their art. New selves cut off old selves. Sleeps soundly when sleeping like a child . . . Eye of Horus designer scarves will be in the fall line.

Forever desirous under a pyramid.

B: She confessed affection for him and he made a tattoo of her. Enough of this god damnit. Tell me once and for all.

WHO is dead?

A physically magnificent person. Whichever one yielded to opportunistic moments. Have to stepfetch and sort to find out. Someone who was rode hard and put away in a wet heap on the floor. We really don't know if HE'S dead or SHE'S dead. A decomposing body in the pushcart is all the evidence we have. They thought it was Roxine who made him a fortune on Post-Impressionist water beds but the smiling sucker-puncher turned up the other day. Now they think it's a transsexual in the middle of his operation or a strange mixture of male and female body parts from two distinct individuals.

B: Did you sniff out the intelligentsia with the Fido collar?

You don't know your intelligentsia.

B: Separated for burial?

Hopefully. Like two different people. Separated as much as possible. Commingling has already happened but will be avoided to whatever degree possible before internment.

B: Any clues?

Potato chips on a Birkenstock add up to one clue. Another is ring around the collar. We're involved in the disorder of searching another's home. I'm not at liberty to say much about the state of her body.

B: What do you mean?

Not at liberty. There was a note.

B: Don't make a new alienation an old alienation and vice versa. She was pregnant, wasn't she?

What makes you say that? Why should that be your conclusion?

B: I knew her. Because I just don't get it.

Do you have any idea of her true lineage? Her desires? What was expected of her? Her interests? Her fantasies?

B: She knew whatever she did, family money would bail her out. It was more than money though. Diseased imagination. If we had royalty in this country, she'd be it. Why I must stress whoever's body parts were in that red wheelbarrow, you'd best find out and find out quick. Less and less

people on their way to Saks. A traffic we rely on. We like to
situate ourselves next to the very best shopping. This gal
could tell the time of day from how much her European cut
diamonds were smeared. Tell me about the note.

Nothing to tell. Short funny balding Chicago is, as usual,
full of surprises. In it for control. It stated, "He who talks
with the burning bush is no longer basted in righteous nec-
tars." Poor little rich girl is a flaky fallacy like "the nebbish
schlepper Jew." Try to find me one or two. Hot thoughts
and passion.

B: More like captured, handled, tranquilized, and put in
with the pygmy goats. Hired help DO have a better life.
Rich girls aren't allowed. She had a dream . . . an inner
sanctum of soothing thoughts . . . she became wide-eyed at
the thought of luxurious head rubs, long horse rides on the
cloudy moors, fireside naps without burning down the
house. What can I say?

An Anglophile.

B: Any life is a better one.

One appetite and you seem overcome. Where are you
from?

B: I'm my own dowry. Sin a little. Repent a lot. Girls don't
leave home just because they're thrown out. They leave
home because that home happens to be in Little Rock.
Pimpo of "egg cream fame" happened to agree with me.
Virgin-recall. Cinéastes. Three-moon sky resembles three-
orange sky. Man Ray did something to slit our eyes;
nothing's been the same since his Weber grill technique.
Like Pimpo says (and his lips are moving when he says it),
"They're all bitches." If you know an hour less agreeable,
shake it loose or relinquish it. I differ from Carrie. I like
them excited by their own voice, in from some rattlesnake
bar, wearing crazy Florida pants . . . eavesdropping seams
on their clothing . . . unmarried to their devoted wives. Call
'em "You big yellow taxi." That alone will make 'em grow
full straight. I'm anti-religion cause the new religion is style.
Style became a virtue. Sounds New England. My father was
a maitre d'. Mom was a topless waitress. All we had in our

house were violins and avocado seeds soaking. Culture and necessity. Mom got me off HER back and onto mine. Got me my first job. Too flat to be THAT kind of waitress so my stepsisters and I got into this racket. Three of us posed for this picture—I'm the necklace between two breasts. Our all-American family gossip was over dishes.

That's good. Clean people.

B: Don't you see? A pimp is a carried man who doesn't know or care how far his final destination is. You and I know who carries him: a vigorous-hipped woman giving birth to Bosch in a Circle K. Some things never change. Same woman it's always been . . . paid the same too.

I like a sizable war-opiate woman to relieve trenchlike depressions.

B: Woman runs unstrung pearls in new purple garters for your sugar britches.

Woman properly misunderstood the supreme fascist carrying the madman's mirror.

B: Woman is the muddied sunken cunt of the world, a keyhole visiting the center of each day with a wakefulness in a place where pulled-on eyelashes are never removed.

Woman was one fella's (preoccupied with death) bright idea. Slightly damaged saints.

B: Woman makes her bed the least personal space. Does all kinds of milking all kinds of udders.

Woman dresses careless and disloyal archangels.

B: Like a second sun, woman undresses old passionate and out-of-work Spaniards.

Woman loves to put your ample shoe on you. Toes too personal. Does whack it.

B: Woman is a pretty girl who thinks sausage a most likable gland. Won't mouse with too much meat.

Woman has a nervous bedwarmed composition . . . she responds to certain musical strains. Do you think women start out bandied about by men, then roundabout to be the nation's backbone?

B: Fuck the day. I'm too busy beating off my own death. Afterwards? Buffered by what they're promised in looks and gestures? Bespoke opulence. Turncoats. We am what we am . . . we can think far enough ahead to predict the next john. I pretend this is a church exclusively for women. We number more than one hundred virgins consecrated to religious devotions. Plastic rosaries. I have a question for you. Is it possible a man could be a kind of ants to the shade, flies ashimmer GROUP idea? I KNOW "man" was an idea I had. One thought smudged with rouge idea with or without a roof over its head . . . which sustained me??? Hah!

I know the feeling. Do you enjoy all this sunshine flooding into the room? You must.

B: It cleanses my crystals. It airs out the room to make way for the next customer. I dislike the pungent air reeking of them. Our shocking almost violently pink room was suggested by Zenobia. She said it allows even the most violent criminal to calm down. She has a room like that for her husband when he has what she calls his "psychological seizures."

Squeaky Meeber? Does she have problems with him?

B: No more than she would with any tautology. He roils prehistoric waters. He bit her earlobe once. She is unaware the only problem with him is his matinal shotglass of expresso every morning.

Gets him moving. . . .

PIPPIN AND BROCADE SPEND TIME TOGETHER COLLABORATING ON AN UNUSUAL CONVERSATIONAL LOG ENTRY:

No. 99932

If there is no God (Ego Deus) I'll be him.

See what the little darlins (women) have done now.

What I liked about him? I liked one of his couplets. Or was it an internal rhyme?

He had *spruces* and in the next line *crucial.*

Perfection. The rest of the poem was crap. Double *p*s.

Another thing?

I liked his photo collection.

Must not have been too much to like about the poor sucker.

He had Marilyn Monroe on the coroner's slab. He had Hitler as a baby.

Fine examples of how dying can be an excellent career move.

But we're stiff-necked baldheads to you, the search is in darkness for a friend.

No. I really think you got your foot into something here. City life?

Sedentary life.

What happened to you?

I got mixed up with a literate but scrimping family. Happens to us all eventually. I fell victim to the Western craving for definition. It happened in one of those big chairs pulling on me harder than gravity.

PIPPIN AND BROCADE SPEND TIME TOGETHER ON AN UNUSUAL CONVERSATIONAL LOG ENTRY

  or two:

  Log entry no. 99933

  WE ALL HAVE EXCREMENTAL VISION.

  I mean we all truly believe "death is the misplaced name for a linguistic predicament." Can't argue with it.

IN PRAISE OF THE OLD PROSTITUTE ON THE MORNING OF HER BURIAL:

  Being poor was hardly working. She was the natural order of things; avowed psychic with avowed contacts to dead and dying poets . . . had sex with two guys on James Dean's grave. Yeah she won $—a huge sum—big bucks in court (seance income loss) . . . sure as the stuffing comes out of my chair tickling me into laughter. So what if her Indiana IQ is so low she could be from Arkansas? (Wasn't any lower before she died.)

  She is our fair and final lady. After her, THEY DISCONTINUED THE MODEL.

  Have you read *Hoosier Home Repair?* or *Rats, Lice and How*

They Influenced the History of Western Europe (reading materials found in dead one's room)? I have.

SHE WAS A SOUTHPAW SLINGER OF STONES to an eighteenth of an inch AND WOULD NOT MISS.

I imagine conversations I would have with her if she were still alive:

Do you find yourself weak, gauche, crooked, or maimed?

C: Lyft, gauche . . . mancino? No but I find myself cooked.

Send in the next great audience.

C: Cheerios aren't aerodynamic. Says so right here. When one is thrown, it veers instead of taking flight.

Sugar-frosted. Changes your outlook. When his mouth, my tongue, and my shoe get together—I wish he were not a Cheerio.

C: I like to reminisce back to when we were feisty small fry in bathing suits and high heels strutting our stuff on the boardwalk.

Too bad that, like many other things, NEVER HAPPENED.

Girl (*French accent*):

Now they say I'm world-renowned. I'm fifth generation "circus" with tightrope and bicycle under the bed. (*To someone out the door:*) Is he the one wants us screaming "gimmiMick?" GOTCHA. Excuse me. We had to get *that* straight before she left. Thinks he's Mick and Madison Avenue is somehow responsible for his plight.

Here I am. It all goes back to glamour-pageant stuff, just a skip from cheerleading stuff. All-important growing up in a small Texas town. Realize the horror awakened when your hairs do mutiny! An aside which may or may not rate. Since day one we prepare to tell our story. Off the beaten track. Road not taken.

When I'm in a big city, on the street with several girls, the mission is ATTENTION for the group as a whole. Priority. Possibilities get close, then you want some zeroing in on

yourself. Alone. Line-up competition like a beauty contest.
Some brassy trait will magnify you. Miss America is usually a
dog. Yet selected from a crowd. Am I not right?

You're always a winner. Inevitability is a built-in.
SOONER OR LATER YOU GET PICKED. I had this old
geezer in here today says, "Sweetheart, I know you're not
sweet and you've got but a little tarnished black heart left,
fact is—at moments you got one hell of a hook. Silver,
shiny, and no doubt rusty on the off day, but YOU gotta
hook. Bottle it for the big bucks." Bang for buck.

What the fuck Mr. Bazooka don't realize—no bottle
small enough. Then Mr. Big Man bawls like a babe, "We're
all sons a bitch puppies." Confessed he'd like to but would
never have guts enough to be with me, "women getting
their nails done are the ones we take to dinner, with the *rare*
return on the price of dinner in terms of metered sex. Be as
sorry as I am for the inequalities. I believe it's as easy for
girls like you, all glamour—hard and suffering to kill me as
roll with me."

I wouldn't want to chow down looking at that mug any-
how. Might throw my digestion off. After all this talky-talk
it was time for the usual so I tie him up, put makeup on his
face and my hair . . . he balls me up inside, calling it "my
party." I end up with vital fluids in my ear. Up and over.
Don't ask me how. Wonder of nature.

World don't owe me a good time. Many wicked things in
a past life to get this particular life this particular time. Last
five minutes he advises me in ways would make the Turkish
police blush—how to spend MY free time. He is legless,
which don't interfere with his tuba playing. Plays his tuba
mouthpiece on his way to work. Pacifier. Floating elements
help him compose.

This rambling may be my only chance to put myself in a
historical perspective before I die. I was a girl older women
liked . . . wanted me married to their menfolk. What I was
told. I was appropriated. I wonder did these dames think
they could rule their own unruly by ruling me? Parts of
yourself a mystery to yourself. Solve mysteries and maybe

the answer to that one will pop up. Have another fistful of Teddy Grahams. Four years in the slammer for manslaughter scares the least qualified matchmaker away.

Slammer days? Fights and screaming in many languages. The clientele is not a composed bunch to begin with. On visiting days Carrie showed and wouldn't let me complain. She'd tell me HER gripes: The weather on the Riviera is ghastly, her Lear needs expensive repair, Val stole the baby, etc. Her problems made me want to get out. I was hearing about HER cockamamy life. She'd describe what "theatre" the girls were up to and how (real bad) they needed me for a part. They were in the midst of *Hamlet.* We discussed the female lead "O"—Carrie said Hamlet was expected to make an honest woman out of O, but of course never did. Sent her to the nunnery (same as the whorehouse). If she was a slut, her own father assigned her that position of honor. The heroine defended Hamlet in the most inelegant and inarticulate fashion. I asked Carrie, "O was inarticulate and *the heroine* in a Shakespeare play?" In Meeber's production maybe. Even I know SOMETHING. Carrie could be such a snog at times.

Our discussions were laughable. So we'd have a laugh. A real laugh. She had her own ideas for a play: The life and times of Sang Chong. She wanted Jack Lemmon in eyeliner to star in the movie version. I guess Sang Chong was THE super con artist in ancient China. He dressed like a woman, bound feet and all, offering to teach women's work to the good families' daughters. Impregnated a bunch. Guess they got "women's work" down pat. . . . Funny the things appealing to Pimpessa Carrie. Mind you. Mind your back. This is where I get out.

Bootlaces: One more reason we're close to the banking district. We know bottle-fed bankers pretty well. A generation of grunters. Snorers. Old suit on a new john. When I worked the streets I stole $200 and a watch from a kid who had no business being with me. This is from one who don't steal. Hard to believe? That kind of immaturity belongs elsewhere. If I rubbed his wits like a genie rubbing a lamp, I'd be thinking of Rimbaud's socks into the wee hours. At least his tall radical parents in riding boots weren't dragging him in for what's regarded as the best lesson in life. I have little stomach for eat-the-world people like THAT expecting Christmas lights all year round.

Little snot. Educated in Swiss schools. I did it to teach the ferocious precocious a lesson. First-person account of plastic surgery. Not to mess with us. A little of each and much more. Innocence retrouvé. He'll be carrying a blackjack and revolver under his apron now. I doubt he came looking for one of us again . . . certainly not for his goods. Such anthropological studies cost dearly. I can stop a boy like that from so sorry ends. Death wears blonde braids, lederhosen, and can't get enough foot-stamping, dirndls, and zithers. Rumor has it, death is never losing in the next room. Now he's down the hall far from the "next room." A living nightmare. Sapien suckers can't go home with special dispensation from the pope. Lord knows we can't.

No shortage of business for me. Other worlds step out. Dancin' a bella two-step. Outstep. Our special customers are hooked . . . passion stores itself for us. Call in celebrated wrestling naked madmen. No need for definition when it's obsolete. When it's "the world's oldest profession" I know what you're talking.

Took him home to my two obnoxious squealers (somebody's bastards) and shot up in front of him. I can be a degenerate drug-shooting cunt. He's a little *Shot-putting-with-my-world son of a bitch.* Ragpicker in lotus land. Still didn't scare him off so I took his belongings giving him his life. Easy enough to be a sideshow treating him like an eccentric. Maybe somebody will do the same for my little ones some day. Before nap time there was some whispering about a tango but I'm not sure I care what he said. You simp. You simp. You simp. Now he's allotted two seasons, like in the Bible: early and late fall. Easter doesn't count. Rebirth state of mind.

OK. Show me. Nice picture. Yeah. I know her. Unseasonably noticeable. PRETTY is her game. Right? Before she caught me sleeping with her dictionary, she accused me of breaking her sentence. We countercharged her with "queenship." Didn't want to be demoted to beekeep, especially with African bees. My recourse was to see Denny the Dwarf about multiplication tables. His motto is "If you can't count it, it will hurt you," which beats the pants off the alternative.

Her favorite technique is squaring the circle. KWADRATRAKOLA, like glasnost, is the only meeting ground between the hip and the square. My unsavory attitude is reflected in her favorite pithy saying: "BEWARE INTERSTELLAR SLICK AND URBAN COOL. BE PETALS SPREAD WIDE." A bender and straightener of horse hooves finds the thought process impenetrable. She squared the circle while I circled the square. When you square the circle, you put yourself in a place of insanity, not wisdom.

She flew in this friend from overseas to relate: "Latrine," a purple-haired Polish prostitute whose nickname for men is "kielbasa." We were "the kielbasa holders," rollers and naturally EATERS. She singled me out: "I can see you are among the bald species. You used to have bronze locks. Maybe you smirkingly think I'm redundant, but isn't there a lot to be said for interstellar slick bad taste, however redundant?" Then I knew she was on my side. It was nice. TWO no longer had to be a jungle. She had us drinking this lunatic pink ginger lemonade, a "juicy fruity ass-lickin' drink" she baptized "Butterfly Genitalia." Smooth as . . . you guessed it! Butterfly genitalia.

Pimpessa put the idea of "Mythical Cannibal Woman Night" into his fucking head in the first place. For Pimpo and Pimpessa there was a central celebrating room built around ostentation and deliberate wastefulness (the compost heap). In this oceanic room, celebrations lasted several days in a plush designer atmosphere with "Mythical Cannibal Woman" overtones. This consummate excess validated Pimpo's corporation's rank by displaying symbols of non-inherited and non-inheritable privilege (new fast and dirty money.) There one would find the dancing etc. and performance art if you will. Plus a "Psycho Bitch Day Celebration," at the end of which one is given extravagant quantities of knotted rainbows. Acceptance of the rainbows affirms Pimpo's enhanced status. His grand munificence is immediately exchangeable for trips to Hawaii. The winning girls stay at one of his hotels, where he simply makes more moolah off them. Off us. Our bodies. He's got us sucking milk from cows' udders. Cheap.

NOW I'm a feminist. Had a lot to learn. I move into the penumbra instead of negating. You might think the next step for a feminist would be to get out—wrong. I can do my work here. The lighting's good. It always depended on the meat of the sandwich. After reviewing your haphazard application of lipstick, my strongest urge is to take you to the makeover room.

Please call me Benji. My name is Englebert Humpherifyoucan, "Western intellectual of renown." You know they had some gay dealings. Some experiments. I was one of those customers. When you sign on for a weekly caravan of boys, you get bored. Boys on lease. The women aren't as transient.

Vanity had me sting my lips with bees in my swell-lipped Mick Jaggerish days. Before silicone I was a White Negro longing for banana climates, coconuts, and surfers. I morbidly created my own face. They say I'm likable in a "different, sorry, wrong hemisphere" kind of way.

These relationships could be triangular. I wonder . . . could they be otherwise? We had a choice, which was a relief: we could deal with Strongarm Pimpo or Pimpessa—I believe she goes as "Carrie." They're both experts in what to do with each individual biochemistry. I preferred dealing with her. Professional. Can't ask for sensibilities: it's cold-hearted, IT'S BUSINESS. "Bidness" as we say where I come from. It's a party when Carrie blows up a house. That became less and less common. Pimpo was a civilizing factor working on her.

I'll show you around. The Activity Room is where the contractually agreed upon HAPPENS. The expected is between two people, unless specified in *said* contract which incidentally is ripped up when *said* client departs. No trace.

Lighting is important. Have you heard the expression "invisible ink, milk in the sink?" It uses inkspots in a moat to illustrate a school of lighting. They've called me in to consult on various lighting techniques. Why I'm here. Each room is unique as you will be shown on this tour. Please note the distinct differences in lighting.

Interviewer: Have you worked on lighting for the Kit Kat?

Don't they have bare lightbulbs hanging from a string? They hardly need me for that!

The Neo-Platonic Room's light has to be "extrinsic, radiating, and the main source of all light." Light in the Liberace room is candlelight of course. Millions of candles with sparkling crystal bits hang from chandeliers. Candles set the mood. In the corner is a grand piano constructed of paper, for the "composer within" (screaming bloody murder to get out) that increasing percentage of select clientele.

The lumination goes back to the premise; society has been invented and is constantly being reinvented, relighted. Our fabrication adds to invention. Your hour should be "an hour most agreeable," including illuminations.

The East Indian Room has romantic gaslights with millions of tiny mirrors surrounding a famous ruby-colored crystal. It will dazzle the Western eye, especially if you have a hankering for initiation into exotic, Eastern lovemaking. You don't have to know Asia to partake.

Pimpo tells everybody he's in charge of the medicine. Here's the dispensary. Food and drugs. Whatever's needed to get it up. Some go into the "Cough Syrup Room," as we like to call it—never to return! Each "client" is charged not by the drug or amount of drug but by the hour. Face it, some are ready after one candy bar. When one of the employees has an ache, they don't complain to Pimpo; that would be like accusing him of being pain-free, God forbid. Sometimes he acts like a witch doctor from Borneo. When he got like that Pimpessa ignored him or she'd say, "Get out of my way until you stop acting like an elephant in mating season."

I see you looking at my finger. My mother insisted we keep our hands busy and above the table, etc. My fingers were a little too busy one morning so she chopped one off. The constant reminder is what hurts. . . .

Pimpo doesn't think of himself as a slave trader; he calls the girls "dancers" and talks himself into Carrie's "performance art" idea. Personally, I don't think the girls are stupid as dancers. You know the old adage . . . we employ a certain percentage of our brains, etc.

Pimpo the penetrating savage deludes himself he's got occupational hazards like the rest of us. Original slime, if you ask me. Has pep rallies for the girls. Says how boring it would be if things always went according to plan. Ends with "I'd like my employees to have a healthier breed of invading parts at the end of each shift."

Your Carrie—now there was a gal with ways and ways with words. I went walking with her one day . . . she referred to winos as her "bottle-rich cash-poor." I've skimmed her notebook . . . best parts outlined in lipstick. Did you read the part about "God sends us plagues?" And the one "Poor Tom's thorn is dry." Priceless. I'll sum it up for you: "The fucking fucker is fucked." Framed those hellscapes. Sugar bitches are a trip. I copied one entry out to refer back. Often. She was atypical. Stuffed many a woodpecker. She saw a lot of us as mumbling arguments for the gas chamber. Linguisters united in death. Want to see an excerpt? I have one here. Here goes:

Wear my denims like a badge when I'm not working. No one expects me to be hooking cause girls from the Orient slurp

**their lunch and DON'T HOOK. I'm a walking correction. I
know different. Sometimes I pretend I'm Wonder Woman
or a cop out of the ant hills. Out of the invaluable into the
ridiculous. Plop myself into dumb stuff. Rub it all over.
Legitimate. On my days off. At work, I'm the rewrapped
ragpicker with charge over another moved or moving from
the center of his desires. Escape for moments. Then I think
how can I get the sucker to shove off premature? I lump it.
Heap earth on it. Plant a pansy. Torched that A on my hairy
chest but the smoke and char make me want to puke and I
despise constant reminders.**

Talented madcap, ain't she huh? Enfant terrible. This
door leads you to a unique offering Demolition of Man
Room . . . used to be the livestock room. Livestock stam-
peded on payday when their "lost respect" wasn't paid out
in bucks. OUTTAHERE!

This place satisfies a demand. People come here and kill
themselves. Or murder a loved one, acquaintance, stranger,
or celebrity. Serial killings are big. The whole thing is acted
out.

The client can bring in the actual person or Pimpo sup-
plies a stand-in. Realistic playacting. Seems most in-house
performance art has panned out. Investment-wise, hands-
on violence often arouses the client, who is consequently
moved to the next room of his choice. Helps psychological
well-being. And the bill goes up. Each week Pimpo works
with a chemist and mechanic to concoct a special death at
Filene's bargain-basement prices. Last week it was a corro-
sive creosote solution guaranteed to leave the victim twist-
ing and foaming at the mouth in excruciating pain. All
"happenings" are filmed. The best deaths are preserved on
video. Rentable. Voyeurs can watch other people acting out
their death fantasies. Sometimes that's all THEY need.
There's a sign-up sheet and waiting list for *Before During and
After Death by a Hangman.* That's the most popular one. Customers don't want to wait for that one. Need it quick when
they need it. Hear them taking orders?

"We're here at your toss and call."

"Cute! But you too must wait your turn."

In the whole history of this place, the only troublemaker was a heart and brains financier; a regular Tin Man dressed in a tinkling suit of flattened tin cans, espousing his God-given rights. That was one scary moment. He was screaming what sounded like "DADA. Is you is or is you ain't my baby?" Torched his "having lumped it part" to end all circumstance. Rather gruesome stuff.

The thing you had to like about Carrie darling was she never felt defiled by her white European antecedents.

Prostitute:

I don't work for Pimpo. Says he gets along with me like a house afire. No time for happiness—that none-of-your-business asinine question. Left me blotched and shivery every time he left me. American. Smoked Luckies. An hour at the most. Not like I'm marrying him . . . the way he scratches his licey head. Know what he likes for breakfast— eggs Benedict. Eggs Buckingham fountain. Comme un oeuf dansant sur un jet d'eau. Don't think I didn't know those letters were written for somebody else. I could give you a sob story then hop in my red Testo with the bumper sticker "I'D RATHER BE WEEPING."

Englefred knows I like seeing HIM. We play games. Why is your back to me, lover? Ye olde ice-pick shoulder. He'd say ice pink. Baby. Then I grab to fling him ass-backwards. I unbutton his shirt after savagely ripping it, rape him just the way he likes it. Same rape as always, no surprises. Love the way he puts my shoe on. Then I drag him behind a large dusty cranberry theatrical curtain and scream bloody murder. Tell him to fuck off. Once a month. Good regular pay. What jollies. Shovelsful. Goes back to his boyfriend feeling like a just-been-raped-man, etc.

If, but I should say WHEN I smell dank, off, and of crustaceans, I shower. Like to do it after my last job. Thrills 'em to smell the other men on me. My new unmonastic feminist inclinations tell me women aren't in favor of rape but men are. The crowbar's untapped strengths have been doing a number on chickadees all along. Let 'em think they're Christmas in your mouth when you're just kicking back a black tubercular hack.

For the longest time I thought he was on the swatting bugs SWAT team over in Port Valmouth. Now I know he's into interiors. Think he'll advise me on what we should do with this joint? Last place I worked, I wouldn't wash my black sneakers in the mop sink they called a bathtub. Twits and plumbing men produced THIS little Broadway production of ours. Many of my present customers used to get serviced by Carrie at Pimpo's . . . like Scarface over there. They know what they want. Unfortunately, they want Carrie back. See the half-broken bottle sticking out of that one's face? Indication his wife's around. Her fatness makes them incompatible. She's at home tearing at her cheeks with her bare hands. Or some goon's hands. Blood's like mud. Thicken till it hurts.

The performance art aspect allows some dancers to cross over—hey, wherever the bucks are. It worked for Carrie. C'est la vie! I used to do a special services act—first with a rodent, then a mongoose, and lastly a falcon. In my old age, believe me THIS is more appropriate and more lucrative. Saving up to buy a Dunkin' Donuts slash Exxon.

Yeah. I do fortunes. I did Carrie's. Yeah I have copies. OK. Here goes:

Scorpio's Horrorscope—A Naturalistic Head on a Byzantine Body
I see you a helium-headed SOMEONE busily trimming lamps. Your best friends call you "Hammerhead nose." You would like to be a long-haired starlet, but you have your head shorn and shorn again. The second of November you will put on a flute-catching dress. What's the German word for descendants of flute players? It's important to your life, so find out. Your children will be Anglican combinations. Different fathers.

You refuse to be a F.A.T.-chested woman. This is a biological impossibility. A woman? And at the same time less than F.A.T.? Chested?

There is a man. His mouth is cut on your sword's-point breasts. His sexual fulfillment is to suck. Calls you tub chests. It's an insult to his body, not yours. Impeded creation. Man of Elfin neurotics. Elfin states of mind. Elfin erotics. Avoid Elfin storms. Elfin aspects make bop poets trample yellowed paper. Underfoot. I see you a Kennebunkport bag lady. You will carry empty refolded bags. Of whatnot.

I'm blocked. Whose olfactory what? The smell is a sad end of summer. Confused me. Missed beauty by precisely twenty-two hours.

I see career advancement. Your job will involve monogamous swans. None of you will inhabit the Limpopo region.

There is another man in the distance. His visage is reflected in antique mirrors painted over black. When he sucks your breasts you will want to thank him. Don't.

I see your life: unmade hotel-room beds, thirsty unmade days. I see two more men in your life. They wear pump-me-up sneaks. Red. Does this have of any significance?

These men will eventually found the Zippy Peal Pocket Fisherman Co. One of the men is the sexy Slesh Klug, who will play an important role in your life.

Do the initials D.X. mean anything? The two men again. One says l'chaim. The other says hi. If you've never trucked with a Hampstead witch . . . then you will.

If you've never donned a priest's robes and argued with another priest over who preaches from the higher of two pulpits . . . you will.

The two men are furtive dunkers. Of donuts. They keep male popinjays as pets. I see you primping your long hair in front of movie cameras saying, "My hair is titian."

Someone you knew died happy. Very recently. All your toenails turned black and fell off. If these events have not occurred already, prepare for them to happen within six months.

Someone close to you is into betrayal and recrimination. Both your marriages end with the throwing of carrot juice-spotted Cuisinarts.

Great talking to you but someone's pounding RATHER suggestively at my window. Remember I'm the one like Billie Holiday, only I smile.

    I: When I'm back at Pimpo's, with whom should I speak?

    The pimp and one more of his young ladies: "Marie Tussaud III."

Marie: Hi, sit over there. I know you and you know me. I'll spill my guts. Next they'll let you see Pimpo, who is descended from so-called reasonable people. About Carrie . . . I used to spend a lot of time discussing *the pleasures of the unmade bed* at her home. The decor was simple. She espoused the Italian futurists, so naturally I thought speed, color, and light would be reflected in her decor. But it was stark. Almost Japanese. To look at it you might think Italian composition had never been invented. Guess where the speed and the light went? Translated themselves into her writings. I'm sure you've been exposed to some of her writings by now. Joke and comic books covered her bookshelves. Very literary. What she read embarrassed her and we agreed it would embarrass us—so under wraps it went.

    She had some fine art. A Léger for pride and joy. That purchase was dedicated to one of her "moments of class." Over the desk in her office is a poster stating "You said you would grant me genius—well, where is it?" The makeup area, complete with adjacent dressing room, were two simple yet elegant rooms. She sat at the vanity shaping to nothing her eyebrows—unhappy until she looked between a eunuch and Apollinaire.

    An exhibitionist streak surfaced when she was most unhappy and just the opposite on off-hours. Remember that concert not too long ago, the Bald Aztec Dogs were jamming when the manic guitarist went up in flames? Said she

wanted to go the same radiator-babies way. The sex-dog
guitarist (lead Bald Aztec Dog) had asked her to be one of
the three dancers on stage that night, but she declined.
And they all fried.

In the off, all the girls would talk about less "active" pro-
fessions or getting "out" in some way. Not Carrie, who
would say, "Pig's ass. I was born an old maid and it's taken
me this long to get over THAT." Then we'd fall into discussion about whatever preparation was needed to deal with
our next client.

Can you give an example?

Marie: Sure. "I have to dress as a schoolboy begging for a
whipping. I play choirboy to his 'spike.' " (Anglo-Catholic
ritualist partial to equivocal relationships.)

Then we'd complain. Pet peeves. "I hate it when they
want your back wings outspread in order to drum you to
death." Some aspects are more difficult than others and
some situations, you find out pretty quickly, must be
avoided after only one time out. The proverbial rough time
is FACT. Happens to everyone some time in their illustrious
career.

Pimpo requires notes, so we all become writers to an extent that is a hoot. By the time a client is a regular, many
meetings have been taken dealing with his or her individual
problems . . . similar to any psych ward. Expert care COSTS.

I remember Carrie complaining, "What pisses me off is
them rampaging in here, chomping on some pea doves,
soberly drunk cause they're 'talking.' Fuck that. Geeks end
up trashing the place. Fucking jerks . . . why don't they drag
their pity and irony elsewhere? Find someone else to relish
them a crumpet or two."

Her rule was the house rule. "Don't let them in. Never
befriend a trick. Have another set of friends handy." Some
clients want to get close to you . . . figure you out. Lots of
fright-dicks. No one cares if a wobble-legged working girl
gets blown away. Happy to see you go. Another bottle of
Jack. Kiss you g'bye. Fall in love with you like you're their
therapist. Think you can do something for them outside.

Unhealthy. She drew lines. Never altered in those professional . . . is *dichotomies* the right word?

Sure.

Marie: The architectural setup here at the Kit Kat is an attempt to make us less vulnerable. Less wide open. Have to protect one another. Twenty girls work in this particular house with one mattress on the floor in each room. Doors remain open all the time. If we hear something, we run to help another girl get out of it.

Carrie hated to see a new girl coming in. Not because they would be competition for her in any way—but she hated the thought of it happening all over again for another "unknowledgeable nubile." Trouble is they THINK they're knowledged. Got the nubile part right. Carrie talked down the amount of work it involves to outsiders but talked it up with the new girls. Hoping they'd bail out. Saw herself as a kind of lighthouse, WARNING! Impending danger. To hear her sometimes you'd think we were rolling in our own—or worse—someone else's excrement.

While we wait we philosophize, chat, beautify, etc. . . . have some fun. Sit around brushing each other's hair. Talk lingerie sales or Persian rugs; polyester and wool differences, etc.

Did you ever get the feeling she should get out?

Marie: It was more than a feeling . . . I used to think she had BEEN out, that she had the station wagon, 2.2 children, and doctor husband. We'd be fantasizing about normalcy and she'd pipe in with it ain't all it's cracked up to be like . . . old hat to her. Dignified . . . the way she held her head unconsciously . . . unstudied and dignified stuff like that comes from somewhere . . . nice. Not from a deprived background . . . fallacy that most of us came from shit. Pretty balanced bunch in the successful corner. One time she confessed herself the runt of the litter. On the contrary, we knew her to be quite a voluptuous full-figured woman with a toned physique.

Once Carrie said life taught her to look into the eye of that "apple pie hallucination, THE AMERICAN WIFE, who

is more concerned with her husband's indigestion than
politics." Strife, wife, and motion. She said the smartest
people know when they're not welcome—and locomote. I
suspect she did that.

Picture-taking came up once—one of us needed her picture. I forget why. Carrie said if we were cyclops, or a wife,
or an actress, we'd be just as photosensitive as she. She said
"No."

Did she talk about her dreams?

Marie: Her dreams were less than ordinary, they were
mundane unless she was serving up ironies. "I WANT to be
put out to pasture in my old age, superannuated, and innocently retired from, say, K Mart." Under the illusion her life
would begin THEN, in that distant future, she could be the
quirkiest.

Her clients?

Marie: Her favorite client was Silly Linguister, fresh out
of pudgy elderly citizens' jail. A repeater . . . jailed for painting and thereby shaming the Statue of Liberty. The second
time they nailed him as he approached the monument with
"unabashed artistry" (must have been wearing a beret) and
his can of dripping paint. His insides smell like rotten tapi-
oca. Now that she's gone, lucky me, I've inherited him.
Sour Stomach himself. Her log will get me through our ren-
dezvous. There are two chapters on him. Nobody can do it
to him like she could. I hear that often enough. "The best."
He talks about her all the time. Asks me can he pretty
please get in touch with her? I thought I needed her as a pal
but she's really better off. Seeing her go makes me want to
really go. No kidding. I deserve better too.

Are you sure you can't tell me anything about your boss?
Anything I should know on or off the record?

Marie: Naw. He'll be straight with you. Next room.

Was Carrie, in your opinion, capable of murder?

Marie: I've known so-called murderers—killers. Some no
different from me or you. One certainly can't tell by looking . . . boy-next-door serial killers. "Such a nice boy helped
me bring in my groceries"- type thing. She had a pensive-

ness. There was other stuff going on with Carrie which won't cut and dry. In that respect, she could have murdered. In retrospect, quirks in her personality may have been omnipresent. Hindsight . . . now incidents pop into my head and I see she raced strangely to certain finish lines. Let's hypotenuse her into the type of person who murders. If she did, it was without anger, she won't try temporary insanity—premeditated all the way. Calm and cool. Premeditated 'cause I've seen that chick pushed to the brink time and time again when she coulda shoulda. Didn't. Pregnant with fatal calamities, she weighed carefully the consequences of every weird little iota. Don't think for a minute she made a rash decision. All decided. But what the hell do I know?

Thank you.

Marie: Step over and in to (please not into) the boss for your next interview.

"I have to tell you going in I think you've got to be the stupidest race on earth," said pockmarked Pimpo, clad in silk, watering orchids. Blood stained the beautiful material adorning his crippled body. "Excuse my mess. I was out back killing carrier pigeons . . . one thing cowboys without parentage do."

I'd like to ask you a few questions . . .

"Thought you might. I hate all them bitches as a gender if you must know. Not happy unless they're stirring it up. Enjambed last wearers of rouge. Most women know that stuff isn't good for them. She had a monkey's tail. Freak of nature. Otherwise she couldn't have sold tickets to her own show. Had three breasts . . . not uncommon. Some of the new ones are impressionable. Poor and hungry is the way I like 'em. Not her. Not her buddies. Maybe some of their clients, though. Look, I inherited this business. Tell you what I know but it's no good. Hate to waste your time. Aren't we busy men? A beer?"

I'd love one.

"She wanted to bring gerbils into the act. I said OK. We tried it. But we had all these furry little dead carcasses around and guys taken to the emergency room, it got messy. I wanted to fire her monkey tail ass but I let them talk me into letting her stay. She had it out for particular clients, if you know what I mean. A following. Main Street America might still be innocent if word didn't get out big time. We end up defending these girls in two completely different ways. Aw, forget it."

Her ideas?

"One idea was to sun-fire without burning each man's door knocker. Panned out. We've got that one still in operation. Her data entries were excellent and to this minute invaluable to the other girls. Lots of innovation there. Carrie Innovation Meeber.

"She took distortionist classes and brought in a hands-on artistic group. One idea was multi-hueing members. The paints were edible and pepper-flavored. Don't you just love it? Tribal. Gotta give her credit. Wasn't afraid to fall flat on her back, so to speak. She organized lucrative tours: art groups in to have a look at our 'tainted women.' She didn't respect us though—I was an 'evolved baboon.' Personally, I wasn't asking for respect.

"She was a woman with a business sense and more than your average interest in doing something to penises. Most girls have it to the 'Where's mine?' point of negotiation. 'Where's mine?' is the beginning and end of their business acumen. Like 'See you tomorrow, Chump!' "

We're told she often referred to the lost tribe.

"That's what she called this paint project. It distanced a lot of the old guard. Beaver-eaters beware. Please excuse. I love you too baby. The girls like to kiss me when they're babies—fresh in. An entrepreneur wanted to marry Carrie once. Eurotrash. But he started getting so fat he finally blew up or something. Happens. The strangest things happen. Wasn't she already married?"

Valmouth?

"Yeah. The hypochondriac who gave her the baby boy fetus in a jar? Have you seen that?"

Yes.

"This profession is hard on a marriage. Think about it. Everybody who picks up a sexually transmitted disease returns expecting doctoring by us. Absurd. Now they must sign a waiver on entrance. Won't use their real names anyway. Our girls take every precaution. But I sometimes wonder if she didn't catch something."

What makes you say that?

"A former beauty contest judge's wife dropped him off once a year for his Christmas present. This past year Carrie talked about him like HE was her yearly Christmas present. She was getting things really mixed up towards the end. All sufficiently mad enough to want it."

You allowed her to continue?

"Carrie was here before me. Grandfathered in. We let her do some strictly forbidden things . . . like allowing her to grant clients voyeuristic moments, which believe you me is usually a no-no. Some pea-pickers think squawking gawking beats going to the movies."

Squawking gawkers.

"Carrie could get up two fees for half as much work. Most of the girls would do it if they could. Won't allow it any more. Problems arise."

Thing is, there are psychos acting out serious problems.

"A lurking wife nobody minds. We like to spread education. It's just the weirdos."

Are sandwiches still available?

"Sure. We have a special on that today."

Bestiality?

"I'll admit to the gerbils but that's over."

Did she partake of drugs?

"I don't think so. Maybe when she ran with Valmouth. I'm usually the first to know. I make drug runs if we don't have whatever in stock. I do remember she called someone her educated spoon who in turn called her 'my educated banana'—I assumed it was their love-langue. Let's look that john up in the log, which goes NOWHERE WITHOUT A

WARRANT. She has an impish sense of the ridiculous . . . nowhere is it more pronounced than in her log entries. But if you think it will bring you total insight into her character—think again. She talks here about his proud posterior. 'He shaves his face so as not to ruin me with ouch his stitched-on lips.' Have to go through the whole thing one day. Not that I expect it to make much sense. Too literary."

Would you have her set apart from her contemporaries, from her fellow prostitutes?

"She set herself apart. One couldn't help but see her that way. Absolutely. At the end, but I guess it was coming for a long time, she was unavailable, which infuriated everyone. Especially me if I'm supposed to be her boss. Some women you just gotta let 'em go. Standing by her man or something stupid. The guy sent her here, didn't he? Jerk. Deserved what he got. She commanded great fees. Once she understood the monetary facts, she absented herself and kind of hired out other girls as deputies; distributing the loaves and fish. A pyramid in my own place. Shit! She gave a lot of other girls a start—only if she was sure they couldn't be talked out of it. First she tried that. Talked quite a few out before they were in, which actually made monetary sense for the establishment in the long haul.

"Her girls BECAME her. Nobody knew the difference, so long as the substitutes had the technique . . . what's on sale here. Faces are not the big thing. Like Hemingway said, 'helpful hands.' I retrieved that from her notes.

"She was odious and regularly absent thereby all the more odious. Resentment built up towards her. But go figure women—she would light on the scene and the girls didn't want nobody but her. Shadow to their leader. Her 'all go' still echoes in the halls.

"You know how we started in performance art? She organized a kind of rifle troop of fuckers. Professional fuckers. It got to the point where she was in town maybe twice a year. She would have the girls line up. People paid $500 a head. What you have to remember is that audience participation with one girl at a time was encouraged. I'm hoping I can remember one of their procedures. Each direction is at a rifle volley.

"Here goes:

The group advanced in line and fucked.

Threw back its left by the file movement and fucked.

Took ground to the right by open column movement and fucked.

Brought forward its left by the echelon movement and fucked.

Changed its front to the rear by the countermarch of divisions by files and fucked.

Reversed its front by the countermarch of divisions to the center and fucked.

Advanced in line and fucked.

Advanced in open columns, formed behind two center divisions, and fucked.

Formed a hollow square and fucked.

Advanced in a square and fucked.

Formed line on center by the echelon movement and fucked.

Advanced in line at the open order—general salute.

"Walk this way please. They were good choreographed soldiers, man. Beautiful to see. Herculean in effect. We're talking one talented group of women. Perfecto! Would you care to see another piece she wrote? It's being performed in the Liberace Room and here . . . we . . . are!"

CURTAIN UP ON ACTORS IN SLACKS AT GOLF TEES.

"Vaudeville at the Inferno" is written in white chalk on a blackboard stage left.

One golfer does a monologue: "Watch that chick with the big rear," she tells the viewing audience who are, in fact, staking out a chick with a big rear. So who needs to be told? She's a persnickety pachyderm. Didn't she have hereditary syphilis and beg the doctors to kill her? Excuse me, she's from a smeared and dirty people, whose lives are bound up with their own pachyderms. She dates a chi-chi who has his hair done for him by another into a ravaged topknot.

I ask her to discuss the development of the area over the past years:

(Golfer does reenactment solo.)

Kind of vile. Fancy, opulent, wasteful.

And on being the working WASP?

More than the work ethic. Chinese and Italians cook. Ethnicity has to do with . . . the finer things.

Please accompany me downstairs to the bomb shelter. Or shall we continue where we . . .

A female enters and says: Back to what WASPS eat— how's the road-kill Marmot?

Golfer 2): I eat it . . . then it's nightmare time. I have one where I'm onstage by myself. Quite some time goes by. Then I'm visited. This Yale graduate comes on and says, "If I could find a white boy who could sing like a nigger, might make us a million dollars." What does the laughing do for you?

Golfer 1): The kind where I'm accompanied and we're rolling on and off the floor weeping unashamedly in and out of the fetal situation? That's the big IT. Why, in your opinion, do you do what you do?

Golfer 2): When I'm not checking the china for lead, I regard myself as a teacher with direct access to the minds of the children of the ruling class.

Golfer 1): Expatiate "ruling class" please.

Golfer 2): Those who enjoy eating their own.

Golfer 1): Angry?

Female: No, I just like hitting. I like hitting people.

Two golfers: OK. Not just dead and white. We're male. You like hitting us?

Female: Learn it in order to play it to end it. Boring piggish dead white males are, in fact, very much alive. What must end.

Golfers: And yet you buy into us and all we are "about" to a certain extent.

Female (*aside*): To the extent they speak to me. They're right sometimes. At it long enough. Always better dancers than we think. I want to succeed. Don't I? And the drink?

Golfers: Pabst Blue Ribbon!

Female: Yeah.

1): White-boy shoes?

2): And black-boy shoes.

F): Both want the black-leather dentist chair in their prospective living rooms, and decor falls into place around it.

Golfers: Same things for different reasons.

F): Reasons of aura. I find huge comfort in the crowd. It's animated. You can be swept up in it. Gives you something to hate. It's like any asshole with whom you don't want to spend the rest of your life. Fun to abscond with his energy. A laugh at another's expense makes you feel whole.

Golfers: Sounds expensive—keeping time with you. Asshole to make you whole. Asswhole?

F): People like to think you're just like them or beneath them. Nicer. REALITY—gets 'em in the ego. That hurts more than the wallet. I get the impression, correct me if I'm wrong, you expect to be discovered any minute.

1): Any minute all my life. Looking back on my life, I can't pretend it hasn't happened. Little moments of recognition. Not the way I coulda thunk. Woody Allen should show up at the library (I peruse) and want us for realism. Little moments of recognition.

F): It may send the person on his way in disgust.

2): Your failings?

1): I dread my inefficiencies. I'm married to them. Makes me a bundle of what I wasn't. Anything worth winning is like—oh let the other person win.

F): And you're the big golfer?

1): To win you have to go up there and give them something they want. Nothing's worth that. Totally inconvenient.

F): Don't get me wrong—I've played the hunter, always lost in that role. Doesn't suit.

F+ 1) +2) = God must be replaced.

Curtain down.

Glad that's over.

Pimpo: Kind of excruciating, isn't it?

How did folks bandy her name about?

Pimpo: Differed depending on the time and place . . .
you would think they were discussing totally different
people. She was "prude," "studious," "trying to sell," then
"bon vivant," and finally "murderess." *Nothing left to lose* philosophy.

And you?

Pimpo: You can ask any of the girls who will say I left their
honor intact.

I'll tell you what they SAID you called her: *The Cutest Ass,
Dead Ass, A Girl, Fresh Daisy, Insidewalk Cowboy.*

Pimpo: She drew attention to thunder lost in herself.
Her friends wanted men with money for her. One sugges-
tion was an MBA graduate.

Did you ever find her interested in recipes?

Pimpo: I'd be lying if I said no. I'll cut you a break
(though you might not see it that way) and let you read this
questionnaire section of her log.

Carrie's log no. 3343. Conversation #999.

False perceptions of various stages of behavior like being
labeled "mellow" seem drug-related and not at all true. I'm
perceived as mellow yet I'm eaten alive. It's very difficult.
Composure is something I aspire to. Actresses are compo-
sure-embodiments because it's all conjured and totally
false.

I don't like dry, kiss-ass behavior, stained or rotten teeth,
speed or acid, drugs in general, peeling nail polish, loud
sloppy chewing, rat droppings, birds stuck in air ducts, al-
lergies, what you HAVE to do.

When I find someone satisfied with their lot: (I really
don't find that.) Most people aren't as satisfied as I am. For
a year, it was just the one thing in my life holding me back
and now that's eradicated.

Will contentment last?

Does anything? Own up to the full knowledge you put yourself in it voluntarily. In these United States anyway. Do you understand buying and selling? I'm not going to change their worldview. A joke when they think it's a new idea. It's how you combine the ideas out there—what you take for yourself—what you abandon. Cleaning is a constant VIBRANT thought.

Interviewer takes a lunch break and returns to find Luissette with Pimpo. He waits until they finish talking.

Luissette with Pimpo:

He: You gotta Heva like Eve the Arranger.

She: You mean she was guaranteed no more than average intelligence?

He: We were guaranteed she would not be above average. Kisses easy. Kisses stolen.

She: Believed only by the thief to be stolen. What about welfare mothers?

He: That's the proper line of thought. What about the murder?

She: Murder by neglect.

He: What do you expect from high school call girls forbidden to attend the exhibition of art rejected by the Third Reich? You have a full understanding of the icons we talk about. Will you represent us?

She: Who is "us"?

He: Peace.

She: The old "fuck you" times two?

He: Not, at first glance, much to look at. Arranger.

She: You want me to be your arranger?

He: Were we falsely led to believe history is your profession?

She: Onanism.

He: How many does it take?

She: Aristotle and me. One.

He: He was a bald man.

She: And a millionaire.

He: Scroptophilia is only triumphant feminism.

She: Exactly.

He: Why face away from me? I know the way to take a woman.

She: Because you call my vagina "Babushka." And won't stop barking at me. Stay put. You will roger me to find you disappear inside me. Don't you feel partially erased when that happens?

He: Yes. I have to dress up like a German emperor with an active vocabulary of dog commands.

She: Your penis represents you like a child inside me. You're another Cabbie.

He: Kinch is inside you.

She: Bargained for this while looking at the snow and wolves outside my window. If we hadn't been in China this never would have happened.

He: We all have bargainers' faces.

She: No more operatic peeps. Rains this time every day. Need a gamp. My old chum Kinch.

He: My old chum Luissette. Water warm soft. Tell me about the gamp. How did that poem go?

She: It went in the trash. My old chum Took Took. Seeming real.

He: Or really seeming. Do you feel my entire weight?

She: I do. Tiny red brute of a thing.

He: I want to almost smother you.

She: That's normal. Homo Vulgarus.

He: Luissette your real name? Your mouths are enlarged. Do something.

She: With your crowbar? I want to please you. Everything swells and is not swell. Use this Pepsi bottle. At this point in time you have two distinct possibilities—sticking it up or strapping it off.

He: Buss me.

She: Roger me.

He: Manhood found here.

She: Enter but do not enter.

He: You're talking chemical suicide. Vessel.

She: Do not drink.

He: No paternity suit.

She: And you get to take home what you brought me. I don't want it. Take it home to your everlasting bride in celebration of your everlasting first night.

He: "Opening night," so to speak? Taking home the gamp?

She: You're working my mouths pretty good. Lavish-limbed me. Even though my hair falls out around you. You will be classified "trick with ambiguity." Not many of those. Go now to the men's room.

He: So busy with half a foot of cane. What's around it?

She: Your sock.

He: You make it look like an oboe.

She: Told you it swells like a once-embottled genie. Broken in to. Work for the night is always coming. Why I pop prunes.

He: What about her?

She: Always ends up riddled with bullets and robbed. Fractured pantaloons get to be a bore.

He: Touch you where?

She: Buss you where? The very place. Where are you lonely?

He: Nerveless on featherhead mountain. I'm a lot like you were, which makes me cover up with cabbage leaves.

She: Life in an unmade is cracked up to be a big red bedsore. Scratch yourself in it often enough.

He: What about my hat rack? What about your skirt duty?

She: My hat's off to you Mr. . . . De Kock. It has something to do with the sincerity of your socks and shoes.

He: Under old-fashioned sofas. I'd like some heart of yours up and in. Sacred Heart with a flame severing it in two.

She: Fecundity in your trousers. My vagina has been re-structured with wire and chicken bones. Job-related surgery.

He: Bags-ful. Workman's comp, I surmise. What about the murder?

She: If I tell you about that, I'll be ruining myself perhaps for life.

He: Tell me. Underwear with complications?

She: Tell you so you can tell him? I'll tell him myself.

Luissette with Interviewer:

She: Carrie called herself the second sex and liked sailors fresh in who needed it desperately as she did . . . never liked paying customers. Cared not a pin who they were. She was an old-line nightwalker. So were they. They didn't have to walk far if she smelled a landing. She felt like mothering, teaching. Liked them young. Wanted them off on her . . . dripping down her stomach. Had ways of forcing them to wait. Until her turn. Said it gave them willpower. She was so in love with willpower I thought she was going to name her son that. Will Power. She had to beat them back with her built-in fists while her body was a million foreign-country body parts mixed like a cubist painting . . . her vagina on the sole of her foot. Used to say, "I like to make a mickey stand then see HOW LONG he can stand." Contests with a secondhand watch. Forced participants to choose "Eater or Eaten!"

Liked hair-pulling and biting. I saw her leave with the blue suede dress on. Showing off her white dusted bosom. She added a slight glitter polish. Said it would sing up at people even if she became indisposed. After meeting one man, she pulled out some ice-cold butter, saying, "Let's think about the oldest way known to man to melt this slow." Put her on the job to find out if a sailor's seatbelt works. If he knew whoop, she would record it: either the sensational or funny. Helluva hobby. Chile with wile. A female animal with fantastic muscles defined. Uncommonplace passions.

Shh. Here comes Pimpo.

(This moment of revelation is interrupted when Pimpo enters:)

Pimpo: I've got a few words to say about Carrie: pleasure

became work. She got a pale smile. That won't sell a girl. Don't get me wrong, I get the bitches in here. Nothing wrong with that. I was whorehouse physician, if you will. We drank and drugged to no avail. Suddenly she was miscast. Capital became her everything. Lust just beyond her, that outboard motor had no gas. When it's his money, a guy can smell it. Ripe for a fall. No longer every little sailor's misery. Kicked the fellows right in the pants, so to speak. I blame that amputee she carted around.

What little (not a wealth of information) the girls know about the guy was told them by her friend. Reputedly red, religious, and hot, his seed was split. You know how that goes. His wife was the ever-present and indubitable fatal problem. Carrie went swimming in his blue faience tub filled with heated black spiced tea. The experience intoxicated her in such a way she was never our little arranger again. We just got a new one today. Luissette over here has minutes ago agreed to my stipulations.

This guy was proud to be self-intoxicated criminal garbage. I only saw his Oriental roast-beef face once. He kept the buffalo you see across the road. Ate them for sandwich meat . . . and buffalo burgers. Said Italians kill a woman the moment she puts down tuna glop expecting it to be eaten. Had this THING about tuna glop which was an amazing concept to him. She was allured. She didn't HAVE to intoxicate him. He savaged her. He had many bubbling body holes like you see in my nose. A freak. "In all my days I have never" . . . you know how that story goes. Exactly where the toreador pants come in. You know all about that. In those days everything was on the house. We all went through the same mill. Together. The long-suffering wifeliness was hard on us. She rubbed our faces in it. To us, she had become a hydroponic vegetable hanging in space. From Such-A-Much to hydroponics. All my women started looking tired and sad. And the men were out of work. Nothing else to say about them. Sad-looking bunch. He broke into my home and stole the linen off my bed. What the hell does he want with that? This is the company your precious Carrie keeps?

Orm Gamulson is related to him by marriage through
. . . what's her name? Kimothy his first wife. Have you questioned her? You guys can check on that. Gamulson is employed by the art gallery/bar down the street. His self-pro-
claimed "anti-profession" is "uglifier." If anyone cried or
was moved to an emotion while observing his art (no matter
how inane), he would see to it THAT portion was de-
stroyed. No longer open to public ridicule. At times subtle
and imprecise, at other times subtle and precise; sum him
up as a subtle subliterate. Anyway, I digress.

Interviewer: We've been there. He has shared his
thoughts.

She: Carrie's man didn't think a woman could be ruined
by marriage. I know, we had a long discussion about that
the time I met him. His ailments got the best of him and he
gestured madly with his hands out of control as if I planted
a whopping steaming portion of tuna glop on his tray. What
started out as wonderful dead art by spillers of paint (from
tequila-hearted worms) became lungers spitting blood into
their own recipes.

Word got out and people stayed away. Loyal customers
would no longer partake at the restaurant. Imagine folks, if
you will, a death wish for friends and innocent off-the-street
customers.

Carrie nicknamed him Priss. He cultivated in her, his
lovely Gypsy, everything sacred and utterly profane. Made
her repeat all of it two or three times a day. Sniffed her out
to know exactly who she was with . . . never tortured her in
full view of an audience. Her homecomings were black-
nailed and bruise-lipped. What the hell were we supposed
to do with her looking like that? Always said she had a great
time. She was into the casting-couch scene. He made that
easy for her. Couching it was his hobby. Another case of the
elephant holding the leopard at bay.

Interviewer: Does "this man" have a name other than
"Priss."

She: They also called him "Interloper." It has been al-
luded to that Carrie and her earlier man Valmouth made a

fortune in ear-globes. They started manufacturing a decorative paint magically held together with baby urine. It smelled awful (only while it was being applied). It made people sick. It was a very noisy factory . . . all communication was written with the "ear-globe paint." Each reader lost strength with every written message. They lounged by the tub all day. One day he pulled the chain out of the tub. POP. They sneezed. Then came across a rhyme—I don't know how. The rhyme was an accident. Incidents and accidents sent their lives in a totally different direction. She became a fugitive flower . . . disarmingly helpless (like it said in the papers). They got a poetic license plate. Got a car. Took one drive and then another, returned to the house after the second drive, walked in the door to find the urined paint had thickened into a light plastic goop. It was an adhesive worth millions for various industrial applications. They were rich. Adhesive barons. Overnight. Panderers were called off. That's when they opened the Shy Club. A few hundred ear-globes actually came to full production and are now invaluable collectibles. I think Saks had the exclusive on them.

Members of the Shy Club wore skirts of ribbons. Salaries were the only glamorous subject considered worthy of conversation. Haven't figured this out yet but I was told one key to the recent murder is "a suicide can't be buried in consecrated ground." Any fool can have his dog and pony shows (animal tricks with HulaHoops, etc.) over sacred sites.

Plastic goop worth millions bruised his head. And it bruised her head. Goes to show you one man gathers the split gash of another. He was into class distinctions: one class could blow bubbles while another couldn't. She could blow bubbles.

He saw her as an Oriental stallion full of "josh" and "kid." She fit well into the company of mothers, friends, old maids, you name it. The thing turned him on was her bringing azaleas into the house. Naturally, his other girlfriends brought azaleas but they left them at the front door which to him is somehow less disconcerting. They had been professional ladies and he tried to believe them but . . . could not.

He: This female stallion in some way empowered him?

She: The power of *king* given by a woman to a man makes him and keeps him king long after his scepter is relinquished. They would fight. We would arrive at a specified time and he wouldn't be there. She would explain his absence like so: "He's in the dungeon filling another military mailing crate full of my azalea-motif belongings." Then he would appear sulking as if summoned from an angry punishment.

He: What for?

She: From what I could tell, it was to further encourage her collecting. Their reconciliations calmed all fury. He valued her bulletproof eye for collecting. He held her hand when he wanted her to love him . . . all the while behind her back, he hocked her choicest ceramics. Duty to himself. His gifts to her were major collecting trips (when and where she would make her discoveries). Her astronomer's eye was tremendous. Sometimes he would go along on these trips and sometimes . . . decline. Transactions and closings had everything to do with *both* of them.

Pimpo: Now *this terrible thing* has happened I'm reminded of a game they often played—let me try to remember, a feather was involved. There was a weight of measurement. She threatened him by saying, "When the feather weighs more than your heart, the crocodile devours it." Is that a clue? There was a lot of talk about eating hearts . . . more than in your average run-of-the-mill household. At the time we assumed it was allegorical or symbolic, diffused or removed in some way from reality—but now I'm not so sure. Other organs were pretty much left alone.

One day he caught me alone and confessed she was godawful, but the best he could hope to OWN. So they married. I attended the soiree after dressing myself as "a German on his wedding day." We toasted them with spicy alelike mead. Triple morns passed and on the third afternoon, they reminded us we ate live bull, which had been hopping around in a delicious soup of mud, stalactites, and tapwater served out of the Egyptian (replica) turquoise-colored tub. The black tea was blended with bull's blood. Gory but delicious. We suffered lost minds . . . lost three days of our lives. The stock market crashed as we slam-danced amid squirts of blood and razor blades. Beaten begun. Beaten end. All the guests have permanent scar tissue to remind them of the connubial celebration.

Toward the end of the night, a serving girl came out carrying one tray with two severed heads. The hair on each head was a mass of red peppers spray-painted with silver ends. On closer look, I saw one head was Mishka and the other was Alexander. I dropped to the floor. Cold faint. Mishka revivified me. "The heads are art." I was reassured. "Likenesses." The wedding party was forced to participate in the auctioning off of this art. I was entirely scandalized by the whole thing, especially when informed I won in the bidding. For 20,000 rubles, I owned one head. Mishka told me his vanity was being severed and displayed. He who "lives in his own face" is taught something—ways of redemption— which could be a comfort to us all. I wandered . . . wondering . . . whatever to do with my winnings. It was getting late. I found . . . wretched little reason to depart. The longer we stayed, I feared we would spend the rest of our lives at the Miami Fountainbleu. When I can't shake it—I'm still there. Never-leave syndrome.

Holding on to my head, I found a bereft group violated in more than one way on more than one occasion during the festivities. We all confessed to having participated in some unmentionable act. All I can say—it was throbbing then sank. And . . . it was unintentional. Sensational. The guests were walking victims of a fixed idea. This ineffable union ruined us. Ruined weddings for me. Now if a wedding is mentioned, I wait to see if both parties live for a year and if they do survive it, I send them a fragile Fabergé egg and tell them "Be very careful in this fragile predicament."

They each (Carrie and "Interloper") had their own separate receiving line in separate rooms. Every guest was told

"Embrace me for the sake of life" once by the bride and once by the groom. Dinner faltered then went bland. After cake each guest (victim, if you ask me) was officially asked to reinvent society . . . (bunch of peach sieves we were) . . . couldn't come up with much. (Regular society was looking pretty damned good.) There was a last speech by both bride and groom before we were "released."

Her speech took us on a reminiscent, chronological, thoughtful search for a mate. What she had previously wanted in a marriage partner was a millionaire. She went to all the best places but all the millionaires were in K Mart buying socks. We were told when to clap, when to yelp, and when to hiss. Messages came up behind the speaker in neon letters. His speech, entitled "The Wonders of Hemp," dealt with clothing, wood pulp, and the fact Levi Strauss made his first jeans from hemp, etc. Then we all chawed on hemp brownies smothered in Cool Whip.

The couple, connected to each other by tinfoil chains, departed in a Rolls. The guests were handed rhymed couplets and expected to chant something about "Who is clanking his chains." Everybody sounds different when you remove the commas so I had hope for their marriage . . . is either one alive? Did they ever happen in this world? Answer me something . . . did she stink?

Interviewer: Every killer does not stink.

Luissette: I should have known when I saw her wedding gown—it was some horror's idea of Las Vegas style. She believed the old adage "a husband's funeral is a wife's true wedding." He was a decorative nobody if you ask me.

Interviewer: Could Interloper and Valmouth be one and the same person?

Pimpo: Silly Willy, come over here. We're seriously branching off into performance art. Would you like to see a practice (that which may occur)? In here. Carrie discovered this guy.

An artist covered in melting whipping cream says:

SNAGS. RIP-RAP.

Curtain up behind him.

Artist #2: No need to fear, my urine is pure. My MOTHER IS OMNIPOTENT. And I am a man, sensuous not vulgar. Leather subculture is mine. Tall and blue-eyed, I am able to trace my ancestry to Viking rulers such as Gorm the Old, Harold Blue-Tooth, and Svend Fork-Beard.

Artist #1: I take photographs. A photograph is a gift from the person IN the photo. I've adopted Latino death-cult subculture. Pop stars pick me up. You can make me sit here in my chair like an overboiled leek, or you can open the doors and let the whole family in to enjoy me.

Player #3: The boss said, "Frankly, your telegram to the agency worried us not a little bit." (*He reads telegram aloud:*)

"AM BEING CHRISTENED HERE TOMORROWSTOP

"IN THE GANGESSTOP

"DO NOT WORRYSTOP

"AM NOT A BELIEVERSTOP" (*stops reading*).

Artist # 1: I said not to worry. No need. Like talking about Gene Kelly's singing voice. Who cares? His phrasing is perfect. His diction and clarity have desire. He has all the quality we demand of someone WANTING a song to be sung.

AND I PROMISE, YOU'LL FIND AS I DO, THE CAMEL RACES QUITE DIVERTING.

Curtain down.

Pimpo: Reminds me, for some strange reason, of the young man doing dishes next to a sink of soapy water, with his hat and vest on. Like he ran in from an organized cockfight, saw what needed to be done, and got down to serious scrubbing. Necessary impossible projects.

Interviewer: Whatever needed to be done?

Pimpo: So happy and smiling about it.

From a member of the audience (*practically on stage*): Yes you can develop your movie negatives in the love canal . . . I'm smiling the whole time.

Pimpo: How do you feel?

Interviewer: Fine, and yourself?

Pimpo: Like the postal system: worse and worse.

Interviewer: What we've got here is unlarded failure to communicate.

Pimpo: Let's keep it that way, shall we? Admittedly he needs to work on it but we're branching off into other rotation of bodies entertainment fields. Thanks to bitch goddess Carrie. Sole reason to thank her. My vote goes for an old-fashioned burlesque hour. The best-looking girls have learned to strip off ornate costumes that come away in eight or nine pieces. My favorite strip-down ends with a clown face on each breast lighted up from behind by remote control. I'm lucky enough to have a gal who eats sparingly enough to wear it.

Interviewer: Interesting. . . .

Pimpo: Look, Buster, you come into our Tenderloin District and it's like you've got this poet, artist or, yeah, why not say it—Irish attitude. It irks the fuck outta me. Are you all of twenty-five years old and a man living on or should I say OFF a trust fund?

Interviewer: Say whatever you want. I want you to realize you are a suspect in this case.

Pimpo: Suspect? You don't even know who's dead! Is it Val or Interloper or Carrie? Is it all of them? By the way, what's your sperm count this minute?

Interviewer: And elenchus goes on.

Pimpo: Cross-examination. Next they'll have their way reading Plato in the pulpit.

Interviewer: Reel yourself in. We know enough about you and your beliefs to be concerned.

Pimpo: I know more about you. "Concern!"

Interviewer: We know you think you're a Shirley Temple reincarnation.

Pimpo: A reincarnation of someone who isn't even dead?

I: You've been scared of your fate since your classmates had you strung up.

P: Too prissy to do it themselves. Scared of my fate since I had prophetic qualms and wanted to be a fashion-con-

scious white girl in an Issey Miyake bra and platform shoes
. . . though it was easier to make Botticelli stop painting Ve-
nuses than to pull that off. Easier to be a man controlling
many lives of many beautiful women.

I: Listen, I have to go now and really want to set up another meeting with you. Are you free November 11th?

P: Let me get my book. November 11th. Warbug Day.
That's George S. Patton, Jr.,'s birthday. I am sorry and have
plans. My friends get together to be vainglorious fellows.
We dress tough. No Pindar the poet costumes. Stars and
stripes. Only time of the year we can forget the "horrors of
peace"—did you know Patton not Pindar was an undistin-
guished student? A shock. Maybe larger than me, yes, but
not more beautiful.

I: How about the 12th?

P: The 12th, the 12th, the 12th. Let me see. . . . Oh I
can't. It's the Tunisia Tree Festival. Free men will not per-
ish.

I: Do you dress up like a maple? Pretend you're a tree
doctor eradicating Dutch elm? Doesn't that make you one
notch beneath the scale of animal nobility?

P: Let's just find a date and a time satisfactory to both of
us. Thank you.

I: November 13th?

P: I'll be in New York. Holland Tunnel Celebration.
Opened on that day in 1927. This tunnel is a justly famous
green organ.

I: November 28th?

P: I'll be in England. William Blake's birth anniversary.
Over Christmas I'll be off on my annual six-day bicycling
adventure with the Society of American Youth Hostels.
Messy.

I: January 1st?

P: I go to Canada for the Polar Bear Swim. New Year's
Day icy celebration. Technoplatonics. Full gear.

I: January 8th?

P: Hmmm, that's Midwife's Day in Greece. The men stay
home, look after children, and do housework. If I'm caught

out on the street, I'll be stripped and drenched with cold water. That might be the very day. I'm not anxious to go on the 8th this year. Made the mistake of doing it last year. Thought Midwife's Day was . . . well . . . something else. My lucky day is always August 31st: "Janmashtami"—birth anniversary of Lord Krishna, who is the reincarnation of Vishnu and author of the *Bhagavadgita*. (I find it not at all coincidental that it's also Malaysia's Independence Day. Brilliant Truths Day.)

I: January 8th it is.

P: January 8th.

I & P (*in unison*): Settled.

P: What's with your wild potato nose? Hoping to create a bit of cinematic excitement?

I: Always and forever.

P: Ruling-class interviewer.

I: Sex dog. Don't "Pindar the poet" me.

Interviewer: May I raise a slight question here? Pimpo's establishment is a different place depending on who paints your picture. Goes from twenty to one hundred employees depending on who is retching. I've been guided through two "firms." One has a neon "Kit Kat Girls Go-Go" sign and inside rooms are equipped with mattresses. Period. School-age children are in baby-doll pajamas twirling each other's hair waiting for customers. The second is an upscale place with decorated rooms. Women look like Wall Street executives. Everything is by appointment. Are they both Pimpo's places? Can this be explained?

Narrator: Surely. The small quiet one is a moneymaker. Different clientele: students, country folk, and pedophiles. Pimpo is most proud of the second, which is based on an exclusive bordello. Very hush-hush. The Kit Kats are ignorant about the second place unless they're being promoted into it. At which point, if they have further contact with a Kit Kat or Kit Kat clientele, their contract with Pimpo is terminated.

Interviewer: Where do the rest of the Kit Kat girls think the girl is going when she leaves for such a promotion?

Narrator: Home. Marriage. Jail. It's tied in to their history. They don't just vanish one day. They act it up a bit and say their so longs.

Chapter 9

Oblivion on a Plate

I: MR. BIOFF, IS IT TRUE you told Carrie about your upbringing?

Yes.

Would you care to tell us what you said?

It went like this:

I (Chuck) said: Seriously understand my father, he is stark raving mad. A one-eyed Jack, and I'm the only one (living) who will testify to having seen the other side of his Joker face. Then I stated his beliefs (to the best of my memory):

1) Life is great when it's you inside the tent pissing out.

2) Admire the guy who orders every entree, a half bite out of each, chooses one then sends the rest back.

3) Let this be a fat and happy free world.

4) Crush attempted coups, THEN return your calls.

5) Sit behind a heavy piece of real furniture playing with your "Predator's Balls."

And then Carrie said: Brass monkey balls?

In his own mind, what are your dad's major achievements?

Chuck: Susie Ping asked him for her first dance on her Bas Mitzvah night. Was school mascot in high school. Sexual conquests at twelve or somesuch refuse.

Carrie: Be content he did not become a doctor.

Chuck: Swings his imaginary scalpel anyway. "The Unbridled Philanderer" eventually touches all. Yes, you too shall be touched by him . . . he owns the police in Valmouth Town. His SWAT team practices running up and down cellar stairs. Joke is we have maybe three flights of stairs in the whole town. Flights of fancy.

Carrie: Would you give me an example of his idea of a baby story?

Chuck: When I was a baby—or "toy to his manhood"—I went over to a strange lady, touched her leg, and whispered, "Pantyhose," rubbing her ankleted ankle all the while.

Carrie: You can tell a lot about a parent by his idea of a good baby story. Virilis. You doubt his veracity?

Chuck: Indubitably. Good old Dad, I can hear him now, preaching, "We should die appropriately Roman." I was born on the birthday of Dad's hero "Lord Ronald" who "flung himself upon his horse and rode madly off in all directions."

Carrie: Did he help you with your feedings?

Chuck: For my daily sustenance he threw my pear up high reciting, "Time to catch sustenance, choke on it, and nearly die."

Later, as son and ward of the court, I was weaned on Louisiana hot sauce, cold eggs, and dark chocolates (after the best crème liqueur fillings had been picked out with an artful fingernail). Then I was bounced home again.

Hours on end this father to me spent watching the arrival of ships from the gabled window and widow's walk (which inspired my mother to invent what is very close to "the pepperpot roof"). Dad talked up his desire to be buried under the shade of a halfway tree. My parents—when they weren't chasing me down the road for stealing something to eat—got me a job fitting doors with small pieces of bright colored glass. "Shadow Creator" they called me. Had a few roofing jobs too, until I broke my mother's heart.

She sent me in to be on the receiving end of quite the birds and bees lecture. It was slightly more biological than most little boys can handle: "Queen Bee (female) leaves the hive once to mate with as many as twenty-five drones shooting the crazy breeze nearby. Each drone who participates explodes his genitals onto the Queen's body, dies, but only after leaving quite the clue he was there. The Queen's little men's sperm fertilizes four million eggs."

This was my dad's (he gave the sex lecture) roundabout way of talking about Valmouth's case. It seems Valmouth wanted to be but was not present at the conception of the one who soon will come to be known as his child Chuck. Christ Child Chuck.

Years after our "little talk" I cast off my hobnailed shoes and married a woman from a historical family. Seems one of her ancestors was awarded the house and land for his part in the regicide of King Charles I. Remember that one? Mistake to name our firstborn Kitty. You can figure what they call her in school: "Kingkiller Kitty." Excepting their cruelty, children are complete people.

Before the first time we had sex, like a good drone, I prepared to die. Thanks Dad. Good thing my wife knew what the hell she was doing. So you're wondering how we got mixed up with hog-packing money from Chicago . . . I poke my nose into things don't concern me. Devolving.

All my father's children wanted some way to finally defy him so we tied boards to the frontal bones of our own children in order to present Dad with flat-faced grandchildren. Protection against slings of arrows. Misfortune. In the nursery one day, one scalp-scratching child of mine bounced a heavy sword right off his brother's little head. Ping!

Asked for response? Pop swore he would strangle all his grandchildren—mark of a special favor. No need for uglified creatures with his name . . . he got busy impregnating the countryside's sore-backed women. Wherever we went lewd little ones waved to us calling us "brother."

You may very well wonder about my mom, before AND after I broke her heart (women can die from broken body parts). Her ancestors fled the Inquisition. Didn't have an "in" with the queen. She was monogamous as *Peromyscus californicus* (the California mouse, which is the only truly monogamous species in this world).

Mom used to arrive in an empty K Car. The only other thing I have to say in her regard is she blew her nose more (or is it less?) charmingly depending on where she was. She said things like "Smell of thy meat. Put it to thy nose." She believed "sex is for darkies" and marriage for white ladies. You would find her, as always, fat and knitting.

I: Would you explain how you got mixed up with the Valmouth plan? Where does Pimpo figure in these convoluted matters?

Chuck: I wish I knew.

I: Did it start with Carrie and her influence over Pimpo? We realize she held sway. Or vice versa? Was it a deal Valmouth made with Pimpo? With Carrie?

Chuck: When the authorities figure out which one of the group is dead—maybe we'll get answers to the little Chuckie question. He's my biological son and Carrie's the mother . . . but how the whole thing got started? Not privy. I was never in the inner circle. I could have been' duped by all of them. We're all dupes if you ask me.

I: Do you feel you gave up everything for Carrie?

Chuck: At times.

I: You introduced Carrie to your father, did you not?

Chuck: I did.

I: Your father happens to fit Orm Gamulson's description.

I'm happy to be here. An honor. I will chat with this one or that one about what THEY'RE interested in. Morality levels of most people bother me. So I find myself in doubt when it comes to "trust"—a dirty word that either means nothing or too much. Ninety percent of any conversation is in the speaker's best interest. At this age—if you can get a word in edgeways. I told Carrie many times there are so many you don't want to be stuck with, seen next to, that she, also, should beware the proverbial "exchange of words." She became a fine actress. Left 'em somewhere between laughter and tears. I warned her about ankles—just a little too sexy—too private. She's a good girl. Listened to her mama. Brilliant elbows and long arms run in the family. If I wasn't her mother, I'd still say she was hip-hop. Her profession is the family profession. Actresses all.

And the prostitution?

Hip self-parody.

What did she cherish?

Things I cherish. You think it's better to chance it. I never had those choices and neither did my baby. She studied acting every day on the street. She let them describe themselves then stole from them whatever was useful. Stored it up. Future references. She never had a companion warning her not to stare fulsome into a man's eyes.

Have you been to Pimpo's?

Certainly. I find the working conditions confining, same as Carrie. We're accustomed to the out-of-door life. It's an adjustment. Now vacations have to be saved up for field trips. Movable perimeters.

Did you have fears for your daughter?

Fears for a girl with all that talent? No. Can't protect a child. Their forecast for her was inclement weather for the rest of her life and that's long after I'm gone. Remember: climate is what you expect. Weather is what you get!

Please describe your daughter's typical dress and temperament.

She dressed like an Englishwoman in the countryside. Cashmere cardigan and pearls. I stopped in daily to find her seated at the breakfast nook with all her finest silver. Used her silver every day. We read the paper. She likes the *Christian Science Monitor.* The last day I saw her I said, "I have a decorating job after this. I'm leaving shortly."

Carrie said, "Who for?"

An Englishwoman whose husband left her, etc.

You haven't seen her since her return?

No.

No more questions.

Would you please answer some questions about both Carrie and Val? I understand you know them both?

Certainly.

Did you ever see them together?

No. I guess I never did.

Did that strike you as strange?

You get used to it. They were always talking about each other so I knew they spent a lot of time together when they weren't doing other things.

Describe Carrie please.

She wears tramp shoes and winter pearls. She is a dirty, soon-to-be-clean ashtray. Call her pimples. Call her CAR-BOHYDRATE QUEEN. Call her God with bad posture. Slouching. She has burn marks on the underside of her wrists and forearms from frying foods' splattering grease.

Describe him.

He wears paisley suspenders and purple tuxedo shoes. Dandruff humanizes peloothered him.

Any striking similarities between them?

Precious little win or fall. Val is what Val does (drugs) eight days a week. Cranks out half-moon collars. Is a white half moon. He's a licker of lead pencils who perceives Carrie in the neighborhood of *jaded goddess* when in fact she is a chewed plastic pen. Chawed on . . . sometimes he finds her all the way scandalous . . . I like the way he favors the guy with the finger in Chapel 16 . . . in spite of the fact bowler hat production's on the upswing, I know she would never marry a clotheshorse or any HALF TRAGEDY in an empty sack.

Meaning him?

No.

Are they the same height?

Possibly. Could be. Never thought about it.

Were any of their features similar?

People start to look alike. I'm sure if I saw them together I'd see the differences.

Do you remember anything he said about her that might help us get a clear picture of the relationship?

"Emphatic revvings are friends. Superfucker—Carrie. To be superfucked is Carrie's only artistic progression. All offers are to be accepted. Grace traveling." He said things like that. They both had this "on my way in" solo attitude. Not to be brushed against. Not to be intersected. No minuets to sturdy rugrats in chickenshit size. I summed her up as a

Kensington Garden ratbag. He begged, as any man masquerading with free time, on his way up, to differ.
Did you contribute to their relationship in any way?
Unbeknownst to me, yes. I taught peloothered him how
to spot a real lady . . . by the Monopoly toys dangling from
her ears. They just happened to be within her budget *and*
haute couture.
Did she say anything about him?
Thought it cute, more than twice, "the way his dummy
parrots him." She confessed to me, "The unloneliest moment is circumnavigating a man." My response was: *If you're
talking Pimpo or Val, I must agree.*
Do you know anything about a child?
We used to tease her, hers would be unkillable Kryptonite kids playing Goose Goose Swan. Holes in their socks,
same as their dad. No one would ever be able to locate him.
We'd be giving "Mystery Man Dad" attributes, accolades,
and excuses, like "holes in his socks and Irish pretense
KEEP HIM AWAY."
Do you know anything about Carrie's education?
Carrie was considered ineducable to a degree. We believed her children would be the same.

Narrator: INEDUCABLE Carrie. Hah! That person is a liar.
I know all about a relationship between two distinctly separate individuals—Carrie and Val. You can't refute "His
Omnisciency" the narrator! Some people would have you
believe that Narrator 2 is Narrator 1 pretending to be an
expert. I happen to know that Narrator 2 is just as qualified
as I am and is only asked questions in areas of his expertise.
Whereas I'm asked every picayune thing.
(Ten years ago) Sister Carrie strikes up a kickword dalliance with Valmouth. Warm with the fancies of youth approaching thirties, pretty with the insipid prettiness of a
less than formative period, possessing a figure, wait a cotton-picking minute, "eventual shapeliness?" Questionable.
To no way. This is the girl they call board-breasts. "Shrivel-

tits." Car headlights were gifts because friends felt she could REALLY use them. Sorely. Her eyes—they WERE big like whosiewhatsits.

Whosiwuzzits to be exact. A fair to middling example of the American middle class two generations removed from the immigrant. Reading and writing were not beyond her interest . . . they WERE her interest and source of her problems. WHAT SHE READ. Girl from a scrimping literary family. Her feet were boats covered with elf shoes or cowboy boots depending on the state of brain cells in the morning (whether she had banged her head repeatedly off some hard flat object). The tendency was to "take her boots off" though IT WAS RUMORED she never did. She and not she alone was interested in her charms. Less than quarter-equipped "little Knight," she ventured to reconnoiter the city of the big shoulders, if need be, ripping somebody's fig leaves off TO DO HER INTERPRETATION OF THE SCANDALOUS BANANA. Men were merely phallic pencil erasers or spear-throwers when she did her Creole Love Call.

She was opening doors for people. Nobody would open her any. The look was virginal and sex became hygiene. Something she should do. She had a bra, a red sundress, a black jersey dress, big French clown pants, and a Woolrich coat. To play the interview game she suited up in a borrowed monkey suit. Munchkins or piggies fit (squeak) into tight-fitting highly polished shoes.

A *no show* for "said" interview. She took a bus to Lake Titicaca to sunbathe instead. Thought about what she would have said as job interviewee: "I knew a guy once who filled his cooler with ethnic treats before setting out on a hot journey. He had to keep an eternal flame of incense burning under his anus. To light his fire. He met with me because I was blondish or blondly. I'm a big blonde Dallas girl by birth. He would make me come and wanted me but with boobs and less slanted eyes. Said it would only cost him $3500 to buy the boobs. Changes would be made. Boobs being number one. Don't worry, hon, we'll use saline ones or

148 SISTER CARRIE

peanut oil ones for durability cause I tend to get rough. Yeah I want this exact woman. With a couple minor changes."

Sunbathing, she met Socrates Valmouth grunting and drinking from a dirty glass. He was the tintype rags and bottle picker who dropped his strength into her more than a few times. He dropped his strength into her five times on his way home. And he dropped his strength into her often on the jaguar couch.

The man would have her works translated into six languages. So she gave him her volumes. Autographed. She liked the imbecile bohemian, especially around the mouth. He told her he sometimes awakens to the grand allusion he did it his way. She said sometimes I awaken to the grand delusion I'm Caroline Meeber-Sister Carrie, or the grand illusion I'm not totally alone. He said sometimes I awaken to the grand delusion I'm Saul Bellow and, married or no, I zap the creative youth of this country like Zoro. Why I go as a surf Nazi in beige lipstick. As if you had any doubts. Are your walls covered with asbestos for TRULY decorative purposes? He then proceeded to zap her creative youth though he was no Saul Bellow.

Women, women, women, whether the remaining inexperienced women (Valmouth claims he has known) had it sewn up by the Horse Doctor of State Street . . . or is that Hate Street? It's not something we'll ever know and frankly it's none of our god-damned business. Perhaps they just became hardworking at weaving and channeling that frustration (also none of our business). We know Telemachus was not a true hero, just a boy trying to pander his mother. WHATEVER gets a kid a new daddy. Think about it. Think about Val in this light.

Think about Mucky pup Monsieur without a tail. Athletic suicide. Another trip to finishing school if we're not careful. The point is . . . Socrates Valmouth thought Caroline was different: "I find she falls into any pose to satiate lust. Hers and mine. How refreshing! Like a baboon. Yes," he said, "like a she-baboon."

Asked was she a spectre of another age and clime? Asked did her aunt collect unimportant literary men? She said, "What the fuck? Yeah, I am. Yeah, she does. Who wants to know?" After her cold grouse and coffee, no one wanted to know. Her shirt climbed out of her pants. For five minutes she was placid and stable and imagination atrophied. Every shop door she opened mysteriously blew up. Though she wasn't married to "the Frog," she was, after all, that same polyester ribbon around that same "nucular" bomb. Easy to understand relationships like that. Try again next day. Worth many a try. His extensive metaphor: THERE'S A MOD SPACE BETWEEN YOUR LINES. THOUGH YOUR JEANS ARE RAGSHOP UNDERNOURISHED SECONDS, YOU ARE A CHIC, CLEVER GIRL. AFTER YOU REMOVE THE TEN FEET OF TOILET PAPER FROM YOUR BOOT, MAY I RIP A HOLE IN THE KNEE OF YOUR JEANS?

She thought: "If he rips them I'll bill him fifty bucks. Dinner tonight. As if he had disembarked on Sappho's isle of Lesbos. World with a baldy-sour hairdo. Lost his mind already, so what's a little baldness?" The decision to dissolve the large psychic distance has been made. Fifty bucks a rip. Dinner. This cow-town's babe.

Shrivel-tits, no longer a plump placidish person who had been to Lake Placid (where towels were nicely, quietly steaming), removed her space shuttle hat. From poll to "whatnot" it had a power of its own. The pertinent question goes: "After you whip me with strips of goatskin, then what? And exactly HOW would that promote the Eden-evictee's pregnancy?"

THEY DID NOT SHOOT THEMSELVES IN THE MOUTH AFTER KISSING EACH OTHER GOOD-BYE. The surgeon who sewed her and countless millions had his man ring her doorbell (expecting once again to be refused entrance). While the surgeon pulled the light carriage rug higher about his knees, she, to his chagrin, asked the centenarian in. Seems the cosmos had revealed itself again.

"Would you call it rose-leafy?"

No he said.

"Remove it altogether?"

No he said.

"Centenarians common as Reese's Pieces. If I didn't know you better, I'd think you were MOCKING HUMAN frailty."

No he said.

"I say it fills our sail it fills our sail it fills our sail."

No he said. Dogs our fate. Dogs our fate. Dogs our fate.

"How do I know you're really here?"

I have a plate in front of me don't I? Must be.

"Got to be somewhere."

Might as well be here. Long as a housewife is a scrubber and duster.

"How did you come to be lost?"

It will all come out in the next deposition. Sick and tired of your back-chat. If genius be, in Emerson's phrase, a *stellar and undiminishable something* whose origin is a mystery and whose essence cannot be defined, then I've never met one. But I remember a time long ago—they ALL used to be geniuses. Long as I am.

"But I'm taking interior decorating."

With Zenobia Zooker?

"Can't you tell? Have a look-see. Our going rate is $150 an hour."

I do notice we're near a jaguar-skin couch.

"She was my mother some thirty-five years ago."

And no girl then.

"No girl then."

I thought she was mine some seventy-five years ago. May she rest in peace.

"She's asleep on a cot upstairs."

May she rest in peace. Would you load that dripping nipple into my mouth?

"I don't want it bruised like the sky today."

I won't chew.

"You have no teeth left."

Suck not chew.

"Suck then."

Suck suck suck suck suck. Squirt squirt. Suck.

"You remind me of my first boyfriend who would rip his toenails off with his bare hands or teeth. In the pure joy of the moment."

He knew the only good meat in Montana was on the hoof.

"Hard to get at."

If the animal's restless.

"Let's deep-six her."

ZENOBIA? Okeedokee.

Narrator 1): She's got the surgeon agreeing to "deep-six" Zenobia? Then what happened to the surgeon?

Narrator 2): He turns up again later as a psych. specialist with halitosis. We don't know if Carrie or Val hired him. The facts would help us get to the bottom of this.

Valmouth (*hiding behind the jaguar couch*) and Carrie found themselves in cruel irreversible desperation.

Narrator: Is that an anti-social erection I see? Their goings-on:

C: Shall we artichoke-tint our hair tonight? It will lighten my mood and promise us we'll be alive forever.

V: Okeedokee. After we rat the tar out of it and spray some hell into it.

C: After we look into the center that bore procreation.

V: That COULD take hours.

C: Then let's go to the Rodeo and gum daisies to the stem.

V: Okeedokee.

C: Look me in the eye when you say that.

V: Okeedokee.

C: Across from sticky Mike's Frog Bar, up above the satellite dishes, the little old moon looks scratched.

V: Yeah. Like a kitchen-cleansered opal.

C: Yeah. Rising. Look at your turquoise ring and make a wish.

V: I wish we could read some choice John Bunyan after-dinner bits.

C: AND Thomas Carlyle.

V: Oh yeah.

C: Then let's drag our curled hammer toes in pilgrimage to . . .

V: To the armorial gates of the Academy! A word of advice for you on this Halloween Eve—wear borrowed shoes to fool 'em. VELVET SANDAL THAT I AM MAN.

C: "Man," she whispered wearing her prosperous yet pink Lyndon B. Johnson Oriental smile as she carried the rhinestone purse over to him. She avoided his eyes the entire time.

V: Yeah!

C: And the darkness?

V: We're wonderful folks. "AMERICANS" if we made it through titanic cedars wearing velvet sandals. . . .

C: Okeedokee.

V: Let's bet on the come. Catch my temperature in passing.

C: Would you care to discuss the competition?

V: Remember your aunt?

C: The one collecting unimportant . . .

V: Yeah.

C: The one who liked to look gorgeous visiting her husband in the hospital?

V: Yeah. "Let 'em believe YOU think they're coming home," she said, and then gave him $26 to outdo her sister who cleanly gave $25. Their brother says, "My sisters are like a bunch of wild horses."

C: F. Scott said, "We have two or three great moving experiences in our lives—experiences so great and moving that it doesn't seem at the time that anyone else has been caught up and pounded and dazzled and astonished and beaten and broken and rescued and illuminated and rewarded and humbled in just that way before."

V: The implication being they had?

C: Right.

Narrator: "Us four" they called themselves though they always add up to two. Forever pointing with an unfinished monkey on a leash. Does it all leave you feeling a touch lonely?

Narrator 2): Like, FOR COMPANY, you're the one with the electric screwdriver at your side. Monkeys never finish. When I look back on their lives I'll say the wives gave great sermon but were not always helpful. They know who they are. Shhh!

C: When I look back on my life, like Hitler, I never allowed any servants see me in my underpants. Battering ram to battering ram. I entertained myself in sport. I watched and rooted for chickens in chicken fights, I drank my favorite drink "Sex on the Beach." The baiting of bears was my great pastime.

V: What part of your body ARROGATES TO ITSELF ALL REFINEMENT?

C: You guess. Carnality has nothing to do with our prayers that begin BUT DOGS AND ALL MEN.

V: So talk religion. One man's *junk* is another man's . . .

C: When we girls had downtime in school we had interesting conversations on a variety of subjects like "family religion," one went not a little like this:

Huge pig and a pig's family in the road.
Talk Trinity of quality. It's on a mountain. As years go by, there's a gentle rounding.
Add trees.
Green cliff. Raw cliff. Some weather.
My people (people who have found favor with an angel) vs. the people I would like to be my people (YOUR people) —used to be such nice girls.

V: That's a Trinity?

C: Yes. In order to order America all to ourselves. Can't expect gospel for a few measly bucks.

V: How can you lead people "sensitive" to what should be done?

C: I went and stood by the door with hand outstretched hoping they would get their drunken flaky selves off the bed. Doubly alarmed, they said they didn't want to hold my hand. Badly controlled puppets.

V: Equals the amount of my joy, which is to say NONE.

C: DECOY.

V: SHELL GAS ASS.

C: Red-haired Irish Catholic nurses saved my life twice at a blues concert. I don't know their names.

V: Water lapping. Lap. That's the future squishing between your toes.

C: Hold that Waterford bowl as if it's your duty. Is it an ugly and tiresome burden?

V: With the silence of a Kleenex box, I put Zeus and Brilliant together and still didn't get IDEAL LOVERS. Here COMES SORROW THY NAME IS WOMAN.

C: SUNDAY IDEAS.

V: Her gravestone says "Famished. Split for a burger."

Luissanne: The old man at Jimmy's fish fry reminds me of Starvin' Marvin. Old, skinny, and stuck in Firenze. Shuffling around the block twice to gawk at me. The Yugoslavian café. I stuff my face, which is obviously music to his ears. My sister goes to Italy to diet. Then the toothless smiling old fart is next to me rubbing my arm. Yucko. Do I swim? Is the pope Catholic? Where's the pool? Bet you do. Miniskirt allows thighs to touch. Thighs touching the wood. Wood of the original crucifix. Don't need to worry about lulls in the conversation. He'll make passes at the waitresses in our downtime. Tinned tomato. Posturing pig. Thinks I'm twelve.

V: Describe the blood.

C: Winey. Spanish. Meaty. Bloodlike sauce. Missed bloodbath. Orthodox to have blood on satin. Surprise them with Fifth Avenue blood. Prime sausage. Needlework. The man handed me #4 strength and accused me of being the only sunbather in the house. The only one for miles. . . .

V: Name it and you'll be seeing it again and again. Holy Roller.

Narrator: In my day, the whole package would have been assembled by fax. Lest we forget DOGS AND ALL MEN. They'll try to tell you that Carrie IS Val and Val IS Carrie— hogwash! How could they talk like this if that were so? You know what they're trying to make me.

C: Improve or escape it.

Narrator: How did Val give her a job in advertising if he never existed? This is what I saw and heard:

Val: Chuck brought it to me. It is a genuine sale. No chenanekin! Charranada. I like what you did with this. Foot apparel for all participants and whoever belongs to each set. Come aboard! (*He reads aloud:*)

1) Slipper-mules with pom-poms for incomplete butchers' wives.

2) Gold lamé fuck-me sandals (all heels and toes).

3) Boar leather oxfords (waterproof) for famous allergic men.

4) Canvas sneaks with the toes ripped out for total comfort.

5) Roller Blades and kneepads for monkeys with tin ears.

6) Hushpuppies for when you're really cookin'.

7) Reeboks.

8) Orange plastic ballet slippers with large painted metal daisies over toes.

9) Birkenstocks.

C: Let me get this straight. You want me to work for an advertising company. Me. Carrie Meebs. I give you back the list you gave my mother, with a few minor changes, and Presto!

Valmouth: Do you think for one minute I want an ignorant slut protected all her short life from what you know so well?

C: Barely out of one snake pit and into another. I was beginning to have some control. I like it. I want more control. I'm an aging broad. If I did this . . . whatever makes you think I would? If I do this—I want bucks. You suits all think I want to be respectable like nothin' else. One man's respectable. Shit.

Valmouth: I wanted to get you into dealing art, but unfortunately no major collector of my work was kind enough to die in the last quarter. No great properties on the block. This is merely and appropriately my second career choice for you. Why, you're visibly shaken. You upset Hon? Carrie?

C: I want a change. Tired of verminous rags. Before I'm declared a saint and lie in state some sacrosanct somewhere . . . promise me they won't tear me up for relics? I don't want to have a sliver of my bone in some fat ol' nun's crucifix or parts of me in a turkey fan fanning some pope I don't even know.

Valmouth: Not to worry. You know all about notoriously lavish entertainments. You know the type of mentality. Sans artistic illusions, you understand a bang for a buck.

C: Bang for buck. A conversion. Not skin-deep though. Dip me in flea bath.

Val: Then you'll do it! Compatriot!

C: Return to the slime. Advertising agents always return. Like poets. Hardheaded. This may just do me in. Stress-death. You get to wear my ashes in little crocks of funerary jewelry. Celebrate. If I get a casket I want one of those high-gloss auto-body ones. Low-rider purple. No unnecessary embalming. I keep getting this claustrophobic feeling there's a biographer out there watching me . . . one thinks about every move. I'll write a book about me and coincidental life circumstances shared with my invisible biographer. We come from Scranton. We tap-dance. We are cinéastes.

V: You'll do it?

C: It would be an exercise in poor judgment. It would be my expression of the realization of a neurotic impulse. If I get fat it's your fault, Val.

V: Mine and the banana fudge ripple—20,000 gallons. Think of it—for the first time in your life you can afford to indulge in a personality cult.

C: Afford. Afford. Affordable mistakes.

V: Do I look like the victim of a deep neurological disturbance? No mistake.

C: Does the air make you claustrophobic in here? Like you're breathing in the exhaled air of someone who made all the correct advertising decisions in the twenties and went home to his jaguar couch and died at least a decade ago ?

V: You were born to back-cracking wealth, Carrie. You

don't overuse your posh accent or your title yet can't hide who you are. Wealth is everything whether you've got it or no. Now, would you please get to work on this account for me?

C: Actually I've been working on it. Doublemint needs a fresh new look. The product's advertising is old-fashioned. The answer is recognizable *American Gothic,* with a new twist. This ad could be used anywhere since reproductions of the original piece are found in grade-school and high-school textbooks. The lettering of the written message is broken in order to grab the attention of a younger audience (who might skip over it otherwise). Realize this . . . after you've been through a shoot with live snakes and elephants, a bunch of guys in Armani suits and haircuts fails to get your attention away from the work.

V: You're an engine.

C: Arthritic and stoned deaf.

V: God must have cared enough about you to punish you in a previous life.

C: Don't scandalize to titillate me then present me with a Thanksgiving turkey. Promise me when I go to trial that a thousand souls in twenty different-sized groups of recognizable people won't be allowed in for ten-minute intervals to view my courtroom struggle.

V: Blood oozes from an abdominal wound and you are without sympathy for the brutalized aristocracy.

C: Voluntary bloodletting. Boiled Grace in the last town in America. You won't be there.

V: There already. Let me tell you about our fair city of Alarcon. Stars end the spires of our churches . . . (fingers inches apart) . . . the Castle is here. You will love to visit and love to work here. It overhangs the River Formaldehyde. All the windows of all the houses glitter in the sunlight and are reflected in the glass in the Castle—you know the rest. Got it reading your buddy's log. Welcome. Easier route less taken. One warning: don't fall into liking the modern for being modern. It's a long bumpy fall down.

KEY FACT

DOUBLEMINT is a unique blend of mints. The gum has a pleasant clean gentle taste.

PROBLEM THE ADVERTISING MUST SOLVE

Consumers are bombarded by exciting new gums. They are overwhelmed by variety. We want the consumers to remember their old favorite.

ADVERTISING OBJECTIVE

How do we make the product HOT? We want people to try the taste of Doublemint again.

CREATIVE STRATEGY

PROSPECT: BABY BOOMERS—MEN AND WOMEN 30+ who remember the soothing taste from their childhood.

ADVERTISING PROMISE: You will not be let down by the taste.

REASONS WHY: Taste is as good as you remember.

Do a **DOUBLE**TAKE
On Wrigley's

DOUBLEMINT GUM
TRY OUR UNIQUE BLEND OF TWO DISTINCT MINTS
TRY OUR UNIQUE BLEND OF TWO DISTINCT MINTS

Chapter 10

Ruby Keeler of the Moment
In 2 It 2 Be Happy

JUST BECAUSE THEY GOT Surgeon Somebody to agree to deep-six Zenobia doesn't mean they did. If they did deep-six her, it doesn't mean they did it successfully, and if they did it successfully, don't think for a minute she won't return.

Your name, please.

Zenobia. I'm Carrie's mother. I want to thank you all for allowing me to come here on this day of inquisition and speak today. I need to talk about baby Chuck. Carrie's baby boy is in my care. I'm hoping to say a few words about the child, which may allow you to deal more favorably with Carrie. When she is found, my hope is you will go lightly with my daughter. She deserves it.

This child had to be born. I feel very strongly about that. Spending time with him, I feel less a grandmother than an explorer of humankind. You know all the circumstances that brought the child (who had been very well cared for by his mother and specific others chosen by her) into my care.

It is quite clear to me the child is content and secure. Chuck is very mature. Extremely. I'll give you an example: I can go to restaurants without a problem. He is the perfect young gentleman (for a toddler). Recently we did just that and he entertained himself prancing about the restaurant interesting diners on the facts of his wee life. It is ironic that singing his grandmother's praises is his favorite pastime in such situations. Moments before he begins, the diners get the premonition something wondrous is about to happen.

Why do you dress Chuck in black?

He dresses himself—always choosing black from a myriad of colors. Naturally I don't object. We were in mourning, of course. Don't forget we thought Carrie was dead.

Chuck has an aura like his mother—I truly believe that's what got her into trouble in the first place. Black encloses vibrations making him less attractive to kidnappers and what have you. With his aura cloaked, the color black acting as an insulator, I feel we can lead more productive normal lives. In order to raise Chuck properly, I'm sexually refrigerating myself (temporarily) and wearing monastic black . . . simply helps. Chuck is my Honiest Bunchiest.

How long do you think you'll have these responsibilities? Who can tell? "If anything was ever finished," as they say. We will not be overactivating his cranium . . . where we went wrong with Carrie. I'd rather have Chuck rebel against us and our boredom by overactivating his OWN cranium. Rebellion is the greatest longest lasting motivator. Child-rearing works in perverse yet predictable ways.

Certain governments will want to accuse Carrie of every crime ever committed. A mere matter of time before she's accused of serial killings. Chuck and I are patient. We know our heroes (Arsenio and Frida). Some days we have that and little else to hold on to.

Ludmilla: Pregnant. Yes. I'm saying that's what I thought my niece was. Her letters home were hormone-laden and weepy. Had to get her out of that convent school. She wasn't getting the proper education. One spring break I drove out to New England to bring her home. I have to describe it as a latter-day hippie hotel with more than many openings for staff. Christianity on some kind of retread rebate deal.

Lawyer: I don't see what this has to do with our case. But proceed.

Adolfina: I can describe it myself. The day Auntie showed, Mother Superior comes into the marble hall yelling, "Mop it up." Days later, Ludmilla's waiting for me, I'm anxious to return with her, and I say to Sister, "You can't turn me in just for following orders." See it? I mean, what did I know about the character of Jesus? Mother Superior

wants me to tell her. So I answer, "Jesus Christ jokes are vulgar and always make me leave a party early . . . I excuse myself from any table to avoid them." Sister said, "We expected one man to come and put everything right. Still do.
We will call for little to no change. Instituting all the while,
nothing BUT. One day when he feels rested, I promise you,
he'll get up and do a little healing." That's where Ludmilla
came in the second time.

Ludmilla: On we talked. Into the wee hours. "Harmless
dove" misconceptions and "doves as parasites" were areas of
PURE KNOWLEDGE by morning. The crone wouldn't let
her go. Every time Adolfina completed one, another punishment waited. "Headmaster" fetched his old-fashioned
black-leather doctor bag. Told me everything was in there.
Pointed and whispered, "Violence is the backdrop for any
peaceful altruistic action." I thought not only do they need
a new headmaster (his doctor bag was all wrong for the
spring collection), they could do with a democratic vote for
a new Mother Superior. I vowed then and there I would put
Adolfina to work myself. Outta that school.

Lawyer: You had a money-making scheme?

Ludmilla: You could call it that.

Lawyer: No more questions.

Jes duit.

Wherze at?

On Bidnis.

Doan see you beatin no hot trail to Bidnis!

That Man: I don't have time for this. My job is to throw
any obscurity on it. She was feeling most inviolate. . . . Let
me ask you, folks: what kind of a prostitute, with a boy's industrial taste, wears Birkenstocks around the house? The
most Chicago of Chicagoans. A mentally wronged one. Like
I said LARGE chunks missing. She was like all the Young
Republicans I met that night—eyebrowless and screaming
Ronald Reagan is a "Gimme Mick Jagger" to her. She
swooned. Wasn't Mick Jagger kicked out of the SS for wear-

ing a Chlorox bottle helmet as a fashion statement? Didn't
somebody of that ilk make a pass at a male talk-show host?
Gives me the kick-screams. She said Reagan is no rock and
roll nigger. Personally, I liked Reagan best when he was a
hairy mechanic with no aspiration. Helluva second Irish
president. Somebody tries to make dog food outta all of
'em. Not unusual for kids Adolfina's age to admire our
generation's notorious enemy. So: Hitler as role model
doesn't surprise me. It's really perfect in a despotovich full-
circle way.

Ludmilla's niece clued me in on Carrie. She and her
aunt were paid to do a number on a "friend" of Carrie's. At
first they knew very little about Carrie and mostly inconse-
quential stuff, like Carrie drives a truck with a fake Rolls
front. Just as big. Just as rusted. Has bright yellow mustard
in her fridge for her child . . . a minor clue. Can hide a lot
behind her cacti fence. Ouch. Milquetoast spots all over
her body.

I can tolerate Adolfina. I scratch her back. She has the
nerve to wear that little number—the red lion-tamer's coat
to remind us of the Irish goddess—"the Morrigu," feeding
on conflict (when not feeding on her young).

As Carrie became their main "project," Adolfina told me
what Carrie is into: "Her people know what it means being
the ONLY victims of nuclear weapons in known history."

Had me there. Wasn't John Wayne also a victim? I sat
across the tea table from Carrie once. She loves tea pots and
I love tea . . . she was bald. It was right after she and Val
spent time at their favorite bar. My favorite bar! Her buddy
Yolanda Kelly the Irish Cuban had enrolled in beautician
school minutes before (might have helped if she attended a
class or two) so free haircuts were offered at the bar. They
were drunk and signed on for two baldy sours (hairdos
come with the drinks). No more flaxen locks for Val.

Narrator: Best beloved Saul says we need that human
touch so he gets his cut between marriages.

That Man: When Pimpo was told the score he said,
"Gotta tell your dreams before breakpoint or she won't

serve again. . . . " I had to agree with him, however reluc-
tantly—it's an act of violence when you shove dirty white
sneakers under the nose of another. Pimpo also said, "Val's
perception of himself is 1 percent of a really big deal."

Carrie according to Adolfina: Pimpo needs Carrie or
anal nitrite to loosen his happy muscle. Winds of color.
Then Grandma's cake powder to nightly finish him off.
Where I come in, though, he denies it. Mentally wronged
Mathildas always been up his alley. She was, like, demoted
from nanny to sockless maid. Ruined again. Takes one to
wind up P's wind-up toy.

Narrator: Carrie traded down from the Porsche and
made the auto page next to her old mechanic. Could barely
afford a concept let alone an idea—one of those Robocops
used to glisten as her lifeguard. All this time friends were
busy winning what they thought was a war. Turned out to be
a conflict with no survivors. Saw it on TV. I believe her father was the newscaster.

That Man: I was particularly interested in how the whole
thing started with Pimpo and Carrie. This was all Adolfina
would say: "Yeah, who doesn't remember when they met?
Their comfort zones were equidistant or some such." Except for a crazy aunt with "jobs"—Ludmilla—Adolfina had
no family of her own. They kicked her out because they
were into Chanel lipstick and she was into grape-flavored kissing potion . . . kicked out after they followed her in and out
of Montgomery Ward's one day. To verify her purchases.

She was dating this moron who, clap or no clap, stuffed
his mouth with kissing-potion kisses. He smoked five packs
of cigarettes a day and, let's face it, had time for little else.
So he called her little Elsie, saying all the while she did not
in the least resemble a cow. Together they drank Winn
Dixie brand instant coffee. And the stuff is exquisite. They
met at the Wildflower dancing one night. He was an older
white-haired man with black wraparound sunglasses who
lived on Strawberry Pop Tarts. What really got to Adolfina
was his ballet stretches sans stretch bar. I should know, I AM
THAT MAN. She has since told me of my past effect on her.

No tragedy . . . yet. Wasn't hungry to go out and manufacture a tragedy like many others of her station do. But if she stumbled upon one . . . she might fill a void. One guy used to put a bag over her head and accompany her only when she had tickets to the Celtics. I should know. I am that man. Then early one morning she was walking past an apartment building and got hit in the head with a missilelike flung object. Ended up with the book and little else (in the way of brains). *Ulysses,* first edition.

When she dresses for Halloween (favorite holiday) she inevitably wears her own shoes. Halloweeners know it's her. Last time that happened the man whispered, "And I change my voice to talk to you females." She scared easy and ran. I should know.

When I tell about her parents I say they were Irish royalty, a priest and a nun (Latrine Luissanne) who gave it all up when she was born . . . quite a while before they could bring themselves to look at her face. Remains beside her man, unlike so many of today's modern women.

Now Adolfina is a sixteen-year-old millionaire who knows which of her friends aren't. Told me if she had a baby she wanted to name it like those winds they name: Sirocco, Mistral, Harmattan, Chinook, or Sikavei. Here's Adolfina now. Talk to her yourself.

Adolfina: I had the baby. We agreed the baby's name would change depending on the prevailing wind. Sikavei with head round for rolling wears a brimless hat, is the wind, and is unstable love sitting on the scummy dirty couch. He has been told repeatedly NOT to dirty it. So his back is broken again. Dirties it and is shot. My monkey's IN. The couch was stinking filth before he sat on it. A moot point to the drunken hunter and owner of said couch and lover of Winn Dixie coffee. Blinkie's visor's still blinking at the bottom of the lake. Tyrolean visors. He was The Tall. The Manicured. His suits fit. Would be buried in one. Used to tie his pajamas around his neck so as not to look down. Always doing things that would prove later to be instances of pure Dada. Called us "une génération fichue." It's for-

ever the next morning and we're forever situated in front
of the same window. He goes to the vespasian and nothing
happens. Instead of leaving and returning and leaving and
returning he sort of stands guard there in case something
comes gushing out. Rebel with a . . . poor bastard of prede-
termined extravagance! Wanted to name the baby Janis
Joyce. Joyce would have preferred something Italianate.
Such ironies leave me alone with my silent chuckles.

When Ludmilla said anything to my distaste, I would say,
"Don't you own something or other?" At these times and
these times alone, she wanted to kill me or tell me I was a
foul, inhospitable Bog-Mistress to my uncouth Bog-Lord.
She wasn't told about the latest wormholes or termite problems. All was considered forgiven by Rat and Latriss so after
a while even Latrine, my mother, went along with the majority. I was what you might call a man. What you might call
a woman. Lady for lack of a better term.

I taught Carrie how to do it too. Become a man or a
woman. That's why I believe them to be one in the same—
and by that I mean Carrie and Val. Nuts and Sluts. No one's
ever seen them together. Except Carrie's best friend (unreliable witness). I believe they're both unaccounted for at
this moment—are they both dead? One body with two sets
of organs between them. One isn't dead without the other.
That's all I'm saying.

When she was Val, telling mother-in-law hysterectomy
jokes, I could listen all day to such tomfoolery and monkey-
shines. Yo it be my man. Her abilities and agilities would
astound you. Pretends she's from Outer Baroush. Which is
exactly why she needed a guy like Chuck wearing a coat and
tie since kindergarten. Needed for procreation and don't
think for a minute it wasn't all planned by Carrie and
Pimpo before she left. She wants something of herself inside herself in perennial conversation. I saw Chuck Bioff
kissing her toes and blowing on them. He could also
despotovich like a pro . . . it was something to see. Carrie
thought one husband per woman was pure antic sidesplit-
ting wit.

Pimpo has recordings of conversations from the island at that time. Not much of a role model. Huh? Let's pencil him out for being too tall. Too busy putting people off their lunch. Then she took the *Queen Mary* home. Chuck got wise to Carrie; things like why she returned to Cabrini O'Greene and why she poignantly named her child Chuck when it should have been Samantha or Whitney.

That Man: Before Adolfina's arresting tale was arrested, I interjected, "Chuckie Bioff's not a GIRL!"

Adolfina: No, Chuckie is a boy but he's being instructed like Carrie was—how to be both . . . all things to all people. Flesh of all flesh. Ain't feasted upon. She feasted. Joke is, she had Chuck feeling like he was in cahoots with Pimpo when it was Carrie in cahoots from conception.

That Man: Actress Carrie, if you ask me. The worst that can happen to me . . . is . . . it's all over when the picture-taking stops. Her Sicilian summer of love is over and my minutes of fame approach demise. I'm an ex-carnival barker, no longer universally recognized as a sacred incarnation.

Adolfina: I have one more thing to say about their lockstep child. I'm very friendly with the librarian who has Chuckie in her story-telling classroom. Here goes: when asked what kind of book he'd like to take home, that child wants books with "the guts" . . . blood with blackened hardened stitches. This particular sideshow is fini. See you again when Ronnie (who?) Reagan mounts a diamond on his front left tooth.

Narrator: Carrie knew all the while what she was NOT doing. . . . That is, listening to the sound of her hair turning gray. Said she was killing the twentieth century (she found the nineteenth taken). Rode the age into the ground then sold it for glue children could sniff.

Adolfina: You take a score of Eurotrash looking to develop into something; the usual thought suspects for rounding up, who more often than not believe themselves at their obsessive best to be some kind of New Age proposition, you take them to the bellybutton of the planet where

they ARE "instructed." Simple. When you finish with them
they're finished for life with New Age safaris and whatnot.
Lucrative.

Narrator: She had an easy start because (this is the secret) America never existed for her. We always had to prove
it and I don't think we convinced her one iota.

Adolfina: Their infamous road trip was adorned or the
telling was adorned . . . more like marching with a crooked
staff than driving in a fancy sportscar. She was a beautiful
woman wearing dirty shoes. Her brilliant broach was a Cub
Scout badge smeared by a wanderlust dervish in the sand.
She left Val and picked up with some other man. "Interloper." Chose nothin' when the choice was between
nothins . . . she had to have a question before this one could
be her god-damned answer. Said she felt he was a huge bar-
nacle growing on her back . . . kept getting bigger and
heavier, making her less human.

That Man: Oh yeah, this reminds me to speak of God
who built his shack from the remains of an old railroad car
and heavy machinery cardboard crates. His accoutrements
consisted of a mattress and a small black-and-white television. The only reception brought in two channels: one with
Baptist preachers, the second offered twenty-four-hour yodeling.

Adolfina: She found herself saying this mantra: "Jesus—
on him be peace." Her partner turned out to be the number one son of a Jewish accountant from Kiev. She was sorry
for herself when she discovered his head hard as the floor
of her basement back home. She didn't trust the oblivion
he offered her. So what if it's on a plate? He was her howl-
ing-backwards custodian. He decided to let her go—came
into the shack and said, "Carrie, I wouldn't blame you if you
took the next *Queen Mary* home." She said she would go if
he promised she would never be looked upon in hindsight
like slides from a trip abroad. Like that picture of God cre-
ating Adam.

Narrator 1: Later he thought *that's exactly what she wants
me to do.* Close to being right for maybe the second time in

his life. Past burdens.

Narrator 2: This "one of these days" girl I know types all day wearing huge weights on her wrists. You are there for her stories about New Age safaris, so you don't have to *be there* type circumstance. It stops many "one of these days" types from becoming macabre. People surround them sans unhappiness. Dead stones really do speak. Every "one of these days" people is on the "finding his own palace" route. Everybody asking how do you like it? Typical response: "It's a palace." When all the while you thought it was a mica and mahogany basement. Sit rock and roll. Join us in a bottle of White Electricity. Think of it as sweet white grits all over your body.

Adolfina: Let me explain Pimpo: his brain, mapped out like a desk calendar, is why he functions in this particular appointment-oriented business. Gotta think like a calendar. Every notch in your brain is an empty square with room for a date and message of daily intent. I guess you're wondering why Pimpo went along with Carrie on this. Why he sent Chuck and Carrie down there. At her urging. He owes her. Let's also say he would be loathe to admit it. Guess he had taken his railroad engineer pants off one too many times in her presence.

Narrator 1: I realize you must explore Carrie's historical context. Lied if she told you she's from Bucketsville, Pa. Her eyes were zulejos—Persian for disposable contact blue. She liked to have ALL the ladies over for tea parties. She'd use pioneer pots and kettles—ugliest things you've ever seen, from which we drank authentic wildflower tea. We'd sit out in the yard protected from the wind by Oriental rugs drug across the prairie two hundred years ago. They'd be thrown over a clothesline in a square surrounding us. It kept the wind out so we could talk freely. A teenage girl looked after the young 'uns in the house. A rest from the world breakin' my back today. I was in charge of caviar and champagne which I could find nowhere. So I brought fermented "dry as antiquity" bean paste, white-chocolate-covered pretzels, and sardines in hot sauce. Little did I know

I'd be an anachronism based solely on my hors d'oeuvres.

Adolfina's husband (That Man): Like we tried to tell you before, she scared easy and ran. Some women plumb ain't smart enough to run.

Narrator: Adolfina and her (murderer?) husband play a little family game:

Shall we play a little game of Simon Says?

SS you're Dr. Jazz Goebbels, busy thinking jazz is Americano nigger kike jungle music.

SS boy this is work.

SS Nazis burned the Talmud in Skokie.

SS my name is L-Dopa Jon Cliffe.

SS paint yourself into a corner with surfboard minimalism.

SS my nose hurts.

SS that fat lady has orbits 'round her body.

SS prepare all your life for the greatness of one poem.

SS spread playfulness and certitude.

Simon sent us to Utopia and we wanted (you guessed it) to go home.

Simon said we were fruitful germs in order to rope us in.

Simon agrees microwaved white men aren't as bad as warmed over Toaster Pops.

SS I'm a Czech jazz Gypsy Jew.

Regarding ideas, SS "holders hold few to none."

SS (with genuine surprise) you're just having me on!

I said to Simon, "Pea soup fills me with intellectual red herrings."

Nailless wonder that he is: Simon says he'll be happy when he's living peacefully with great expectations in the subjunctive mode.

Narrator: How many steps before the Queen?

SS five.

Narrator: May I?

SS no.

Adolfina: Once a toady always a toady. Carrie "Amen Charlied" Pimpo to the point of distraction—ours. She was upwardly mobile and it was quite a show. Very humorous.

Same old misery.

Maybe we resented her. Most of us figured her out. She was a swingin' door Susie on *our* side of the saloon door. Learning so little this late. Slow moans. Whenever Pimpo arrived, her suddenly countersunk or wall-mesmerized eyes shadowed him. All her climbing and picking made me claustrophobic in such sycophantic presence. He listened to one of her ideas that worked and before we knew it he was no longer self-reliant.

Power. In the privacy of our cubbies, she was a cutup. In his presence she was a dismally pure drone. Pimpo saw her as Oriental with Germanic overtones; in other words, "efficiency incarnate." They split the work load. Dream time. It became her time for literary aspirations and his for criminal aspirations. Partners.

Off the record please: Pimpo is a mega-bastard. I should know—he's my dad. Carrie was a bastard too. Machiavellian. We thought our velvet season was over. Then we realized her god-damned point. She rallied for us. Our lives are better. If there was any splitting and division—we went with Carrie. World of womanity. We're different subservient blood all on the same clotted mop. Pimpo better not try to take away the "thanks to upwardly noble Carrie" strides we've made. He'd be temporarily then permanently out of business. Inertia ain't his life force. Not Carrie's. If she's alive. I hope she is alive.

(Carrie's friend Latrine Luissanne, now living in Germany:)

Yes, certainly, of course. I met her long before I came to Germany. I met her on the sidewalk one day. She was with Val, who I'd known for years. Little did I realize how one simple meeting would change all our lives so completely. I let him believe I thought we'd see more of her that first day but her behavior didn't cohere. She bored me so, it was hard to make her interesting . . . something we all had to be in those days. The power and the stupidity. Frankly, I was more surprised than anyone at the peace she brought him. His crow's-feet vanished when she was at his side. She was the least bourgeois person. Oriental redhead. She had this habit of leaving her body. Resembled always a girl on her way to luncheon . . . her knees or some physicality always stopped her from actually getting there. She was like a small barkless dog (why my nickname for her is Alcos). My present relationship with her consists of Christmas card interface plus a phone conversation a couple times a year (much more than I would have expected at first meeting).

When she was new she was green. A used buckaroo. Thyroid eyes. Michelin lips. Her companion (Val if you just look at the snake), affected by her wonder, felt it was contagious . . . thought we could all benefit from her presence. SOMETHING was contagious but he was hugely mistaken. It came to be understood she would get herself into one of the great keypunch businesses until something happened to take her in a totally different direction. No one knew what. She wished NOT to resume her lawn mower. No one figured on "eventual" promotion and marriage was out of the question. Nope. Metropolitan air was calculated thick as clams and yam goulash.

How could we know she was quoting Kafka whenever she mumbled, "Peachy keen?" Or Proust when she spat, "We didn't do it!" It's grimly amusing now. Like grinding one's teeth.

The gulf between poverty and success is wide and deep and hot enough to cook some yams. She knew what people died from near Val Town Hall. Jealousy. Val wanted her to be struck by the wealth that she was oblivious to, all the while she begged him to let her model. He took her where there was not a person on the street worth less than $200,000. In winter the furs were ermine-edged. The fad was fake chartreuse monkey tails trimmed in black lace. Carrie had to have one. And yes, it was June all right.

Bodacious, he audaciously scouted the boulevard. Ran into two old colleagues, Peggy Laugher and Mai Heaven. They were hardly Caroline's cup a soup. Got their monkey

tails wholesale and wondered aloud why Carrie was without.
Carrie turned away to talk to herself and whispered for all
to hear:

"When I was an amber-freckled girl, before I had my eyelashes and brows scraped off by my psycho-surgeon, I didn't
need to be blessed with prehensile monkey tails, but had a
real monkey for a pet . . . fed him pail after pail of clams and
stir-fried yams."

I joined the happy or miserable group making it a happy
AND miserable fivesome.

I had to ask Val about her:

L: Does she know what people die from around here?

V: Jealousy.

L: Her opinions on wide and deep?

V: The city's center is overawesome and abashing, calculated to be thick as unlucky generations.

L: She does have the bloom of a rose. This might pass by
you, Valmouth.

V: Not in one who believes as I do in the helpless and
rude. She believes the Blessed Virgin conceived Jesus
through her belly button. Virgin birth.

L: I would like to have her dress one of my Barbies.

V: Thought so. Her greetings are vaguely contemporary.

Puts me of a strange mind. Primrose in the Wild West
End. I know what Carrie was thinking because I could read
her mind. While these words crossed our lips, Carrie
thought, "Just take a look at the snake." Those who passed
greeted her with vague cognition and still vaguer saluta-
tions. She continued to wonder how Val got the city (actually a whistle-stop) named for him. His namesake was decorated in monumental Art Deco with huge fountains, pools,
and pastel-painted statues. Busy indifferent streets would
have to be her refuge.

She became drained of vitality and soothed. Bits of our
conversation floated her way . . . like . . .

We'll make a heroine of her.

Victim first.

The funnest part.

She needs barbarizing.

Then debarbarizing.

Carrie? . . . Is it a push you're after?

She answered: I sit astride the jaguar-covered board of a
hammock swing, attached to a wooden platform painted
with black and white cow spots. Therefore . . . must be a
push I'm after. Yes.

Told you she was a bit of all right.

May I push your children on it?

No, Carrie.

She mayn't mine.

MAY I PUSH YOUR CHILDREN ON IT?

Yes. Push Grouse DuBelly. Where do you see yourself at
the end of all this, Carrie?

When all's said and done? As a woman of several facets
. . . no specialties. They said all LEADER OF THE PEOPLE
jobs were taken. . . .

Are you fond of animals?

I don't, as some do, find the country warping. In my
homeland mares consort with bulls, giraffes seek after the
few remaining rams, and one species in particular does curious things in and among itself.

You must be from Arkansas. You intrigued by amorous
energy?

Using her soon-to-be-famous "triste far" look, Carrie responded: Let me put it to you this way—last night I awoke
in a cold sweat brandishing wildly to discovered but as-yet
unnamed planets . . . an empty bottle of Sardo Oil.

Brandished the bottle of Sardo? Where did the smelly oil
go?

I have answered enough questions. I would like to witness your avowed indulgences. Much mush is done for reasons of romance.

Carrie, on my way here today I met a youth who had
plunged heedlessly into amusements which would have
been more seemly, more becoming, had this youth been
the offspring of a career diplomat. I see you too as one of
the unkillable sturdies.

I would like to meet him. Diametrically opposed to privileges I would deserve had I been a cradled child of fortune?

He had not the courage to enter. Fled to other climes. You will speak out for yourself on one topic only—PLEASURE. Carrie, my observation is: YOU ARE SILENT ON ALL ELSE.

If I enter, my unnatural timidity in all things relating to my advancement will be mitigated?

Curtailed. Your natural timidity combined with power and resource, frees you up to masquerade as you will for reasons of romance.

Debarbarizing?

Debarbarizing.

I want to work out-of-doors.

I'm sorry. We've decided against barbarizing. Carrie, you were listening to our conversation earlier. What I said about Seth, I trust you overheard?

Yeah.

My disclaimer: As he turned, I saw it was not Seth at all.

Carrie didn't look surprised.

That's how I remember our initial meeting. I felt she was asking the king of Spain for just two of his eyes. When you hang with men you hang also with their women. She was his. Back then it was always Valmouth and Carrie. It's unfortunate I lost touch with Val. Last time I saw him wasn't too long after that. He was running an errand. I said, "Is that egg on your head Val?"

"Probably . . . Carrie often wipes her hands in my hair while cooking. I'm off to buy more chicken fat."

I like to feel that was the last time I ever saw him though in truth I saw him many more times. My mind, very appropriately, makes it the last. Symbolics.

Lawyer: Her avowed indulgences? Did you ever get a straight answer about them?

I know somebody else who did.

Lawyer: We need to know about this person, but first will you tell us, Luissanne, about your relationship with Val before and after he met up with her?

One thing you can't hide from is the Great Politburo in the sky. Can't float over the flamingo-crocodile state for long without having to land. Battling climates. He asked me which way to the Wall. (Berlin.) Carrie never knew he came to visit us. Thought he was visiting his cousins Angoisse and Tristesse. Understand my relationship with him: he made me in his own image. WYGARBOWAC: a method for re-fashioning coarse animal skins into elegant leather. He found me sulking for keeps over here with my husband. That was certainly our last meeting. My husband, old enough to be my grandfather, was present the whole time. We all wondered *who would write letters home?*

My history is irrelevant but I see you want more: I left my convent high school a semester shy of graduation. Got permission from someone else's mother and motored across the Mojave Desert in a yellow roadster wearing a powder pink suit with matching hat, fishnets, lipstick, and gloves. More regular than regular. A Vanna-be quality, if she was born yet. I gave Val a ride. My nose, rearranged by muggers a decade before, smelled not a rat, though Val was a common cheat and cutpurse. Hope gushes eternal in the female breast like the delicatessen down the street, incapable of getting a lunch order straight. A dream had me so I sent home a chirp from under my right breast. Chirp of joy. I can no longer do that. Other fish to fry.

Psychologically, I know I took up with him due to my up-bringing. Those blueprints never fade. One gleans LES-SONS IN CRUELTY suffering through them. I understand why Carrie took up with him. Carrie and I weren't that different back then and THAT more than anything explains why we still do the Xmas thing.

I was just as boring. I did boarding school in Europe. When your mom is raising you, you never think she'll make it as a tap-dancing game-show host. I could never take my mom with me on a trip overseas. She claimed she needed four passports. One for each name: her acting name, poet-ess name, dancing name, and lastly her holistic name. We solved it calling her a performance artist. When one of her performances was over we'd say, "Let's go home and beat somebody up."

Mom signed her letters YOUR DOG. YOUR COMPLETE DOG. If I ever have an heir she wants me to name her grandchild Sam Beckett "Barclay." Scatologics. Like kufologics. I was brought up to say "Good show!" instead of hello. Expects me to pick up the bill the way Sam did.

Put value in silence. However, as we approach silence . . . we meet the necessary slime on the way. No use for beauties. Warned me against ever becoming one. The beauties were sauntering lies with skin she met at a Mary Kay party. A wicked bunch to get in with. Slime. Mom had little use for them. "If man hadn't moved outta slime (so he had to search for it the rest of his life) where would he be? Whatever we move outta we search for indefinitely. Occam's razor." Fact-fitting explanations. Dreams had me . . . Carrie too . . . good men looked pretty awful . . . never cared how many inches a gentleman.

My mom was Kafka with outfits. We used to say: "If she's sleepy she takes coffee. If she wakes up at night, coffee sends her to sleep. Sleeps because it's no longer fashionable to die." Her life had something to do with a Turkish officer with a flowerpot top his head and long wounded monologues. When I need her advice and she can't be reached, I pick up Samuel. What he advises, she agrees with: "When you're in the last ditch, there's only one thing left to do—SING." I always try to remember that one. As an Irish person twice removed I often think about the Catholic Church and the English and then, of course, Sam, "Ils nous ont encule la gloire." (They buggered glory into us.) Yucky they are.

Mom kissed me on both cheeks then dashed my head into the mythic behind of Cuchulain. Those of less stature would feel free to bring their orange boxes to step on. Right now she's making her pilgrimage to Dublin's General Post Office. Gone dressed as pedagogical Eros with unspoken subtext sex. Mom's way of saying a thing is hierarchically a step above the thing said. And Dad . . . stopped the

game when she told him how he could kill himself . . . with
knives and forks. What scared her was the thought of becoming some beaver-eater's white woman. Loved him to
stand up at the table to expose his gospel pipe. Yet we tried
to discourage that behavior. Mother did not run away from
home. Father did? Father did not beat me. Mother did?
Shem's white boy. Preoccupation with the revolting. Life-
long occupation. All us women "mooning about."

Mouthfuls of much obliged and handfuls of . . . so like I
was saying it was because of my mother and my upbringing
. . . my father, etc. . . . I picked Val up. We went on the trip
to wet each other, to pick the cactus prickles out of each
other's hands . . . throwing up falling down running into
walls . . . that kinda thing.

Val thought people were running after him. The United
States is such a big country . . . he's such a little big man.
Warrior. We beat drums, had mud fights and bragging contests, then urinated on trees together. The Jungle Jim
thing. He was no longer married to Heidi with outfits.
Hadn't met the little soldier of fortune yet. He surely is paying for that particular crime of the century by now.

Let me give bildungsroman examples: I needed to take a
leak. I tend to have this need. Occupies me. Driving
through New Mexico smack in the middle of nowhere, I
pulled all the way into a gas station and haphazard-parked
to the rear in front of the ladies'. I looked to my left and
saw two Ho Jo two dips staring. Timed hints. Incredulous
chicken-fried-steak eaters. This delayed my thinking about
Russian Basil the Blind and how I'd have to remove my fur-
lined pelisse and how I'd leave the radio on, etc. I saw the
female version run for the ladies'. I can wait my turn. I was
relieved. Maybe they weren't staring at us but at the door—
"Who would get there first? What are the odds? Which is
the men's?" That type thing. My honey, who was "the very"
to me, went to the pumps to compare gas situations. It became my turn for the ladies' and I took it. When I returned,
the car with our worldly goods was locked and the other car
gone. I looked into the dead buzzard tree over my head to

find a squirming live thing in a plastic bag tied to evil branches. A wriggling animal thing. A strango's idea of a Christmas decoration? Decoration from the devil. Determined to shut out the normal feelings; alone and abandoned, I shut my eyes. Good to shut your eyes three minutes a day.

The long gone had kidnapped my honey in the American southwest. I knew how but why? On whose verandah was he sitting? How cold was the mint julep in his hand? Was he in or out of his captives' praises? Who would sew on my buttons? I took out my spare key and climbed in. All belongings were intact. I drove down the road and there at the side of the road was "the very," a little roughed up but no worse for wear and tear. He assured me they had the highest opinion of him and we vowed never to speak of the incident, chalking it up to "the weirdo (his kidnappers bathed in nightly gore) Wild West."

Next we encountered two dressed in livery enjoying themselves in the power booth.

"Sit down," they said.

No.

"At the table with us," they said. "See that couch over there? You two will be spending a lot of time on it."

Will not.

"We'd better cover it with plastic so we can hose it down regularly. You have to learn the power thing. Let 'em wait hours to see you then tell 'em come back tomorrow. When you visit a friend you MUST be recognized. We'll pay someone. After clearance from security, you'll be stopped by an adoring fan. If you go absolutely unrecognized, we need to know. Do you understand?"

We played their game . . . the money seemed good. I put so clumsy Valmouth in the limo but he kept falling out the other side. Slippery seats. I had to kiss the woman's lovely fat little bananalike fingers. She had the best regulated mind in the free world. We called them PRESIDENT and TREASURER of the CARP AND SUCKER CLUB. They brought up guests and WE entertained. I liked the fisher-

men best. I showed off my knowledge. I knew the top three
lures: Sputterfrog, Buzzbait, and Pee Wee Wart. Fish give it
up and jump in your boat when you have the right equip-
ment. They sent us Chartreuse Flake Mister Twister Poc'it
Hawgers for some skinned rabbit's birthday.

Comes a time in your life when you learn to make your
own compost, grow worms, etc. It was that exact time.

They got us mixed up in their religion, though we never
believed. They were our bread and butter for three years of
entire summers. Garden of the Goddesses. Nun and priest
"habits" were grass skirts. I still have the fallopian tubes and
ovaries necklace. Fertility rites were actually fun. Dancing
around the maypole. They took our babies though. Bum-
mer. Fertility only did THEM good. I still catch myself
clutching my womb to beseech the fruitful goddess within.
Wailing in fevered pitch is fine. I won't tell what we were
instructed to do with the crystal penis. Most unpleasant.

I longed to see Valmouth but they had men confined at
solstices, equinoxes, and Groundhog Days. That's when Val
became interested in marketing research.

The enemy of course was and is Madison Fucking Avenue—where they all used to work when they were young,
smart, and beautiful. Yes they HAD been in advertising.

Anyway we left the Goddesses and traveled like I said to
the desert and when we got back we didn't want to spend
time with each other . . . already a lifetime. That's when he
became Carrie's. I'm sure that was yet another lifetime. I
have no problem with that. I'm no brood hen. Carrie's a
coppernob provoking accidents, in my humbled opinion.
He's a man who knows his Far East . . . Val has said, "A
woman is not a valise." How loud they are in each other's
praise is equal to the quantity they denigrate.

Lawyer: Is there anything else you want to say about
Valmouth?

Yes, he told me when he was a genial child, he was forever bringing those big eyes in with him. He would suddenly stop in his tracks and yell "Grandpa," only to discover
the scream erased Hitler's numbers on his grandfather's

arm. But the branding always returned. Eventually.

Lawyer: Carrie will be phoning shortly. Would you be willing to talk with her?

Of course I would.

Lawyer: As you know, Carrie is in hiding. We will both be questioning you about baby Chuck. Is that satisfactory?

Yes.

(Carrie calls and the three are hooked up for teleconference.)

Lawyer: Can you take a moment to explain YOUR interactions with said child?

Latrine Luissanne: Unbeknownst to you, Carrie, Val visited us in Germany; his main fear was that his child would never know a glockenspiel. He never expected to hear much about his child, let alone see him. Long before the arrival of his bouncing baby boy, Val had perfected a repertoire of cartoon-character noises. He wanted the child's first instruction to be his own rendition of farm animals. The progression would be: Porky Pig, clicks, snaps, whistles, and the grand finale—Tweetie. Tweetie-perfecting was in the infant stage, if you'll excuse the expression. Val was one "More Than Willing to Babble for His Wee One" DAD. Said when he squeezed daily oranges for you, Carrie, he sang a little ditty about fruit flies dropping like fruit flies when they drop. He claimed you both knew whoever got the child would either watch the kid throw up or fall asleep and little else for quite some time.

It's not like he had any future delusions about chatting with the heavy-brained adolescent about the moment of his conception. Val simply was not present at Chuck's conception . . . he was first to admit that. Couldn't insist the adoptive parents be baptized let alone baptize the child. That debauches innocence. Ate days. Listened to the roars. Felt exponentially falling clumps of heaven. Hoped to stare the child into wakefulness. I didn't envy Val; I can still hear him ask me, "What if the woman who comes for Tweetie Sweet Pea Chuckie is a despot?"

The woman the lawyer sent WAS a chest of drawers. Test-

ing her, I asked what she thought of this football season.
She said, "Remarkable, of course. They all are." She is in
the pizza line. Delivery business . . . the pizza cooks in the
truck. The woman married Slomo Iscariot: one half of a
semi-famous two-man band. They play dulcet jars to sooth
the savage beast. I am truly sorry for all parties concerned,
Carrie.

Carrie: What did she look like?

Unforgettable. She had deep cleavage and stiletto heels.
You wouldn't think she drives the pizza truck but she does.
I feared that baby would be lost in pig holes in the dark.

Lawyer: Are you of the same opinion today?

Of course not. I see her here. I realize we've all been
taken.

All present look at Zenobia (in flats).

Günther, can you take a moment to explain YOUR interactions with said child?

I was hoping all talk about Val was over. We knew, that is,
Val and I knew Carrie was in Germany, his main fear that
his child would never know a glockenspiel. We had doubts
about it being his kid . . . said he never expected to hear
much about his child, let alone see him.

His cartoon imitations were dreadful. I shot holes in his
boots to make him stop practicing his "repertoire of cartoon-character noises." Nothing would stop him. Porky Pig
was pretty good. We can all do clicks, snaps, and whistles.
Tweetie-time was shoot-the-boot practice time for me. Behind his back we called him one "More Than Willing to
Babble for His Wee One" DAD. He was a fruit fly. Couldn't
insist the *adoptive parents* be baptized let alone baptize the
child. That debauched innocence.

Heaven fell in exponential clumps. He hoped to stare
the child into wakefulness. Poor Val. Latrine said Carrie
used to say, "Aprons say a lot about you whether or not
you're anyone's woman." He kept three in our pantry. . . .

Lawyer: Have you been coached on what to say about
Val?

NO.

Lawyer: It is remarkably similar to testimony we have heard. Do you see the person who took the baby here?
Yes.
Everyone turns to look at Zenobia.
Günther, can you take a moment to explain *parental* interactions with said child?
When Val visited us in Germany, it was just after I joined a two-man band playing dulcet jars to sooth the savage beast. He said he feared his child would never know a glockenspiel. He didn't expect to hear much about his child, let alone see him. Long before the arrival of his bouncing baby boy, Val had perfected a repertoire of cartoon-character noises. He wanted the child's first instruction to be his rendition of farm animals. Then he thought they would move into Porky Pig, clicks, snaps, whistles, and the grand finale would be Bart Simpson. He hadn't perfected Bart Simpson. Hadn't got beyond that curriculum. He was more than willing to babble for his wee one.
Val told me when he squeezed the daily juice for the expectant Mama Carrie, he sang a little ditty about fruit flies dropping like fruit flies when they drop. They knew whoever got the child (didn't know who) would either watch the kid throw up or fall asleep and little else for quite some time.
Val knew he would never be able to chat with the adolescent about his conception. Wasn't there. Ate days. Listened to the roar. Hoped to stare the child into wakefulness. He truly enjoyed slaving over a hot child all day.
Tell us about Val.
My first visit, he traveled around the United States with me. We started in New York. He quizzed after-game subway clientele with, "What do you look for in a woman?" An eighty-six years and three months old Yankee fan and participant needed time to answer Val's (perhaps important young man) important question. Ten minutes and five participants later, Geezer Pee Wee ambled over . . . CHARMS.
What?
Her "charms." A WOMAN'S CHARMS.

What do YOU look for in a woman?

One 718 area code male volunteers "MOISTNESS," as his gal is delighting in her slip-on nails.

MOISTNESS we all cried, like suddenly we had an answer for the first time in our lives.

I know a few Vaseline-toting guys. Dehydrated. D.T. guys who beat one another to a purple pulp once in a bull market. Roomies. Corner of La Salle in Chicago. Arms entwined. Off for a once or twice beer. Val was genuinely pissed at me. Blood ran down my nose onto my Gucci tie. Stomach bloated to pitterpatters. A cycle. Cyclical representation. Bridge and tunnel girls used to be teen mall rats. Now we found ourselves fighting over one.

It was yupper puppies joyfully ripping apart old muscle in order to build stronger new muscle—ripping regeneration. "Heart muscles?" you might very well ask. I said once again and perhaps for the last time, "What the fuck motivates you?" He said, "Babes with the right blood type."

Carrie: Screeching America and its habit of coming to the door got us into mixing infants. Second Fall. The priest assigned me an Act of Contrition for cursing in the Confessional . . . "Please Mister God" . . . . Latrine, aprons say a lot about you whether or not you're anyone's woman. I have three left over in my pantry . . . which is all I'm at liberty to say at this point in time.

Narrator: I've heard THAT before.

I'm here to speak my piece on behalf of Sister Carrie. I too had to leave in the middle of THE ASIAN GAMES or Snootsful. I likewise feel it is my duty to be here. Maybe I could clarify some one of her pithy sayings and whatnot . . . perhaps explain our theater?

Our mutual friend is a man of the theater. His name is Ippolito de' Medici. I believe you have talked together. According to him, the omnivicarious (joked upon) with or without false eyelashes Carrie said, "The beauty of intangible property is that it's unreal estate," all this while holding up the tube mushrooms from her garden, significantly stepping on centrally stipilate fungi. They were coldly defined by mycologists as terrestrial, fleshy, putrescent, stipilate fungi. Carrie would work all those scientific facts into the part. Circuit-riding in a coonskin cap, she saw herself as the princess of Smolensk, in terms of her long slow sipping a glass of Worcester sauce, which incidentally, happened to another friend of mine (Joe of the Universe) and THAT was as they say the beginning of the end. (Joe was not, however, a Parsee or Beelzebub . . . dipping wings time.)

Ippolito, armed with the FACT that puddle nymphs swim, trusted the echo more than your FIRST OUT words. He's better off than hackish females who barely finish walking plenty of dogs before getting up charity balls to facilitate revolving around punches to stir up neon atomic vomits.

Carrie, on the other hand, was past the olives. Quite astonishingly, that was the role and she got into it. We'd all walk on stage and wait for our cue disguised as a query voiced by Carrie:

"Dinosaurs spit?" (As if we'd been talking stipilate fungi.)

Our rehearsed response was always:

We're (breath)

talking (breath)

herbacious (breath)

herds when he says Spokesnerd?

Then Carrie alights to say, "Duct tape him. Or better yet reclassify him THE CLASSIC DEAD WHITE MALE."

Another rehearsed response by those who remain on stage:

"Sews to be bespoke" (breath).

SUBCLASS (breath).

Go figure (breath), heh, heh, heh (breath).

Thank you for your skillful rendition. In my so-called role of Inquisitor, I would like to ask you a few more questions. Who are you really trying to insult when you say she's nine months and ten minutes apart from her sibling?

No one.

Where're you from?

East Fuck, Texas. Where our pleasures are equine and our desires Alpine.

Would you be willing to give us a profound remark on the concept "LOVE" and what tie-ins that may have to Carrie?

My opinion? It may be a strange concept to you. It doesn't spurn those who abuse it the most. I saw a man pick it up in a fistful, so that alone must have hurt. He hurled it against a wall, kicked it when it was down. I didn't see how Love could live. Love got up and begged for more. It got more of the same treatment only worse. Love is Rasputin. Then Love must have tired and, pulling a knife out of its beehive hairdo, slit the guy stomach to neck. Not pretty. But a clean cut. Now Love must be just as much a lonely stinkpig as the next guy. Meaner 'an hell. What happens when love comes to town.

Don't you know she's a stayer?

I know she is never financially embarrassed in any way. I know Val proposed on a roll of toilet paper. I know a lot.

Hard to escape that baptism. Whine whine nudge nudge. "Love," not an easy name to have dropped on your head.

For the rest of us it's always the day after the night before . . . he put an inordinate value on her head, which put the rest of us in a compromising situation, which isn't, by the way, to say he loved her.

Are you at all anxious to see how she fares?

I'm still picking glass out of my foot from the last time I came to see "how she fares. . . ."

I see your foot glistening.

Yes, the way it moves . . . happy to speak in her defense is all.

(Carrie runs into the courtroom.)

Carrie: I have a witness who will prove there is a Val.

Lawyer: An unreliable witness from a commune is worse than none.

Nurse: Certainly not. I took my $1.99 miniskirt down the marble library steps. To sit in the dirt. There was a jazz band

on the corner. They're the talented ones. I'm the one DIS-
COVERED. A patient next to me building paper airplanes.
Flew one my way. Distraction. Pegasus. Horse of another
feather. Interesting little birdie. I found myself lacking communication I would ordinarily be so easily rid of. So many
levels of understanding. I'm used to mischief. This mischief
replaces that mischief. That, this, and so on. Ran in knowing I had no place being there. Looked around until this
weird feeling came over me. Stifled. I had to stop looking.
Anxiety was building. Sewer rat stuff. My mind had time to
justify her gift-from-God position as *Penthouse Forum* answer
columnist. Hadn't she been just like me? Another Medusa-
at-college married to Joe-Grab-a-Sandwich. I don't mean I
don't like rich people—I do. If I ever knew any. But is she a
reincarnation or an impersonation? Universal questions.

Carrie: I was fading in and out. I wanted to throw up.
Heard them come in. My fever made them hazy. I think the
conversation went like this:

Valmouth: She's acting as she was brought up to act.

Talk with her decorator.

V: Didn't the Kennedys pick a nun to decorate the White
House?

According to her mother. Yes.

V: According to her decorator?

Yes.

V: By decoration are we talking about that puppet of
Pope Pius XII with a cardboard arm enabling the viewer to
bless himself?

Yes.

V: At dinner tonight will food be eaten with chopsticks?

Don't be cruel. If you had a little frottage every night,
you'd have very little to complain about.

V: But it's a slippery slope.

Why you chaw your ice so.

V: Dry eye and a hot mind.

Cruel?

V: Public school in Europe will do that.

Your imagination is cruel to you.

V: Get on your motorized tea cart and get the fuck outta there. You're a jarhead cooking meals unfit to serve starving Ethiopians.

According to YOUR mother.

V: If your father is the red roots of feminism . . .

Who is my mother? Right?

V: Exactly.

After frottage there is collage.

V: You attribute it to de-personalization and passivity combined with violence?

No. Manipulative aesthetic education.

V: Don't give me any of your techno-idolatrous jargon.

I'll "read" the river if you "read" the woods.

V: You see our continent as an obstacle.

What difference can it make?

V: Call me at 1-900-BLADDER. My extension is w-e-a-k.

What do you actually know about this joker?

V: She could be reached. What do you WANT to know about this joker?

She knows we can be reached. Val, my teeth are only chipped where I have a hard time getting my fork in.

V: Banging them with your fork.

I'm in town and I'm in a Saint John knit. Isn't that enough?

V: It's still your nurse's uniform.

You love me toting my heavy as a solid gold EMBARRASS-MENT.

V: Nothing sexier than a red plastic wrench.

I'd be donning appropriate George Jetson plus family pants. "Ants on a Log, Sushi, and Fluff-Butter Sandwiches" will be staples. They find Miss Hoboken easy but, I reiterate, NO PIG.

Carrie: I pretended to be stirring to consciousness. I said "Your haircut sends a different message than your face . . . my feelers are disconnected. Different signals." Pure nonsense. Why was his shirt crawling out of her pants? Why was I contemplating going down in the history books? Philistine gifts where friends used to be. Seeing myself good as the ramrod-postured fellas I tricked. Val held my hand.

The nurse with her own explanation: I am the jealous other (my Swiss convent education). It was the day they decided to announce their two-year anniversary . . . I hate to see her in her diamonds. It aggravates me. Some people never knew they married. Do you want some background? Next you'll hear the taped voice of the person who thought she wanted Val more than life itself. She pretended to need him for her children. Lies. It was pure selfishness. She will never believe he is NOT for herself. She nursed Carrie and fell in love with Carrie's husband Valmouth—whether or not he was her legal husband. I am that woman.

The tape: Carrie and Valmouth are scapeface ghosts with a legacy of envy born in the Year of the Hyena; two born airbrushed in their late twenties, partially clothed, clad in the flowing circumstance of a shared Valentino gown. She was a sick girl with a wasp waist who could be/would be helped into communism. (Do any damned thing when they're well.) So busy out wrassling the mule. Empty pistachio shells and wow it's African sculpture. Suited him down to the ground. They dined brilliantly. Exotic wild game dinner.

When it was only too obviously the SPRING COLLECTION like war-blown poppies, we prescribed bromide. When the problem was obviously words—she could find them, all right, but not pronounce them—we let him try to heal her. They danced to exhaustion. Her immune system refused to work, but they danced divinely.

Understand? Their own dark language—they're like twins. OK, forget about understanding. My upper-crust dust refuses to settle. A wife, fast horse, and fastidious hound. Conviction in your best moment. Conviction in all our best moments. Homme moyen sensuel. When Brooklyn came up they thought they had to take a bridge to get there. Didn't care if her Brooklyn predated Christ.

I'm finished at twenty-five. Zooming whom? As if I need to ask. What he had for all of them was a square of light. She accepted that. Studies find cinematics a cure for cretins. I would have chosen crematics in her case.

God wanted to know if he was a man. Man wanted to know if he was God. So the legend goes. Marvel at themselves. Wounds heal over. Break. Heal over. Break. And heal. Provoking more than the rain.

The soon-to-be woman expressed a desire for food. Cooked it. Didn't eat it. Because her husband pointed out this expressed desire, she screamed was he controlling her? Keeping her fat? In the house? Who's zooming now? Twilight's just an institution in our lopsided struggle. Would have been a good sign if one of you could sleep at this juncture. Tantamount to an opportunity.

Who's wrasslin' the mule out there? Such a racket. A lopsided struggle. Getting naked with gardenias. What is it you want? "JUST THE WORLD," he said. Would be unwise to uncage either of them . . . monsters visiting my dreams. Soon the other Muddybear will be in to explain all. It's a mangy cup of tea slurped in the name of magpiety. I prefer wine with great authority and low price. She doesn't have any of those little black hairs in her nose anymore. She's a freak. But he loves her.

I love him. Can't help it if he wants wife-style when I could have given him marriage. Thinks I'm ecclesiastical. I would rule and he would bend necks like rubber. Alas, I wrote a poem in honor and out of respect for his involvement in their anniversary celebration. I'm giving them both up. It's even harder giving up your hated rival. Your hobbies should respect you. I'll be combing Civil War battlefields with metal detectors, searching for miniballs, whispering:

> J.O. Yetta the Satiable is EVERYMAN'S
> dream
> Part of the firmament moves over
> when engaged
> it's loose banged
> in the area of symbolics
> understated
> in that nobody guesses its meaning.

Moved over to the next biggest
finger
less movement
less banging
less nicks for longer duration.
less big
on that one
Superfreak.

Better fit means one less Trotsky falling out
one more tree.
One less Trotsky fixing one side of his hair is no mean feat.
Left at home but not forgotten.
Lessons learned.
Nous sommes.
Do you take many showers my sweet?

Left at home because.
The never-dead stay home.
Last time we seen each other whole.
Nous sommes.

Narrator: Sadie says, "Pinch me. Am I alive?"

Nurse: OK, OK, not so hard. Do you want to rip the tea bag fortune from my earring hook?

Narrator: No.

Nurse: Carrie left ice-pick markings on everything she loves . . . finding infinite reward in that five and dime sense of unreality . . . exposing the treacherous giddiness of the bungi cord . . . being wife . . . being Clerk of the Works . . . gigantic and lean . . . persnickety little piece of undisguised persnicketiness. Just a clap of her hands shuts the lights and television off.

I said OFF!

Narrator: More proof Carrie and Val exist separately and perhaps together:

Off in the distance, in spite of the fact we turned down the volume, we hear someone on television sounding like Carrie's dad. It goes like this: SOMEONE BECAME A PSEUDO-HERMAPHRODITE BY HIS OWN HAND. HE WAS NO ABORIGINE BY BIRTH . . . YET THEIR CUS-

TOMS HE GREW TO LOVE AS HIS OWN—NO I DON'T
MEAN TENNIS. ACTUALLY WE DON'T KNOW WHAT
HE MEANT BY ABORIGINE RITE. ALL WE KNOW IS HE
CREATED AN ORIFICE AT THE JUNCTURE OF HIS PE-
NIS AND SCROTUM. FEMALE ORGASM WAS WHAT
THIS FELLOW WANTED OUT OF LIFE. HE WAS AN
ARTIST SO HE JUST BLED TO DEATH *LIKE MOST
WOMEN DO*
   a little EVERY DAY.

Carrie's lawyer attempting to glean sympathy from the jury:
   I leave it up to you to decide whether there ever was a
Valmouth. If you believe the man existed . . . is he dead?
Did Carrie kill him? Jeeps are entirely too downmarket.
Since we are in the midst of a good long Jacobean silence,
and all fond of dilemma, I will involve you deep and often
in this tale of woe. She was one of the otherwise complete
people at twelve years old.
   We're all in agreement her brother Nick Adams was pretending to be a G.I. Joe (in truth merely a Ken looking like
a Barbie) DRESSING HIS BARBIE. Many innocents came
to be involved in his three-act farce. His family included
Barbie, or Carrie as you know her, and the rest: a long line
of Porkopolis hog-packers. When they retire they become
involved in the ongoing process of itinerant provincials
rounded up and sent home.
   In order to be sent home herself, she asked her brother
(minister and sometimes film director) quite often about
"Christ that psychopath," stating, "The Savior's knowledge
is merely a tragic consciousness of what it is to be alive."
(What they didn't have to deal with. . . .)
   In competitions Carrie had a good stumbly run . . . where
and when she ran into the monsters in a screwing heap.
Reminds one a little of Potapenko, Chekhov's deplorable
friend. Be assured she is an ogre. Be assured it was not she
who tied one single yellow ribbon. Be assured she is not
your friend. Be assured she is a fourth-generation shop rat.

Be assured FRESH OYSTERS will be spray-painted across your railway wagon as it whisks your decomposing body to your native land for burial. And not a minute too soon. Raise your hands if any of you've inadvertently been shipped back for the wrong burial. You have your hand raised. Would you like to tell the jury all about it? Consider yourself, like Carrie, a plucked petunia from an onion patch. And be assured, with a cherubic face like that, you must really gore scholarly and religious oxen.

This pathetic hand-raiser wanted to go to the john:

Juror/ Volunteer: I've been shipped and found it demoralizing and that's all I want to say. How does one secure one's womanhood and one's passage? Do we have to be like potatoes giving birth to sprouting spuds?

Lawyer: Your response to "What was your part in such theater?" is acknowledgment. You had a part.

Juror/Volunteer: Which hardly abates any feelings of inadequacy. Or should it just abate ANY FEELINGS?

Lawyer: Makes you look precious. I call Carrie.

Juror: Thank my lucky stars here comes Carrie.

Lawyer: Carrie, let's go over your part:

Carrie (*whispering*): First I look the pisses squarely in the eye. I say, "He tries very seriously to poison me every six hours." Then I remain incommunicative to the point just beyond rudeness. You see, my underlying overriding unvoiced last remaining fixation (same as the other character) happens to be MOTHERS: "Mothers of anything! Dogs, cats, humans." My uppermost concern. My second line: "Hell is other people."

Lawyer: No, it's "Like green pennies one should BE with one's mother."

Carrie: The rest of the dialogue . . . please help me . . . with it.

Lawyer: OK. Here goes: "What was she pouring slantwise?"

C: Rice Krispies?

L: Interminable teas.

C: Was she sucking . . . and if so WHAT?

L: The substantific marrow.

C: All their spare time spent speaking across borders (il-legally) was one way to kill an afternoon.

L: Do you deny Jesus, a master of knockabout, is the Christ?

C: Yes . . . only if never entirely born. You seem to forget it was me, incognito, in the thrall of Paquita, a rough peas-ant girl descended from Tangiers' patron saint.

L: Thank you for the reenactment of the theater. Inter-esting stuff. Did you foresee any problems working with that particular crew in that particular part of the world?

C: The first day we arrived on the set, a corpse remained in the autopsy room. One simply didn't know what to do.

L: What DOES one do?

C: As always, theories are rampant. We demanded an in-crease in wages. A fact came to greet us in the form of a raise . . . FACT: Tamarind monkeys are notoriously infer-tile. Killing the RAT was our last heroic and praiseworthy act of warfare. Congressional Medals were distributed.

Judge: All fine and good, Carrie, now I will be very happy to sign the release. You are a fine, upstanding citizen. I like being convinced of that. If you killed someone, am I safe saying it was in the role of the mid-Victorian bodhisattva ideal: one who selflessly aspires to realize enlightenment for the sake of everyone else on the planet?

C: Yes sir.

L: I have heard the tape of you spelling out this philoso-phy based on Sanskrit pituitary glands. I need one more thing from you before you will be excused. In one hundred words or less, relay any feelings or thoughts you have about the figure of the dancing faun, who all the while is dancing to high-pitched music no one can hear.

C: I'm not giving away company secrets . . . I have noted his erect penis and the point on his beard remain at the same angle—all I'm prepared to say at this point in time.

THE JURY FINDS YOU NOT GUILTY. Watch it don't come back to bite you.

Chapter 11

Not Exactly an Evangelist
on the Born Again

Carrie runs into an old friend in post office shoes and takes time to explain her moves in and out of the Windy City:

I understand context. Order of Dervishes is a context. I can expound on context. Obsolescence itself. Refer back to my work on incarnation of obsolescence in the Grateful Dead. We're buying into something extinct. Marrying the business. The degree of fanaticism required, and the measure of sincerity we judge and ARE judged, is mathematical-maniacal. Obeisance. I can say that because in my work I'm defining mathematical. One looks for what one knows. Similarities; reference or semblance of a reference to what you know until you are burned and thereby enabled by the burning to rebel against what you now, A-HA, really know. This is omnipresent. I'm talking knowledge of people. I'm talking the color of bad news and good business.

The Grateful Dead was a common denominator, a reference point. I couldn't know he was a combat storm trooper. Not outwardly evident. Every girl outgrows her fascist. Alfred E. Neuman aspects were evident. I wore a pink rubber (bubblegum was the color and bubblegum was the texture) doll in tribute to his pug face. It adorned my Victorian necklace of dripping topazes. The doll was remnant of a full-blown toy, once complete with now defunct plastic parachute—all left by a child for the rubbish it was, on the street. Alfred E. liked the Grateful Dead. Human skull for an inkpot. Cotton balls for brains.

Were you merry?

I deceived myself best. Yes, I was Mohawk-merry.

Were you a halfwit?

Yes. I had the fantastic face of the Sistine Madonna.

Say he is your child.

He is your child. You are his child. But seriously, many times instead of crossing myself in superstition and awe, I should have let Alfred E. or Valmouth and Pimpo go. To cool my lusts I jumped whole hog right into the thick of it. Without a waver. The decision made, this could have been my living to the edge. Kufologists warned it might kill me and I might be a witness to a death. . . . "You'll end up in jail if you stick with blinkies like us."

Jail? My stars and garters. House payments from jail.

Weird things would happen to us. Standing around innocently was "invitation" to the weird. Like Nash Vegas. We waited large increments of time for our stripper to be mixed. Special recipe. One time, I put my quarter in the pay phone to call a customer. This typecast Mafia guy comes running up and pushes me out of the way. He asks me not to mind waiting while he jumps line. Imperative he reach someone immediately. Here's what he said after reaching "said" party:

"You marry the bitch at miniature Saint Peter's and never SEE the bitch? If God is on high and the czar is off with the prince of Smolensk, we're not so bad off after all. Tin horn repeaters. Lovelittle met his earwitness . . . yeah they had diverging tales of woe. Lovelittle came 'round to his friend's way of thinking . . . after repeated clubbings. Where it hurt. They are in agreement that Joaneta D'Arc was drug (dragged) screaming from her hotel. Well yeah. Sure, boss. Illegal for an unaccompanied woman to reside at a Saudi hotel without a police certificate stating she isn't a prostitute. You know that! Whose machete is that? Heard it whizzing by. Yeah. That's what I'm talking about. Think I enjoyed being jailed and deported for letting that woman check in? Blessed are those with nothing to lock up. Once. No longer. I AM the Committee for the Propagation of Virtue and Prevention of Vice. Ordinary people SHOULD be associated with plain food. Why not? WHY NOT? She shoved my fist where her liver used to be. Isn't this animalistic and fatalistic at the same time? Can it be animalistic without being fatalistic?" (With this he turned as if to ask me and a shrug was my only response.)

He continued: "We found ourselves in this garden and there was this tree—yeah, the same tree of knowledge and you know the rest. Stick it to the seasons. All her points are titillating yet moot not mute now. Same woman. Speaking of weak points . . . one of those thingamawhosits. Her adornment was a bronzed IUD around her neck. Yeah for jewelry. Pitiful. Talked tommyrot. Stooped and took it. Happy (for herself) when she could clear a space at the dinette set. Numberless moods. Used to be friends but eventually she PISSED ME OFF. Flaming gas around her Charlie Brown head."

Then he left the phone dangling, turned to me and asked, "Is that a can opener? A grinding wheel? A machete?"

I shrugged again.

He returned to his phone conversation and ended with this pronouncement: "When mother nature is a festering sore infecting like a pus-creating machine, and one takes one's tongue out of the food chain for even seconds . . . I KNOW she did. She worked in some rust bowl city for a perishing sports magazine. Said we would understand her fashion when two years pass, then as a farewell, wished us a big cool space between our toes if we would eat not smoke it."

Click.

He turned around the minute a big limo drove by with a man hanging out. Shot him before anyone on queue could run.

This circumstance made me start asking a lot of questions, like . . . was I hurt? This blank space guy on the phone wasn't from International House but what the hell was he? Where was Teach? Should I always do as I'm told?

I answered my own queries. Teach is in southern Cafeteria. Teach cares about where people come from; their "lineage." Maybe I picked up some same interest. Interest in pineapple upside-down cake. Sprinkle with laughter. Another poet who spent his first marriage at the peep shows.

Who cared?

The city is Convulse-Me-Chicago. We poor plebes are grounded in a specific location. This can be reassuring. A place we know conjures up certain images. Not Cleopatra with pin money. It really hasn't changed in the way it affects your heart as a young girl. City of Algren and big shoulders. If you're brought here BY something, I MEAN something holds you rooted—fine; school, a family move, job, or boyfriend, those can be legit. However, if you've blown in like burnt leaves—and like it, and start to take root—WHERE would surprise your Siamese twin.

I think of Chicago as white vinyl chairs with bright blue vinyl buttons. Backs of chemical heads stain the necks of these stinking chairs. But there's color and lack of color—what you need in an important city.

Television was out. Consumer culture was out. Breaking commandments in. Crashing every party. Fumes, beer, and spaghetti. My body sustained it. Body of a sixteen-year-old (twenty-five) so how bad could a few years' damage be? Paid for in advance with years of exercise, health, and waiting, I was sure to remedy it later with unadulterated maintenance.

Lived unwisely and not very well. Loved stupidly if at all. Ripping at the universe. A Trophy Wife who began seriously marrying at fifteen. Marrying ever since. Now, "love" makes me cock my revolver. Annisette get your gun. Getting beaten up was an interesting phenomenon . . . you're being pummeled, and you think, what I said does not deserve this. What did I say? So you try NOT to say things like that . . . you say something else next time, and for THAT, you are beaten. Ashamed . . . you cling to that cockroach of a person even more. What's NOT to say? Questionable things squeak by. Funny man you are. A brisk handshake, not exactly my idea of ideal affection. Inhibition and honesty are encouraged but wise off to gloomy Potato Head and pow! Cockroach Club person's pleasures are a mystery not just to me. A concrete example of seeing a sermon rather than hearing one.

One time Cockroach Club (C.C.) person was hurt . . . my thoughts consisted of: "I'm not looking at this puss when it's seventy-five years old and uglier. Not worth killing. I'm screwed but not going to prison with a C.C. thought like him on my mind. Deadened myself to the pain on the other side of the coin—deadened to say the verboten. Lined up home owners to vomit on cue. Pretty to think no other man or woman has suffered more than Carrie Meebs.

Gray weed that he was, could have finished me off. I used techniques gathered from the annals of "the Great Sufferers." Pretend NOT to be suffering. He lumped me "like the Irish," who "never know when they are beaten."

No doubt he was the most stupid truly short-assed fat-faced Irishman who never knew when he was dead or who did it to him, too busy counting "dead-asses" everywhere. Good to his plants. His stomach was ironically, inappropriately upset watching a dog owner brutally flog her pet— the eyes got it, then the muzzle. Saw no correlation with his own (without owning a pet) "dog owner" behavior. Who weeps with age last, pays membership dues to various tribes in Kotekas (penis sheaths). Now he's with the boys.

There are fashion alternatives; the way you're viewed by a stranger wakes you up out of your dream state, sometimes for whole moments into the blight. Out of darkness. I had trained myself to throw up on him and did so during an argument atop beautiful french doors and window jams, from which we were expected to untar ninety years of lead paint. A Christian type intercepted. A lecture ensued. I speed-walked home. Where else to go? Walking adrenalin. The Christian was a lean pale egghead character in a typecast farce. None of his business anyway. Color of a voice. Then a wino threw "Crazy Lady" on my face. Plague or baptism? Both.

The apparition that was me:

Nicest way to describe my apparel is to say my shorts used to be white tennis shorts.

Sneakers eaten by paint-stripper displayed two not very fat, unsuckable, hairy toes. Guttersnipe. My shirt's bodice had split of its own accord to complete my spattered-with-paint-and-goo ensemble.

This was one of the times, it doesn't happen very often, you either prostrate yourself over a flaming cross or come up for sunshine. Wearing the best Arab things. Red hands black nails. Terror of ourselves gets in through the terror on the face, in the eye of a stranger. Speed-walked by the bowling lane, people laughed so hard it forced bowling to a halt. Counters have eyes. Beer rings. Cardboard coasters. Deadly flush on my cheeks. Prison pallor. Deafening visions. Desire to chant something to some beat if I only knew how.

THIS ISN'T HAPPENING. TO ME. AIN'T NO TOOTH FAIRY.

Ludicrous botheration when the police came. Didn't come two-black-eyes time. Tickled when they show. A kick to think they would come. Dragnet.

Were you drinking?

Had a Nehi.

Was he a meat eater?

Meat sang in his oven.

Did you go to "dos"?

Some. Ode to his pedicure. Ode to his Christian curios. If you want to dress up a "do" by calling it one. My liverlips conversation, strangely "finishing school" to the guys and inappropriate in its flowery sentiment, made them look at each other in disbelief. What the hell. . . ? I talked to them in their "Yes, dear, you're absolutely right" plumber language. I had my new and exciting explanation for everything, which they were as yet and in retrospect never ready to adopt. I was the chieftain observing the anthropologists, not where they live, where they work in the campsite overlooking the valley where I live. Shoulda/coulda been parlor-bound English intellectuals with a blue-gray stubble. But are NOT. The ones I know live for work on the meat-packing side of town and aren't Brits . . . not exactly "resting for a while" in the recesses of their souls. Depending on your perspective, you might find them bums distributing pamphlets. Resting. Wishing each other little success. Leisured for life? If you want to—call it a party.

I had been warned, "Don't destroy what's best in you. When you touch me, that body of yours, ripped from the universe, will start shaking. Then and only then all things shall be well." After this advice, I vanished into the bush.

I found myself with fine-tuned muscles, smelling of cement, with a weird skin-deep belief in everyone's supposedly special nature; saw good in every "job-in" perpetually melancholy person. Partial account. True luster to be searched out. Right next door, of course, remains a huge capacity for monstrosity in each asylum-seeker encountered. You find the textbook magnetic pull to "types" at any gathering. Vast orgies. After each swindling, I would talk with new people or Jeremiah. My no-strings friend. About any previous love he would say: "Worthless trash, I presume?"

I'd say, "Yeah, threw up on him too."

I tried to leave my rich sexual life out. I worked like a tradesman on a manual typewriter, which contributed to my sculptural feel for pound-beating until I had some foreign object.

ONE

Your writing is short and non-melodic. The future belongs entirely to baby stormer prose.

TWO

You think you're involved in the relevance of contemporary or beyond contemporary verse—you're all wet. Wet all under hundreds of pamphlets.

THREE

Negligible readerships insist on echoes. . . .

I looked in the glass and my likeness never got in the way. Free to portray myself. "Boisterous bloodsuckers" couldn't see me for my likeness. Had to develop out of this stunted personality. Jeremiah tells me practice talking to everyone the way I talk to him. I'm "the humorous new language called woman" singing along to the song "When I Grow Up I Want to Be an Old Woman."

Moved in with the boys. Surrounded by masculine vitality. Was a fight to be heard. Turned from a gray mouse to a
screaming boisterous banshee thing in a house of pantlegs,
car repair, and butchered animal carcasses. Lucky to have
one line *in* with the shrieking clarity of a thirty-second spot
before relinquishing my space. Sound of our own voices.
Long as they pilot the stove. Cocorico. Crows. Care not one
tuppenny button.

Simplified gridlocked undies. Life could be judged by
the type of bathing suit I came to be "sporting." Circumstances weren't too bad the time I found one just my size,
run over by a motorcycle, lying on the sidewalk. Fifty-third
Street. Better than the hand-me-down with no elastic on
top. Criable. When I dove off the rocks at "The Point" into
the cool sewer-yellow water, I was swimming, the water felt
clean. Lead contamination for life. Jeff said, "You look like
shit." Criable.

Not "at home" to him?

Indubitably.

Why is your understanding ass-backwards?

Because I am a member . . . of the pissed upon yet still
undaunted human race.

Are you a gift from God?

A "working station perpetrator tourist" passing through.

A tourist passing through IS a gift from God. We're talking the original Garden of Eden.

We're talking desire to "freeze accident."

What about fate?

Huge amounts of hypocrisy were rampant. General rule
of thumb: Holy Folks with the most vociferous yell for morality need most desperately and most often to be naked
nerve thrashed with their own hypocrisy. Wet noodles.
Soaked in Chef Boyardee for a week. Mr. Mabuse's desire
for "things perfect" frustrated all endeavors. Tended to
drown demonstrated integrity in pulque from fermented
juice of maguey.

Were those your own sought-after impalings?

If it helps YOU sleep at night.

Who's the man-eating Carib who led them to believe in perfection?

Not me. As they say in France, a snake is totally snail tail. I find more trust and solace in observation than authority. Girls . . . yes in the lock box. Nice while you're in there, but little frame of reference makes you crazy later. When you crawl out to write tiny sentences . . . the world kicks you some butt all over. Should one head away from nest building toward the general vicinity of Pariah Peninsula? From there, it's a climb to any larger reality.

Name your larger reality.

He thinks I have lots of guts so to speak. Think about it. Who said, "We never wavered and were never confused?" Nobody I ever wanted to know. Nobody I ever knew.

What about children?

I deserve that years-ahead happiness with Chuckie. It's kind of inevitable. Extortion monies to a barkless dog. They don't in happy bunches take to me like the Singing Nun. I deserve that glee even if it's a delusion or concoction. Beats regurgitating gray antifreeze. It's like the little girl "liked the man part, but why did the lady part have a mustache?"

That unique joy. Solace. Old woman in a shoe?

Something totally disconnected is another psychological speed trap. My friend who's practically German now was vacationing with me one summer. We went to the south of France. We were two Greek-to-me goddesses following the sunshine. Goal enough for us. Some joker ruined our poolside life with a spray can of disinfectant. Much to his pleasure. Men found us to be what they were looking for and equally elusive. Our avowed indulgences at that time in our lives, I will not indulge. I thought by "King James Version" they meant William James. The point is, when we get down to that kind of final precision and say the deed is done, what's been done? How was it done? I hope that's rock 'n' roll. I read something to back me up as if it were a scientific document. Unfortunately it is only another (older than me) wiser woman's opinion. She summed up the men and their great attraction for her, in my kind of science. The gist of what she said:

"It's men. Male society, which means packing us all com-
fortably together within a few acres. This Prince Frederick
thing they have for each other to the exclusion of women
and girls . . . they don't like it, not even the ones who un-
flinchingly accept the primal scream route. Since I am
LIKE a boy, with written homework pockets they'd like to
lie in, they don't have to worry about me. What surprises
me is how they assure me of my womanhood and at the
same time are complementing THEMSELVES. A boy is
what they want. That way they don't have to worry about
Marilyn Monroe for gosh darn sake. Can you imagine how
intimidating a female impersonator like that is?"

Was Marilyn a female impersonator?

Carrie: Should lead to a mad bad wider understanding of
each other. Any approachable play with the paragraph endeavors to show us the way. Westward alcoherent thoughts
prevail. This isn't how Mary (levitating on the shelf) would
have marketed product.

I remember my brother with a friend caught up in the
fact Bro had two sisters. Bro looked at us carefully to find
nothing had changed: he saw his two sisters still without a
single redeeming quality. Isn't it unfair that without one
recent ruinous siege to our female credit, without civilizing
nations, we *females* get such attention? Born female. Caught
from an English ancestor.

I told his friend if we were in "the South" and he were
black and it was a long time ago, just after checking his
machete at the door, he coulda been lynched for "reckless
eyeballing" of me. White women. Black, red. Yellow. Brown.
Powers of womankind.

That's not an oversimplification? You seem to have as-
similated some of that. This death . . . doesn't C.C.'s death
make you a tad lonely?

Back to C.C. person:

Death is a lonely den of thieves. I think twice before boat-
ing with a yachtsman who believes he has nine lives. Business I'm in. Long grass needs trimming. An attention-get-

ting device just being a good girl. That changes. Once again forced to develop a personality. No getting around it. His particular double-jointed jaws contribution was to take my personality intertwined with botanical interests, lend it a green quality, and make me quite the conversationalist.

The old intellectual quicksand. Good old reality. The only perfect thing. Subject to perception. Do you think you have characteristics of fine quality?

Yes. Some places I genuinely feel that. PLACE is crucial in answering that question. Ancient memory has more than a little to do with it. Sleep of mankind. Not to change the subject, but would you be in need of any little gift item with a botanical motif today?

Selling. Selling. No thanks. Rapidity is repugnant to the semi-dozing reader.

To name it is to have it manifest itself. Rapidity made me repugnant in his eyes. Refused to tame his lust. The overt indication was his choice of garb—macaw-feather capes gave it away. Opulence was the message. Symptoms abated. When he chose to dine surrounded by Java peacocks, the telltale signs revealed themselves to me alone. Would not heed the call. If I never eat another banana leaf stuffed with liver-worsted alligator meat, it will be too soon.

Reminds you of your life with him?

My flight upward and my complete leveling off. It wasn't until standing in front of the Yugoslavian consulate in New York, dressed in a little number by Worth, that the answer dawned on me—Solomonically. We've pushed for a smaller world the whole time. A large chunk of his nose is small price to pay for such a wonder. What a prize for my craft guild (who as a class never could stand incarceration) to behold.

He pardoned you in advance.

Yessir. He knew it was the only way to get a girl like me to go along with such pink rosewater foolishness and nervous hands.

And great bobbing breasts. You cynically permit yourself.

I know what everybody thinks. He knew what I'd have to

deal with the rest of my life. He still wanted it. His way of torturing me now and in the hereafter. Ultimate control over the "unable to be watched one." Battle his tantrums until hell freezes then we battle in skates.

You blame him?

We made a deal. He moved in with a suitcase. My first mistake. Conjecture all you like. You know he put me to sleep for a while—exactly what I asked of him.

It could just as well have been the reverse.

What are you saying? He brought me his bucket and feedbag? He wanted us to sport them as chapeaus?

Burlap scooped the fashion world and more than a few missed out. End of the previous step forward.

Greta saw a need.

He was her fever.

She's a Third World reptile woman with her recovered tears. Gets her many with waterworks. Nose a-run. I hoped one day he would twist again his crooked nose and reassure me.

Flammable Man.

Never fell for the gentry stuff. Rude boy in rude health. Can we call it quits for all festivities now? There is no Santy Claus. Where's the milk wagon? Settle on a plastic sedan. Let's be thirsty. Shall we?

Carrie confronts her mirror:

Life of Carrie and other shorts. Right? When I found I had the disease, I freaked as you would. Bleeding from the throat was a clue. My tonsils always feel burned out. Many a saint also died upping the chuck. A hint. One finds oneself perfectly rabid to do any little thing—but of course there's nothing one can do. You feel like you're the only one on the planet who didn't show up for an important meeting.

Two people jumped into and onto my head as possible culprits out of literally hundreds. One raised in Spain blockish guy cried what I thought were tears of joy after we made love . . . like making me was the answer to one of the more frightening queries in his small life. Never quite awake. Ain't lust grand? We had one no-more-tears interlude. It went like this: I was home with my menstrual cycle. Pimpo called and said in spite of his being aware of the circumstance, this guy wanted to see me. I agreed to see him at my house. You break your first rule and then end up breaking them all. We became covered in my blood. I'm a bleeder. We tried to rinse my white cotton sheets in the shower. Then we went for coffee. He was wonderful. I broke up with another guy over him only to have Picasso never call again. In those days I was steadfastly unmarried. Unmarried to any idea.

Later . . . now is later, I think back on those tears, how he never darkened my door either at home or at Pimpo's establishment. I wonder WAS IT HIM? Tears appear and you wonder. In your head you've got three languages pleading for silence speaking one thought quite as old as any hooker's first dollar. Inertia becomes my major motivating force.

The other person who comes to mind was from Finland. A Laplander who enjoyed being housebroken to a certain extent. He had this pronounced goofy foot hatred for his rich father. A singer who couldn't sing. Finnish sounds Russian to me. He asked questions like, "How long before you defy gravity?" I answered three months. His main occupation was trying to get European girls to come live with him in his trailer. A failure by almost any standard, he lived for his bottlecap children and they were wonderful. I wonder why he had custody. I forget. Crazy about having a woman in his possession. Gave up on me pretty quickly. Questioned my choice of outfits. So I gave him a crunchy peanut butter mouthful. Turned him into a certain redfaced gentleman. A hooker could explain.

The Dutch girl who introduced us was an intravenous drug user. Said she kept giving up heroin only to go back hexed for more. Might be dead from this dread disease as we speak. Breakdown of another hoodooed body. Her advice to a client was, "Don't ever lie about where you spend the money." My advice is, "Tell your significant other your money goes to the church. Tell the church the money goes to your wife. And don't bring your wife into the congregation unless she gives info convincing them she's into primal screams with an open, enlarged, sticky mouth."

I was impregnated by an uncalcified mandrake root. All very civilized. I chose pixilated Chuck for the father. To date we have enjoyed two elaborate courtships. He's out this minute buying lava lights to string on the Christmas tree. He's seeing me through. A man.